ISOLATION

I0675461

ISOLATION
A Kid Sensation Novel

By

Kevin Hardman

ISOLATION

Cover Design by Isikol

Edited by Faith Williams, The Atwater Group

This book is published by I&H Recherche Publishing.

ISBN: 978-1-937666-48-4

Printed in the U.S.A.

ISOLATION

ACKNOWLEDGMENTS

I would like to thank the following for their help with this book: GOD first and foremost, since all the blessings in my life come from Him; my family, who continue to love and support me through good times and bad; and my readers, who are the best fans on the planet!

ISOLATION

Thank you for purchasing this book! If, after reading, you find that you enjoyed it, please feel free to leave a review on the site from which it was purchased.

Also, if you would like to be notified when I release new books, please subscribe to my mailing list via the following link: http://eepurl.com/C5a45

Finally, for those who may be interested in following me, I have included my website and social media info:

Website: http://www.kevinhardmanauthor.com/

BookBub: https://www.bookbub.com/authors/kevin-hardman?follow=true

Amazon Author Page: https://www.amazon.com/Kevin-Hardman/e/B00CLTY3YM

Facebook: www.facebook.com/kevin.hardman.967

Twitter: https://twitter.com/kevindhardman

Goodreads: https://www.goodreads.com/author/show/7075077.Kevin_Hardman

And if you like my work, please consider supporting me on Patreon: https://www.patreon.com/kevinhardman

Chapter 1

"Explain to me again what I'm doing here," said my best friend, Smokescreen.

"You're here so that I have someone to talk to if this thing starts getting boring," I replied.

"Oh," Smokey muttered. "And here I was thinking that you and your new West Coast buds just wanted some fresh blood to make fun of."

"No," I assured him, shaking my head. "We made fun of you earlier, so there's no more entertainment value in it."

Smokey chuckled, at the same time brushing a piece of lint off the shoulder of the suit he was wearing, which consisted of a black-and-white pinstriped jacket with matching pants. He also wore a black shirt, white tie, and a fedora.

Taken altogether, Smokey projected the image of an old-school gangster, which was fitting since we were currently at a costume party. He completed the look by carrying an obviously-fake Tommy Gun that nevertheless gave him a slightly menacing air.

"I feel like a horse's rear," he said.

"No, *that* guy is a horse's rear," I corrected, pointing to a skinny fellow wearing the back half of a horse costume. We both laughed heartily at that — perhaps *too* heartily, since our overt jocularity caused a few people nearby to glance in our direction.

As Smokey had noted, we were currently on the West Coast, attending a fete being thrown by the A-List Supers — or rather, their teen affiliate. The A-Listers were a top-notch superhero squad, second only to the Alpha

League (which Smokey and I were a part of) in terms of power and prestige. That said, they had us beat by a mile when it came to glitz and glamour, as evidenced by the soiree where we currently found ourselves.

For instance, a massive ballroom had been rented for the event, which was being catered by a famous chef who had her own television show. The menu included Ossetra caviar, skewers of Wagyu beef, white truffle ice cream, and other dishes that probably cost a small fortune. All in all, it was well in excess of anything I could imagine the Alpha League spending on a party (and again, this was just for the teens).

"Look, your costume's fine," I assured my friend after we regained our composure. "Don't worry about it."

"Easy for you to say," Smokey admonished. "You got the cool outfit."

His comment caused me to give myself a once-over. I was sporting an Egyptian pharaoh costume, consisting of a black tunic, a black-and-gold nemes headdress, and a black shendyt. I also wore gold armbands and matching sandals, along with a black cape and a golden ankh on a necklace.

Overall, I thought it was a good look for me, but I honestly didn't think it was any more "cool" than what Smokey was wearing.

"I wish I could take credit for this getup," I said, "but it was all Vestibule."

Smokey gave me an odd look, although it wasn't completely unexpected. Vestibule was a teen member of the A-List Supers — a teleporter who also had a modeling career. In the past, I and most of my friends had generally considered her to be insipid and snobbish, but recently I'd discovered there was a lot more to her than met the eye.

"So she's picking out your clothes now?" Smokey noted, his tone seeming to imply something.

"She picked out a *costume*," I corrected. "That's a far cry from her laying out my clothes for me on a daily basis."

"Still, Jim, that she's dictating what you wear at all has to mean something."

"What it means is that I lost a bet," I muttered sheepishly.

Smokey frowned. "What kind of bet?"

I sighed. "You remember that big budget mystery movie that opened last week?"

Smokey nodded. "Yeah."

"Well, I actually went to the premiere."

"I know," Smokey stated. "The tabloids were all trying to figure out who Vestibule's mystery date was."

"It wasn't a date," I stressed.

"Right," Smokey droned sarcastically. "You just both happened to show up at the same place, at the same time, and sit next to each other."

"Anyway," I continued, ignoring his jibe, "we made a bet regarding the identity of the killer, and she won."

There was silence for a moment as Smokey just stared at me, and then he burst into laughter.

"Ha!" he chuckled. "Are you kidding me? You let Vestibule hustle you?"

"Nobody got hustled," I argued. "She's a lot more astute than we initially gave her credit for."

"Or maybe she knows someone who worked on the movie and got them to tell her how it ends. After all, she's in good with all these Hollywood types."

"I thought about that," I admitted. "But after getting to know her, I don't think she's any more likely to cheat me than you."

Smokey looked at me askance. "Are we talking about the same Vestibule? The girl who arm-twisted you into a date when the fate of the world was hanging in the balance?"

I frowned. Smokey was referring to a time in the not-too-distant past when we'd needed Vestibule's help to save the planet. She'd used the opportunity to wrangle a date with me in exchange for her assistance.

"Okay, she went a little over the top once," I agreed, "but that's not a true reflection of who she is."

"Maybe," Smokey intoned, sounding unconvinced. "But speak of the devil, here comes your new bestie now."

I followed Smokey's gaze and noted that Vestibule was indeed headed towards the corner of the room that we had staked out as our own. As generally happened whenever I saw her these days, I found myself smiling for no apparent reason as she approached.

She wore a feminine version of the costume I currently had on: a slinky, sleeveless black dress with a gold sash around her waist, along with a gemmed Wesekh collar and a Cleopatra wig with a bob cut. Like me, she had gold sandals and armbands, although the latter was connected to her dress by some colorful material that opened up like an elaborate pair of wings when she spread her arms.

She also sported a bejeweled headpiece, as well as an armband around her right bicep that was designed like a serpent. Finally, her makeup had been applied in an exotic fashion that included a multicolored hue on her eyelids, as well as an Eye of Horus around one eye.

ISOLATION

All things considered, if I was a pharaoh, then she was a goddess. Watching as she sauntered towards us — walking practically in time to some upbeat music playing in the background — it was easy to understand why, in addition to being a superhero, she also had a career as a high-paid fashion model.

"Hey," she said as she stepped close to give me a hug. "Glad you could make it."

"No problem," I stated a moment later as we separated. "Thanks for the invite."

"Me, too," Smokey added. "Although if I'd known there was a couples theme, I would have found someone to drag along as my gangster girlfriend."

"Gun moll," Vestibule declared.

Smokey raised an eyebrow. "Excuse me?"

"Gun moll," Vestibule repeated. "That's the official term for a criminal's girlfriend or female companion. Or you can just say 'moll.'"

Smokey cast a furtive glance in my direction that clearly relayed his surprise. In return, I gave him an I-told-you-so look. As I had mentioned earlier, Vestibule was a lot brighter than my friends and I had previously assumed.

"Anyway," she went on, "it's only by happenstance that Jim and I are matching. Did he tell you about our bet?"

Smokey nodded. "He did, and I'm surprised you didn't make him wear something utterly embarrassing."

"Trust me, I was tempted," Vestibule admitted with a laugh. "In fact, my original impulse was to have him dress as a circus clown. But I decided to show mercy — plus, the costume shop was having a two-for-one special on matching outfits."

"And here we are," I said, spreading my hands expansively.

Vestibule looked as though she were about to make a comment, then unexpectedly cocked her head slightly to the side, as if listening for something. A moment later, it became plainly obvious that she had actually been listening *to* something, as she suddenly reached out and grabbed my hand.

"Come on," she practically demanded. "You're dancing with me."

I had no time to protest as she quickly dragged me out onto the dance floor. A few seconds later, we were completely surrounded by an army of our peers, all swaying, grinding, and stepping to the rhythm of a song I recognized as having just reached number one on the charts.

Needless to say, some of those around us were more rhythmic than others. Vestibule, for instance, was great, and I could easily have imagined her with a career as a dancer were she not a model. At the other end of the spectrum was a kid to my left dressed as a vampire, who seemingly didn't know his right foot from his left and kept bumping into me.

I had no idea how to rate my own dance skills, since it was a rare activity for me. However, my ego got a nice boost when Vestibule leaned towards me and, shouting above the music, declared, "I think I've found my new dance partner! You're great!"

I didn't have my empathic abilities fully cranked up, but from what I could sense, Vestibule wasn't just being kind. She was actually being sincere, and as a result I found myself grinning broadly and felt my cheeks turning red.

Her compliment was enough to make me stay on the dance floor even as the current song ended and another began. This one was some kind of line dance, which quickly became apparent as almost everyone on the dance floor squared off into rows. I didn't know the song, but it was easy enough to pick up on the steps (especially since the moves were all repetitive). More to the point, it was actually a lot of fun — probably more so because I was next to Vestibule the entire time — and it seemed that the song came to an end all too soon.

At that juncture, the DJ made a distinct change in the music selection, because the next thing he played was a popular slow song. People immediately deserted the dance floor in droves, and I had planned to be one of them. However, I hadn't taken more than a step in that direction before a felt a solid grip latch onto my wrist like a vise.

"Oh, no you don't," Vestibule admonished. "You're not stranding me on the dance floor during a slow song."

Before I could verbalize a response, she stepped in close and put her arms around my neck. Almost of their own accord, my hands found their way to her waist and the next thing I knew, we were dancing.

It was admittedly a little awkward for me at first. The only girl I'd had inside my personal space for more than a few moments at a time was my ex, Electra. That said, it didn't take long for me to loosen up.

"So," Vestibule droned after a few seconds, "you seem to be adjusting well to West Coast living."

I raised an eyebrow. "What do you mean?"

"Well, this is what — the third event you've attended out here in the past few weeks?"

"Fourth," I corrected.

"Really?" she muttered, seemingly surprised. "Getting sucked in by the glitz and glamour, are we?"

ISOLATION

"It's not like that," I insisted. "My mom and grandparents are traveling abroad at the moment. The rest of my family is trying to keep me from spending a bunch of time by myself in an empty mansion."

As I spoke, I reflected on what I was saying and — although it was generally true — it was a complete understatement of the actual facts. My mother and grandparents were actually off-planet, traveling the stars and finally bonding as a family unit after decades apart. It was time they sorely needed together, but it did leave me on my own to a large extent (although, in all honesty, I wasn't *completely* alone).

"I assume that this extended family you're talking about is your cousin Avis," Vestibule remarked, interrupting my thoughts.

I nodded. "Yes, but you already know that. You've been at a couple of events that she invited me to."

"Must be cool to have one of the most powerful supers in the world finagling invites for you to exclusive events."

I frowned. I got the impression that Vestibule was trying to tell me something, but in a roundabout way. She had mentioned my cousin Avis — formally known as Rara Avis — who was indeed one of the preeminent capes on the planet. She was also a fixture on the celebrity circuit, with a reputation for partying hard, so getting tickets to star-studded events and such was no big deal for her. More to the point, Avis had recently been reaching out to me since my immediate family had left, probably at the behest of my mom or grandparents (or perhaps even my father, who was her paternal uncle). To be fair, however, Avis's sisters — Monique and Vela — had also made overtures.

"I remember when I was trying to decide which team of supers to join," Vestibule continued. "I must have gotten invites to a thousand galas, movie premieres, con–"

"Wait a minute," I interjected, almost coming to a stop on the dance floor as I finally caught on. "Are you saying that all this — all these parties and premieres I've been getting invited to — are just a recruiting junket? An attempt to get me to join the A-List?"

"Officially, I'm not saying anything like that," Vestibule replied. "But unofficially…"

She trailed off, which essentially let me know that I had guessed right.

"Why are you telling me all this?" I asked.

Vestibule looked away for a moment, and I sensed a small emotional conflict within her.

"You were going to find out eventually," she admitted after a few seconds. "And when you did, you were going to discover that I knew about it, and I didn't want you to think poorly of me."

"Think poorly of you?" I repeated, finding it an odd choice of words. "What do you mean?"

"I didn't want you thinking that I'm only being friendly as part of some recruiting effort. I wanted you to know that I'm hanging out with you because I think you're a lot of fun."

"Well, I knew *that*," I almost exclaimed, grinning. "I'm *major* fun."

"I'm serious," she said, trying not to giggle. "I didn't want you getting the wrong idea about me, which could still happen with your buddy telling you what a selfish, brainless airhead I am."

"You mean Smokey?" I asked. "He didn't say anything like that."

"Oh, really?" Vestibule muttered in a skeptical tone. "I saw the look he gave you earlier — like he was shocked I could string together two syllables."

"Not true," I insisted, shaking my head. "He was just surprised that you knew how to conjugate verbs."

Vestibule immediately started giggling, and I found myself chuckling as well, taken in by her ability to laugh at herself.

"Look," I said after a few moments, "I admit I had some preconceived notions about you, but I was wrong. So whatever I or my friends thought before is irrelevant. As far as I'm concerned, you and I started over with a clean slate, and if you give him a chance, I think the same can be true of you and Smokey."

"All right," she said with a nod. "I'm willing to put forth the effort."

"Great," I uttered. "I know Smokey will as well."

"Good," she declared. "Now, since you mentioned giving people a chance, I thought I should say something: my cousin thinks you're cute."

"Huh?" I muttered in surprise. "Your cousin?"

"Catalina," Vestibule replied, tilting her head towards an area just off the dance floor.

I looked in the direction indicated and saw Vestibule's cousin, who generally went by "Cat," talking to a guy dressed like a cowboy. She was our age and very pretty, and I'd actually met her the previous week at the movie premiere (where she'd been Vestibule's plus-one). However, she tended to do her own thing at events rather than hover around her famous cousin, so I really hadn't had a chance to get to know her.

At the moment, I couldn't help but notice that Cat had taken her nickname to heart with respect to her costume. Basically, she was wearing a skintight bodysuit that bore a cheetah print, along with matching ears and a tail. In addition, she'd gotten an elaborate bodypaint job done that not only gave all exposed areas of her skin the same big-cat semblance, but also made her face appear completely feline. Truth be told, given that even her shoulder-length blonde hair was spotted, it was difficult to tell where the costume ended and her skin began, and the overall effect was so true to form that — had she dropped down on all fours — someone probably would have mistaken her for the real thing.

"So," Vestibule murmured, getting my attention. "What do you think?"

"I think you must have misunderstood," I answered. "Between the movie premiere and tonight, I don't think your cousin's said ten words to me."

"She's shy."

"No, she isn't," I countered, essentially verbalizing what I'd picked up on empathically.

Vestibule simply laughed. "Okay, so she isn't shy. However, I was telling the truth when I said she thinks you're cute, but she was operating under the impression that there was something between us. I told her that it was open season on you — that you and I are just friends." Then she gave me an inquisitive look before adding, "Or did I misstate the facts?"

Her question struck me as peculiar, but I pushed it aside in order to focus on the statement that she'd made about it being open season on me. Frankly speaking, I'd had a girlfriend until very recently, and we'd actually had a very good relationship. However, things had gotten rather complicated when — after a visit to my alien grandmother's home planet of Caeles — I'd returned to

Earth with a Caelesian princess named Myshtal as my fiancée.

I hadn't really had a choice; becoming betrothed to Myshtal was the price of a ticket back home, but my significant other, Electra, hadn't quite seen it that way. We'd tried to make it work, but eventually she'd broken up with me, although there was still a small sliver of hope for our relationship: in essence, if I could find a way to break things off with Myshtal, Electra and I could be a couple again. More to the point, I *wanted* us to be a couple again.

"Look," I said, "I'm flattered, but...I think it's too soon."

"Too soon?" Vestibule repeated. "It's been like a month since you and Electra broke up."

A month, I thought, frowning. That didn't seem right — it felt much longer. Almost without thinking about it, I began doing the math.

Immediately after Electra broke up with me, I'd gone with Rune — another member of the Alpha League — on an odd sojourn to deal with a pressing matter. Ultimately, we'd been gone about a week (although certain repercussions from that jaunt were still being felt). After that, I'd had about a week to hang out with my mother and grandparents before they left the planet. Following their departure, I had spent the last couple of weeks shuffling back and forth between home and various events on the West Coast. All in all, it appeared that it *had* been about a month since Electra called things off.

"On top of that," Vestibule continued, interrupting my reverie, "word on the street is that Electra's already moved on."

"That's not true," I shot back. "A friend — a *platonic* friend — escorted her to a function. That's it."

ISOLATION

"Okay," Vestibule said. "I wasn't trying to—"

She never got to finish her statement, as a gruff voice behind me suddenly interjected with, "Excuse me, but I believe you're dancing with my date."

The voice was plainly directed at me and was accompanied by emotions of jealousy, distress, and agitation. Spinning around, I found myself facing a giant.

It was another teen, but he was at least a head taller than me and seemed to be made of nothing but muscle that had been chiseled from solid rock — literally. I recognized him then; he was another member of the A-List Super's teen affiliate — a fellow known as the Biolithic Colossus, whose body was made of living stone. Based on the scarf that was tied around his head and the eyepatch he sported, he appeared to be dressed as a pirate.

"I'm not your date," Vestibule declared forcefully. "We broke up a while ago, Bee-Cee."

"Yeah," Bee-Cee agreed, "but we can still share a dance."

"Pass," Vestibule stated. "Why don't you go dance with that little strumpet you cheated on me with?"

"Come on," the stone giant said. "Just one little dance."

He stretched out his arm as if to reach for her, and I instinctively stepped in front of him.

"She said 'No,'" I stated.

The Biolithic Colossus looked me up and down, as if seeing me for the first time. "Look, I don't know who you are, but I don't want to make a scene."

"Too late," I asserted, waving a hand to encompass the rest of those present.

Glancing around, Bee-Cee finally seemed to notice that people were starting to stare — in particular, other

13

couples on the dance floor, who were essentially standing still. They were all now watching what probably looked like a love triangle unfolding before their eyes.

He turned back to me. "Maybe I was being too subtle before. What I was trying to imply was that you should step aside, because I wouldn't want to embarrass you."

"That's not likely," I replied, staring him in the eye.

"Okay," Bee-Cee muttered with a shrug, "but don't say I didn't warn you."

He then reached for me. At the same time, Vestibule shouted "No!" and Bee-Cee disappeared.

There was stunned silence for a moment, and then people started cheering.

"That was awesome!" someone said.

"Way to go, Vestibule!" another person yelled.

"Woo-hoo!" crowed someone else.

There were similar comments for the next few minutes, which I initially found surprising. (Later I would learn that the Biolithic Colossus was a bit of a jerk, so his sudden absence wasn't mourned.) In essence, Vestibule quickly found herself being thanked all around for ejecting a boorish lout from the party.

Not wanting to horn in on her spotlight, I surreptitiously took a step back while she was being congratulated, noticing for the first time that Smokey was standing about an arm's length away. At some point while we had been engaged with the Colossus, he had sidled close. I gave him a subtle nod, plainly acknowledging the fact that I understood what his nearby presence meant: if things had gone sideways for some reason, he had my back.

Turning my attention back to Vestibule, I noted that someone — a girl in a nurse's uniform — had finally gotten around to asking her the big question: "Where'd you send him?"

"Someplace he won't cause any trouble," Vestibule answered cryptically.

That was good enough for those present, and eventually they went back to enjoying the party. At that juncture, Vestibule took me by the hand and dragged me to a corner of the room.

"Okay," she said, glancing around to make sure no one was within earshot. "Where'd you teleport him to?"

ISOLATION

Chapter 2

Needless to say, I was the one who had teleported the Biolithic Colossus. Although teleportation is one of the well-known powers of Kid Sensation, no one present (other than Smokey and Vestibule) knew that's who I was. Thus, it was only natural for everyone else to assume that Vestibule was the person who had gotten rid of the Colossus.

"I sent him to the tar pits," I said in answer to Vestibule's question. "One of the shallow pools, so he'll be fine."

Vestibule put a hand up to her mouth, stifling a laugh. The tar pits were a local tourist attraction, ancient pools of sludge where prehistoric animals got trapped millions of years ago.

"That's great!" Vestibule finally gushed. "I was going to dump him in a nearby lake, but that's even better."

"Glad you think so," I remarked, "although it may have been a bit harsh."

Vestibule frowned. "How so?"

"Well, he's going to have to go somewhere and wash the stink of the tar pits off — probably change clothes as well. By the time he's done all that, he'll have missed a good portion of the party."

"I'd argue that's a good thing, but knowing Bee-Cee, he's likely to just come straight back here."

I started to laugh, but then noticed that Vestibule seemed rather somber at the moment.

"What — are you serious?" I muttered.

She shrugged. "It wouldn't surprise me. Making a spectacle of himself is kind of his thing."

"And you dated that guy?" I asked, giving her a dubious look.

"Don't judge me," she growled in faux anger, playfully pinching my arm at the same time. "And if you must know, we were together for a little while, but it wasn't that serious."

"Apparently *he* thinks it was serious."

Vestibule shook her head. "No, he just doesn't like the fact that *I* broke up with *him*. He's one of *those* guys."

"Oh," I murmured. "Well, if he shows up and starts creating a scene again, we'll just send him right back to the tar pits."

Vestibule sighed. "To tell the truth, I'd rather not be here when he comes back."

"Um, okay," I muttered. "I guess we can call it a night."

I tried to sound sincere, but I was actually being a bit disingenuous. In truth, it was still rather early — Smokey and I had practically just arrived. That said, I wanted to be supportive of Vestibule, and sticking around when she felt compelled to leave would have felt disloyal. However, one look at Vestibule's face let me know that I had misjudged the situation.

"Call it a night?" she repeated, looking at me askance. "Like hell we will."

****

Fifteen minutes later, Vestibule, Smokey, Cat, and I were in the back of a chauffeur-driven limousine, which was the vehicle the girls had taken to the party. (I, on the other hand, had simply teleported me and Smokey to the event.) As we pulled away, Vestibule — who was sitting across from me — nudged my leg with her foot, then pointed out the window once she had my attention. Outside, I saw the Biolithic Colossus, smeared with tar from head to foot, racing back towards the party. Simultaneously, the two of us burst into laughter.

After we got over our case of the giggles (and explained to Smokey and Cat what we found to be so funny), Vestibule pulled out her cell phone and started making some calls. With her preoccupied, I turned to Cat, who was seated next to me.

"So, what's next on the agenda?" I asked.

"That's what Vestibule is scouting at the moment," Cat answered. "She's trying to find another party for us to crash."

"We can always just hang out," Smokey suggested. "An actual party isn't mandatory, in my book."

"Oh, yes it is," Cat retorted. "I spent hours perfecting the look for this costume, so all that time is not going to waste. *Someone* has to see how glamorous I am as a big cat."

There was a playful tone to her voice that let Smokey and I know that she was speaking tongue-in-cheek. He and I began snickering, and a moment later Cat joined us. The three of us then began discussing our costumes generally, as well as those we'd seen at the party. Of course, there was no doubt that Cat's getup had been head and shoulders above almost anyone else, and she told a few humorous anecdotes about what it had taken to achieve the look — including the fact that the body paint wouldn't wash off easily if left on too long.

"Basically, I'm the opposite of Cinderella," Cat proclaimed. "Instead of turning back at midnight, I get to stay this way for a few days."

ISOLATION

At that point, Vestibule finally got off her phone.

"All right," she intoned. "The rest of the night's itinerary is all lined up. Let's party!"

ISOLATION

Chapter 3

I had to admit that Vestibule turned out to be an excellent event coordinator. After announcing that it was party time, she had the limo driver pull over and let us out. Then, after giving the chauffeur explicit instructions on where and when to pick us up, she teleported us. (In all honesty, however, I had to negate my own teleportation power, so to speak, in order for her to teleport *me*.)

We popped up at what I immediately recognized as a chic, exclusive event — mostly because the first person I spied, standing only a few feet from me, was a world-famous actor. Not far from him was a singer whose latest hit I'd just heard at the costume party. Continuing to glance around, it became immediately evident that we had waded into a sea of celebrities.

Smokey, plainly noting the same thing I did, leaned towards Vestibule and said, "Should we be here?"

I understood what he was asking. Being teleporters, it was practically impossible to keep someone like Vestibule or me out of any venue. Moreover, some teleporters were infamous for popping up where they were neither expected nor wanted: on stage during televised award shows, on the field during championship sporting events, and so on. Thus, Smokey's fear that we had crashed this party was a valid one.

Vestibule pooh-poohed his concern. "It's cool. I cleared it."

Smokey shot me a worried glance, but I just shrugged, giving him a go-with-it expression. It probably didn't help that we were still in our costumes, so if we actually didn't belong, someone was likely to figure it out quickly enough and call security.

ISOLATION

"Will you relax?" Vestibule said to Smokey, obviously picking up on his mood. "Trust me, it's fine."

Smokey didn't say anything for a moment, then let out a deep breath.

"All right," he said. "If you say so, but…"

He trailed off, suddenly staring across the room as if in a trance.

"Is that who I think it is?" he muttered.

Following his gaze, I looked in the direction indicated and saw a famous young actress named Alita who, at nineteen, already had her own hit television show and three albums that had gone multi-platinum. (It also didn't hurt that her first starring movie role had been in a worldwide blockbuster.)

"I think I was twelve when her show first started," Smokey continued, although it was more like he was thinking out loud rather than intentionally talking to us. "I used to have the biggest crush on her."

"You want to meet her?" Vestibule asked.

Smokey's head snapped in her direction, like he had suddenly come out of a trance.

"No," he insisted, shaking his head. "I couldn't. I don't—"

"Come on," Vestibule said, ignoring his protests and grabbing his hand. A moment later, she was dragging him across the room.

Unexpectedly, Cat turned to me with something I interpreted as a sly look, although it was difficult to tell because of how her face was made up.

"It's just you and me now, big boy," she said coquettishly, taking a sultry step in my direction and leaning into my personal space. "No more hiding behind my cousin's skirt."

ISOLATION

Caught off guard by her shift in personality, I gulped. "Uh…I'm, uh…I'm not sure I know what you mean."

"Sure you do," she countered softly, lightly stroking my cheek with the back of her fingers as she looked longingly into my eyes.

I blanked on how to respond. As I mentally scrambled for words, I reached out empathically towards her. I immediately picked up on a flurry of emotions, including geniality, a slight amount of teen angst, and a strong degree of self-confidence. But the most prevalent feeling at the moment was a rising level of mirth and giddiness, which it only took me a second to interpret.

Mentally, I let out a sigh of relief, then muttered in a sarcastic monotone, "Funny."

"Ha-ha!" Cat squealed, laughing merrily. "I got you! I got you *good!* You should have seen your face."

"So," I droned, ignoring her teasing, "do you pull that little maneater act with all the guys?"

"Only the cute ones," she replied with a wink. "Come on, let's see if there's anybody worth talking to in this place."

Taking my hand, she then began leading me around.

ISOLATION

Chapter 4

Vestibule may have been the more famous member of their family, but there's no way she could have matched Cat's ability to work a room. Simply put, Cat had a talent for engaging with people. Moreover, it didn't seem to matter whether it was someone she ostensibly had anything in common with. Old or young, man or woman, world-famous or completely unknown — she found a way to relate to them all.

Even more surprising, they all seemed to take to her. Of course, the fact that she was still in full feline regalia probably served as a bit of an icebreaker (and a conversation starter), but I had a feeling that — costume or not — people would have found her enchanting. The only other person I'd come across with the same ability to charm others was my nominal fiancée, Myshtal.

As we went around the room (with me essentially following in her wake), I saw her boldly strike up conversations with everyone from rock stars to pro athletes, undeterred and unintimidated by the fact that many of those present were celebrities. She was obviously no respecter of persons, treating everyone the same, and it was more by dint of her efforts that I found myself in conversations with several luminaries whom I probably would never have approached if left to my own devices.

Eventually, however, in working our way through the party, we ended up back where we had started, so to speak: huddled up with Vestibule and Smokey.

"How'd it go?" I asked him.

"It was great," Smokey replied, plainly trying not to sound excited. "She was very nice."

"He's downplaying it," Vestibule interjected. "This silver-tongued devil sweet-talked his way into an invite to Alita's yacht party tomorrow."

"Really?" I blurted out. "That's awesome!"

"It's not as cool as it sounds," Smokey stated. "It was an invite for all of us, and we probably only got it because of Vestibule."

"Nope, that was all you," Vestibule insisted, shaking her head. "I bumped into Alita three times last week, and she never mentioned a yacht party to me once."

"Wow," muttered Cat, giving Smokey an appraising glance. "Guess you *are* a smooth talker."

"No, no, no," Smokey stressed, shaking his head. "It's not like that. I have a girlfriend."

"And you may have a new one after this weekend," Vestibule said with a smile. "Anyway, we ready to go?"

"Go?" I echoed, glancing at my watch. By my estimate, we'd only been at this particular party about an hour. "Where to?"

Vestibule smiled and then teleported us.

****

Ultimately, we ended up going to three more parties, although we spent no more than an hour at each. Like the first shindig Vestibule had teleported us to, each of the following soirees had their own respective complement of celebrities. For the remainder of the evening, however, our little quartet generally stuck together. That said, being in costume meant that we typically stood out, which had its pros and cons.

On the one hand, we were essentially welcomed at each venue, as our presence typically served to liven things up — especially Cat. Her elaborate costume was a hit with everyone and so lifelike that one guy actually went so far as to grab her tail to see if it was real. (That act resulted in Cat threatening to maul him to death, and she said it with such conviction that — had I not been reading her empathically — I would have sworn she meant it.)

On the other hand, being the center of attention also meant that people were curious about us. Vestibule, of course, was a known commodity because of her modeling career. The rest of us were essentially no-names, which was fine with me. I couldn't speak for the others, but I pretty much like my privacy, so I found myself ducking any and all questions of a personal nature, essentially sharing little more than my first name.

Eventually, however, our night on the town began to wind down. We left the last party (which was still going strong) shortly after midnight, this time departing on foot instead of teleporting. In accordance with Vestibule's instructions, the limo was waiting for us when we stepped outside.

"Whew!" Smokey exclaimed as we piled into the back of the car. "Five parties in a row…that's got to be some kind of record, even for a Friday night."

Vestibule and Cat looked at each other and started laughing.

"Well, not a *record*," Vestibule noted a moment later, "but it does get honorable mention."

Smokey merely nodded at this, silently recognizing the fact that, as a teleporter, Vestibule could pop up at a hundred parties in a single night if that's what she wanted to do.

"So what now?" Vestibule asked. "We can squeeze in a few more parties, or just call it a night."

ISOLATION

Smokey gave me an incredulous look, and I knew what he was thinking. I had teleported the two of us to the West Coast for the costume party, but our original time zone was actually a few hours ahead. In short, he was probably starting to feel run down. (I, on the other hand, had merely tweaked my physiological functions, so I could actually go indefinitely without feeling tired, although I'd pay the price later when I switched my biological systems back to normal.)

"To be honest, I'm a little hungry," Cat stated. "I didn't eat much at those parties."

Vestibule turned her attention to me and Smokey. "You guys up for that? I know a great little late-night diner."

I glanced at Smokey, not wanting to speak for him under the circumstances.

"Sounds great," he said, sounding more chipper than he probably felt.

"Awesome!" Vestibule chirped, then hit a button on a nearby panel that operated an intercom for communicating with our driver.

Fifteen minutes later, we found ourselves exiting the limo in front of a '50s-era diner with expansive windows on all sides except the back, and neon lights running along the edge of the roof. Smokey and Cat hustled inside to grab us a booth while I waited with Vestibule as she paid the driver. (Truth be told, she merely took a computer tablet that the chauffeur handed to her and tapped the screen a few times, presumably authorizing payment and a generous tip.)

As the driver pulled away and we began walking towards the diner entrance, I asked, "What do I owe you?"

"Huh?" Vestibule muttered, looking confused.

"For me and Smokey's part of the limo ride," I explained.

Vestibule laughed softly, then said, "You're sweet to offer, but you guys barely spent any time in that car."

"Still, it wasn't free."

"Actually, it was," she countered. "My modeling agency took care of the tab, so don't worry about it."

I shrugged as I opened the door for her. "If you say so."

Once inside, we spotted Smokey and Cat almost immediately, sitting across from one another in a booth next to one of the exterior windows. Upon reaching them, Vestibule slid into the seat next to Smokey, which left me sitting next to her cousin. However, I'd barely gotten comfortable before a middle-aged waitress appeared almost out of nowhere.

"Hi, what can I get you?" she asked in a dry tone. If she found anything strange about two Egyptians, a gangster, and a cheetah sitting in her section, it certainly didn't show in her face (which remained expressionless) or her voice.

"We've got a couple of newbies with us," Vestibule stated, "so how about four of the house specialty, with fries and sodas."

"You got it," the waitress said, then spent a moment getting each of our soda preferences (all of which she wrote on a small pad) before turning and walking away.

"Well, that was weird," Smokey remarked after the waitress was out of earshot.

"What?" asked Cat.

Smokey inclined his head towards the waitress. "You don't think it was odd that she didn't say anything about our costumes?"

"I think you underestimate what counts for weird out here," Vestibule countered. "This diner is a landmark, so you have people flocking here from all over the city, and some of them are coming from studio lots where they're filming movies, television series, variety shows…"

"And they're all dressed for various roles," Smokey added as she trailed off. "So she gets people coming through here all the time in zany outfits, and now she's numb to it."

"Probably," Cat noted.

"Anyway," I droned, turning to Vestibule, "what's this house specialty that you ordered?"

"Grilled cheese sandwiches," she replied. "But they taste out-of-this-world delicious."

"Guess we'll find out soon enough," I said.

Vestibule raised an eyebrow. "You sound skeptical."

I shrugged. "Grilled cheese is grilled cheese. I mean, I like it, but I can't imagine it being as dreamy as you describe."

"Care to bet on that?" Vestibule said, a sly smile forming on her lips.

"What kind of bet?" I asked.

"Just that this will be the best grilled cheese sandwich you ever had," she replied.

I drummed my fingers. "Taste is purely subjective. There's no real way to measure whether it's the best."

"I trust you to be honest and admit it if it is," Vestibule replied. "So, do we have a bet?"

"I don't know. What exactly are we betting?"

Vestibule opened her mouth to speak, but found herself cut off by Smokey.

"I'm just going to jump in right here," he announced. "No bets. You already hustled Jim once with the costume thing. I wouldn't be his friend if I let it happen on my watch."

"Hustled?" Vestibule echoed, feigning offense and laying a hand upon her chest. "*Moi?* I'm just some ditzy airhead. Pulling the wool over someone's eyes is outside my skill set."

"Hmmm," Smokey droned. "That sounds like a prelude to *me* getting hustled."

This statement was followed by a chorus of laughter from all of us. Around that time, the waitress came back with our drinks on a tray; she swiftly distributed them, along with four bamboo straws, then quickly departed.

"So," Cat intoned as she placed a straw in her drink, "what's on the agenda for tomorrow?"

Smokey and I exchanged a glance.

"Well," I began, "we really only came out for the costume party. That being the case, I guess we'll have some breakfast in the morning and then head back home."

"Ix-nay on that," Vestibule declared forcefully. "Smokey's got a yacht party to attend, in case you forgot, and the rest of us get to tag along."

"And if you're staying for breakfast," Cat tacked on, "why not just come by my house for brunch instead?"

Telepathically, I reached out to Smokey. <What do you think?>

<I'm fine with it,> he replied. <I mean, I was hoping to stay for the yacht party anyway.>

I gave a mental nod. <All right, sounds like a plan.>

ISOLATION

Telepathic communication takes place much faster than actual speech, so barely a second had gone by since Cat had asked her question.

"Brunch sounds great," Smokey said with a smile.

Cat seemed delighted by the response and appeared on the verge of saying so, but didn't get a chance.

"Excuse me," I muttered, pulling out my cell phone. "I've got a call I need to take."

Without waiting for anyone to respond, I quickly slid out of the booth and headed to the exit. Once outside, I put away my phone and strode swiftly to the back of the diner.

As I had previously noted, there were no windows at the rear of the building. In fact, there was only a single door that led out to an area currently occupied by a couple of dumpsters. After looking around to make sure no one could see me, I floated up into the air and onto the roof of the diner.

After waiting a few moments, I said, "You can turn off the stealth gear. I know you're there."

For a second, nothing happened, and then the air about five feet in front of me began to shimmer and glow. The coruscation only lasted a few seconds, and when it was gone, I found myself facing someone wearing the armor of a Caelesian royal guard.

The guard reached up with both hands and lifted their helmet, allowing me to see their face for the first time. It was a woman, with long, dark hair braided into a ponytail.

Tucking the helmet under one arm, the guard inclined her head and said, "Highness."

Her greeting was a reminder of the fact that I was actually Caelesian royalty — something I honestly seldom thought about. However, I put that out of my mind and got down to business.

"You wanted to talk?" I asked.

The guard gave me a curious look. "Pardon, Highness?"

"Well, you turned off whatever gadgetry or tech you normally use to block me from sensing you empathically," I explained, reflecting on how I had suddenly picked up on Caelesian emotions while sitting in the diner. "That means you wanted me to know you were there, which implies that you wanted to talk to me about something."

The guard seemed to reflect on this for a moment, then asked, "Where is the princess?"

"You know where she is," I shot back tersely. "You've got her tagged, outfitted with a tracker, or bugged in some other way that lets you know her exact location twenty-four hours a day."

"The question was not meant for my edification, but intended as a reminder that the princess is *your* responsibility."

"Well, Myshtal is fine — I talk to her every day. She's with my cousin Monique and having a great time."

"The welfare of the princess is not an obligation you can foist off on others."

"No one's foisting anything," I muttered angrily. "Myshtal has to develop relationships with other people. She can't be under my wing all the time — it would drive her crazy, and even she admits that."

"Her sanity is not your concern. Her well-being *is*."

"Aren't you people only like two feet away from her at any given point in time? Plus, you can track her within seconds to any spot on the planet. She doesn't need me to protect her. You guys have it covered."

The guard gave me a wary look, as if trying to decide something. Finally she said, "Some of what you surmise is correct, but much of it is completely inaccurate."

"Such as?"

"To begin with, we are not 'two feet away' from the princess at all times. Truth be told, we seldom set foot on this planet. The surveillance we undertake — which is generally limited solely to the princess's location — is done from space. The only other monitoring we do is of her vitals, which we do to get an indication of when she's injured, in danger, or in distress."

"Wait," I muttered, frowning. "So you're *not* always watching?"

"We perform random visual checks, but otherwise we remain distant. We don't watch the princess to see who she's with, listen to her conversations, or anything of that nature."

"So," I surmised, "you put actual eyes on the princess maybe every few days to make sure that she's well and all your equipment is functioning properly, but otherwise you're blind to what she says and does. What about me?"

The guard gave me a confused look. "I'm not sure I understand, Highness."

"Do you watch *me* and track me as well, or monitor me to make sure *I'm* safe?"

"No. We have no such mandates with respect to your person. Our only orders in that regard are to make sure you have not abandoned your charge."

"In other words, when you check up on the princess, you also scout around to make sure I'm close by."

"Or that you are not beyond a reasonable proximity for an extended period."

I crossed my arms. "I take it that's what initiated this conversation. I've been too far from Myshtal for too long."

"Even with your talents, it will be difficult to protect the princess if you're nowhere around."

I let out an exasperated sigh. "As I said before, Myshtal's fine, but if anything happens to her, Queen Dornoccia is free to take it out of my hide."

"Rest assured, she will," the guard declared. "And she may not stop there."

I gave the guard a concerned look. "What's *that* supposed to mean?"

"The princess is Queen Dornoccia's great-great-granddaughter and her favorite. Should anything untoward happen to her, this world would find a battleship the size of a small moon parked on its doorstep in short order."

I simply stared at her for a moment, almost certain that what she'd said was a joke — except the guard wasn't laughing.

"Okay," I finally droned after a few seconds, "this has been fun. Anything else I can do for you before you zip back up to your spaceship?"

"As a matter of fact, there is," the guard replied.

"I was actually being facetious," I declared. However, getting nothing but an expectant look in return, I groaned in exasperation and said, "Okay, fine. What is it?"

"As I mentioned," the guard began, "we can normally track the princess's location, but there is a facility you frequent regularly that our technology can't seem to penetrate."

I had a sudden intuition as to what she was referring to, but merely said, "Go on."

"Bearing in mind that this is for the safety of the princess, we have a device which, if placed inside the facility in question, will allow us to—"

"Forget it," I interjected, cutting her off. "No way am I bugging Alpha League Headquarters for you. Even if I was willing, you'd never get anything like that past Mouse."

"Mouse?" she repeated.

"He's the leader of the Alpha League, and the smartest man on the planet," I explained, leaving off the fact that he was also my mentor. "He'll find any kind of bug you plant before it even has time to send a signal."

"I see," the guard mumbled, appearing to reflect on what I'd said. "However, should you reconsider—"

"I won't," I interjected forcefully.

The guard simply stared at me for a moment, then inclined her head again. "Thank you for your time, Highness."

She put her helmet back on, after which the shimmering began once more. When it died down, the guard had vanished.

Shaking my head in nigh disbelief, I teleported back down to the ground, then went back inside and rejoined my friends.

ISOLATION

Chapter 5

In all honesty, it did turn out to be the best grilled cheese sandwich I'd ever had. (Apparently the restaurant owner had some secret process for making cheese that had been in her family for decades.) I realized then that Smokey was right: I had almost allowed Vestibule to hustle me for, perhaps, a second time. Obviously she was crafty, and I made a mental note to take no more bets with her.

In addition to the meal itself, the company was outstanding. As I already knew from earlier, both girls were fun to hang out with, and that assessment was reinforced as we ate. The conversation was witty and stimulating — almost enough to make me forget my recent tête-à-tête on the diner roof. By the time we finished our food and paid, I was actually looking forward to brunch the next day. (Or, bearing in mind the time, later the *same* day.)

After leaving the diner, the girls gave both Smokey and I quick hugs. A moment later, the two of them vanished, teleported by Vestibule. After confirming with Smokey that he was ready, I did the same for the two of us.

****

We popped up in a two-story penthouse — a spacious domicile situated atop a high-rise of luxury condos. It belonged to my cousin Avis and was generally the place where I'd been staying of late when I was on the West Coast.

The minute we appeared, Smokey stretched and yawned.

"I'm beat," he declared without preamble. "See you in the morning."

Without waiting for a reply, he began trudging up the stairs, heading for the bedroom he'd been given for his stay.

In similar fashion, I went to the guest suite that had essentially become *my* room over the course of the last few weeks, although I teleported there. It was an oversized room which, in addition to a king-sized bed and private bath, contained a sitting area, a walk-in closet, and a study/library.

I popped up in the sitting area and flopped down on a nearby couch. Pulling out my phone, I prepared to call Myshtal, my titular fiancée. However, I spent a moment debating whether to tell her about the Caelesian guard.

As a princess and favorite of Queen Dornoccia, ruler of the Caelesian Empire, Myshtal was probably used to having some sort of protective detail around. It would probably come as no surprise to her to know that she was being monitored in some way. In fact, it was possible that she already knew about it.

On the flip side, assuming that she didn't know about it, would she be upset if she found out later that I knew and hadn't told her? Our betrothal was essentially a business deal, but — that aside — Myshtal and I were pretty close. We'd gone through an ordeal together on Caeles that had created a rather tight bond between us.

Ultimately, I decided to simply play it by ear and then called Myshtal. It was definitely late (or early, depending on your point of view), but I had no doubt she would be expecting my call. (I hadn't been exaggerating

36

when I told the Caelesian guard that we talked every day.) She answered on the first ring.

"Hey!" she gushed. "How was the party?"

"Which one?" I quipped, then gave her a brief overview of the evening.

"Sounds like a lot of fun," she stated when I finished.

"And the opera?" I asked.

"It was fantastic!" she exclaimed, and I could practically see her beaming through the phone. "The costumes, the scenery... It was amazing."

"I'm glad you enjoyed it."

"I did."

"Well, please tell Monique I said 'Thanks' for taking you."

"Will do," she assured me.

Monique was my cousin, the sister of Avis. For the first couple of parties on the West Coast, Myshtal had gone with me. She had seemed to be having fun, but it was Monique who reminded me that — as a princess — Myshtal had probably gone to more parties with the rich-and-famous than she could count. She'd insisted that Myshtal needed exposure to more of Earth's culture than she could get on TV and social media, and could probably benefit from some female bonding.

Long story short, Monique convinced me to let Myshtal come spend some time with her. I was all for it — especially since, with my immediate family gone, it was just me and Myshtal living in a huge mansion. (Also, as I had explained to the Caelesian guard, I think Myshtal and I both recognized that it wasn't good for her to simply follow in my wake everywhere I went.)

All of this was flitting through my mind when I suddenly realized that Myshtal was still talking to me.

"So what do you think?" she asked.

"Huh?" I murmured, unsure what we were talking about.

"Monique said she wants me to stay a few more days," she stated. "Are you okay with that?"

"Sure," I said. "Stay as long as you want."

"Hmmm," she droned. "You agreed to that pretty quickly. Are you trying to get rid of me?"

I laughed. "Of course not. I enjoy having you around, but I do know it's important that you meet other people and have experiences that don't include me."

"All right — as long as you know you're not getting rid of me that easily," she teased. "And speaking of new experiences, we got mugged today."

"What?!" I exclaimed.

"Well, not *exactly* mugged," she clarified. "Some guy tried to snatch Monique's purse while we were having lunch at an outdoor café."

"What happened?"

"After he grabbed her purse and started running, Monique threw her fork at him. It hit him in the calf and he went sprawling, screaming and grabbing his leg. While he was pulling it out and trying to get back on his feet, she just walked over and picked her purse up from where he'd dropped it."

"Wow," I intoned. "That had to be scary."

"Yeah, but that's not even the best part," she said. "After Monique got her purse back, the mugger pulled out a knife. But before he could do anything, the blade just melted. He dropped to his knees, screaming and holding his hand, while Monique just casually walked back and asked me if I wanted dessert."

"Ha-ha!" I laughed. "That sounds just like Monique."

"Yeah, and it was super exciting. I can't remember the last time my heart pounded so fast."

Her comment triggered something in my brain, causing me to become immediately somber. I suddenly had an inkling as to why the Caelesian guard had decided to make her presence known (as well as remind me of my obligation to keep Myshtal safe). Had I been thinking, I would have let the guard know that my cousin Monique — although she relished being a housewife — was a formidable super in her own right with remarkable powers (as the would-be-mugger had found out) and fully capable of protecting Myshtal, if necessary.

That said, I decided against telling her about my rooftop rendezvous at the diner. She seemed to be having such a good time that — even if she was already aware of the guard's presence — I didn't want to be any kind of Debbie Downer.

We talked for a little longer, but bearing in mind how late it was, the conversation didn't last long. After agreeing to speak again the following day, we said goodnight and both hung up. I then went to the bed and stretched out on it for a moment before returning my bodily systems to normal. Exhaustion hit me like a sledgehammer, and I was asleep within seconds.

ISOLATION

Chapter 6

I was awakened by my phone ringing. I grabbed it off the nightstand and glanced at the time.

Six a.m., I thought. *Early.* I then noted who the caller was and bolted awake.

It was Electra. My girlfriend. *Ex*-girlfriend.

I answered with a perfunctory, "Hello."

"What do you think you're doing?" Electra asked without preamble.

"Huh?" I muttered, not sure what she was talking about.

"This picture of you and Vestibule in the Lifestyle section of the paper."

"I'm sorry," I mumbled, wiping my face with my hand. "What picture are you talking about?"

"You and Vestibule in matching outfits at some party last night."

"I guess I haven't seen it yet. It's still early out here."

"Out *here?*" she repeated. "You're still on the West Coast?"

"Yeah, why?"

There was silence for a moment, then Electra said, "I guess you must have had a really good time if you were too tired to teleport home."

I let out an exasperated sigh. "I'm actually out here visiting relatives. In case you forgot, my mother and grandparents are off in space somewhere, so I'm making an effort to get to know the few family members I have left on the planet."

"And where does Vestibule fit into all that?"

"She's just a friend, as you already know."

"So why are the gossip pages referring to you as her new beau?"

"Because they're trying to sell newspapers," I blurted out matter-of-factly. "But I don't understand why you're getting wound up about this. I didn't say anything when Dynamo escorted you to that debutante ball."

"That's different, and you know it. Dynamo and I are just friends."

"Well, you said that you and I are still friends, even though we broke up. Why couldn't *I* take you?"

"You know why," she said flatly. "If we start hanging out and doing things like a couple, then we'll fall back into the old habit of *being* a couple, and I can't have that. I need you to fix this thing with Myshtal first."

"But in the meantime, it's fine for you to date other guys."

"I'm not dating other guys!" she insisted. "But I occasionally have social events where I'm expected to have an escort."

"So it's okay for a male friend to be your date for a ball or a dance, but I can't do the same for a female friend of mine?"

"Ha!" Electra practically barked. "Are you honestly telling me that Vestibule has trouble getting dates?"

"Maybe, like you, she's only looking to hang out with someone platonically."

Electra didn't immediately respond. Of course, she wasn't close enough for me to get a read on her empathically, but I got the impression that I'd struck a nerve.

"Look," she finally said, "I get that you have female friends, and maybe you'll go to dinner with them or a

41

movie or something else like that, and it'll all be purely platonic — just like it is on my end. But not *her*, okay?"

Shaking my head in anger and frustration, I tersely stated, "I gotta go," and hung up.

I tossed my phone back onto the nightstand and lay back on the bed, trying to go back to sleep. It was a waste of time; the conversation with Electra had gotten me too worked up.

Truth be told, I didn't think she was out of line for breaking up with me. It was obviously a complicated situation, and she had handled it well. Moreover, I understood that ending our relationship was intended to motivate me to end my engagement with Myshtal.

At the same time, however, I didn't think she was being quite fair. You don't get to play the jealous girlfriend card if you aren't actually the girlfriend, and she had freely passed on the role. More to the point, she knew I wanted her back. That admittedly gave her some degree of power in the relationship, but didn't give her the right to make unreasonable demands (such as telling me who I could hang out with).

After about ten minutes of brooding on the situation, I threw in the towel on getting any more sleep and decided to start my day. Decision made, I quickly showered and went through my usual morning routine before quickly getting dressed.

It was still early, but I thought that if I hurried I could catch the sun coming up. People always talk about how beautiful sunsets are, but sunrises are just as spectacular in my book, and the roof of the penthouse provided an amazing view.

ISOLATION

Once I was ready, I phased, becoming insubstantial, and then flew up through the ceiling and onto the roof. I then became substantial again.

The top of the penthouse had been constructed as an elaborate rooftop deck, with an outdoor kitchen, a lounge area, and a pergola, among other things. It was obviously designed for entertaining, and I could easily imagine the place full of people, casually drinking wine and enjoying themselves.

Looking around now, I was surprised to find that I wasn't alone; my cousin Avis was nearby. A beautiful young woman with dark, wavy hair, she was currently dressed in a pair of black yoga pants with a matching top that left her midriff bare. She was sitting at a dining table, eating a box of assorted donuts.

"Morning," I muttered, wandering over.

"Morning, cuz," she replied as I sat down across from her. Gesturing towards the box, she said, "Have some. They're the best donuts in the city."

"Thanks," I said, then took her up on her offer, selecting a chocolate-covered donut. "Wow — they're still warm."

She nodded. "Even cold they're awesome, but they're best if you can get them fresh out of the oven. But they make the day's supply in the morning, so you have to get there early if you want them hot."

Rather than reply, I took a bite out of my donut. It was very good — so good in fact that I found myself making a yummy noise, which made my cousin laugh. I was tempted to say something, but held my tongue as I noticed the sky beginning to lighten.

We both became silent then, watching in awe as the sun came up, spreading color and light across the sky. It was a wondrous display of the beauty and majesty of nature, and in truth, it was almost spellbinding. Sadly, it only lasted a few minutes, and when the spell was finally broken I heard Avis sigh.

"No matter how many times I witness it," she stated, "I never get tired of seeing that."

I nodded. Like me, Avis had come to the roof to view the sunrise. Seeing her now, it was hard to reconcile the person in front of me with Avis's renown for being a party girl (which was only slightly less than her reputation for being a super).

"Anyway," she continued. "How was your night?"

"Pretty good," I said, then gave her a quick summary of the highlights, including the run-in with the Biolithic Colossus.

"Glad you had fun," she remarked when I was done. "Sorry about Bee-Cee, though. He's not really a bad guy — just immature in a lot of ways."

"So says the woman who trashed a Vegas suite last month."

"Okay, that was not me," she shot back defensively. "That was some people I didn't even know — friends of some friends of some friends — whom I graciously allowed into what was actually a private party. But this isn't about me, so let's not go off-topic."

"Fine," I said with a snicker. "Staying *on* topic, I was surprised the chaperones didn't jump in once the Colossus started making a scene."

"Those kids are all future teammates. They have to learn to deal with each other, including all aspects of their relationships, and dealing with a jerk at a party is a lot easier than having to do it in the field."

"So, you just let them rumble if they need to?"

She shook her head. "It rarely comes to that, and if it looked serious, someone would have stepped in."

"Okay," I droned, letting her answer percolate for a moment. "Switching gears for a second, were all the parties and premieres you've gotten me invites for just part of some recruiting effort?"

If my bluntness took her by surprise, Avis didn't show it.

Waffling a hand from side to side, she said, "Not per se. First and foremost, I wanted you to have fun and not spend a bunch of time moping around because you missed your mom and grandparents. Second, I wanted you to know that you're welcome here and will always have a place with me, no matter what. That goes for my sisters, too, because none of us want to lose you again."

I simply nodded at this. Her last statement referenced the fact that until very recently, I hadn't even known I had any cousins. They had intentionally stayed out of my life, wrongly thinking it was what my mom wanted, and we had only managed to reconnect a couple of months earlier.

"Finally," Avis continued, "if it turned out that you liked the city, the people, and everything else, I wanted you to see that the A-List is a good group. That way, if you ever decided to weigh your options, we would be top-of-mind."

"Hmmm," I droned. "So basically, from a recruiting standpoint, this wasn't the full-court press."

"Hardly," she said with a slight laugh. "Believe me, once word got out that Kid Sensation was my cousin, there were those who wanted to pull out all the stops to lure you onto the team. If you thought the movie premiere and other stuff you attended were extravagant, you should see the stuff I turned down."

I laughed and then stated, "I'll take your word for it."

"Come on," she said with a grin. "Let's go see what Henrietta is making for breakfast."

"You want me to do the honors?" I asked.

Avis seemed to consider for a moment, then said, "Sure. Go ahead."

Having gotten her okay, I teleported us to the interior of the penthouse, making us pop up in the living room. Almost immediately, we heard voices coming from the kitchen and headed there. Upon entering, we saw Smokey sitting on a stool at an island counter, chatting with Avis's cook, Henrietta.

Dressed in a black chef coat and sporting a toque blanche, Henrietta spied us the second we entered her domain. She was a young woman, maybe thirty years old, with features that would probably be described as handsome rather than pretty, and a smile that could light up a room.

"Good morning, Jim," Henrietta said while whisking something around in a bowl. "Miss Avis."

I returned the greeting and got her thousand-watt-smile in return, which almost made me feel giddy.

"I told you before, Henrietta, it's just 'Avis,'" my cousin admonished as she tossed the box of donuts onto the counter. "You make me feel like an old lady."

"Yes, Miss Avis," Henrietta replied, causing my cousin to shake her head in dismay, while Smokey and I snickered.

"And feel free to take that silly hat off," Avis added. "You make me feel like I'm on a cooking show."

"Yes, Miss Avis," Henrietta said, although I noticed she made no effort to remove her toque blanche, which again, Smokey and I found hilarious.

"So," Avis droned a few moments later, "I see you met Smokescreen."

Henrietta nodded. "Yes, he was kind enough to come introduce himself."

"Well," Smokey commented, "I didn't want her to suddenly see a stranger in here and go into panic mode."

"I wasn't concerned," Henrietta assured him. "Any man who makes his way into this place uninvited is going to have a very bad day."

As she finished speaking, she exchanged a knowing glance with Avis. I got the impression there was a story there, which I'd have to tease out of my cousin later.

"Anyway," Henrietta continued, "breakfast is omelets, and I'm taking orders."

At that juncture, I noticed for the first time that there were numerous bowls on the counter near the cooktop where she was standing. From what I could see, each contained different items: grated cheese, chopped peppers, diced tomatoes, and so on.

"I'll go first," Avis said. "Just cheese in mine, please. I'm going to have enough to do at the gym just working off the donuts I had earlier."

She interlocked her fingers and lifted her arms above her head as she spoke, stretching and bending slightly from side to side. Noticing Smokey looking at her with what seemed like more than casual interest, I telekinetically gave him a thump behind the ear. Wincing, he turned to me with a perplexed look.

Opening up a telepathic channel, I said, <Dude, tell me you were not ogling my cousin.>

<I wasn't ogling *any*body!> he insisted.

<Then why were your eyes practically popping out of your skull? And is that drool on your chin?>

<Funny,> he replied sarcastically. <But since you just *have* to know, she's got, like, washboard abs. I was going to ask her about her workout routine.>

<I bet,> I replied flatly. <Atalanta's going to love hearing about this.>

Mentally, Smokey seemed to gulp. Atalanta was another teen super and someone Smokey had started seeing fairly recently, after breaking up with his longtime girlfriend Sarah. Hailing from a small but wealthy island nation called Argo, Atalanta was a member of a superhero team known as the Argonauts and was incredibly powerful.

<I was looking at her abs,> Smokey finally declared defiantly. <That's my story, and I'm sticking to it.>

We both kind of chortled at that, and as I broke the telepathic connection, I realized that Avis was speaking to us.

"I'm sorry," I muttered. "What were you saying?"

"I was asking what was on your agenda for today," Avis said. "Are you heading back home soon?"

"Actually, Vestibule and her cousin invited us to brunch," I answered, "which means we should probably eat something light as well."

"Speak for yourself," Smokey declared. "I woke up early to finish a paper, and I'm famished."

"A paper?" Avis repeated. "What kind of paper?"

"History," Smokey replied. "Jim and I—"

"Oh, snap!" I yelled, and then teleported.

ISOLATION

Chapter 7

My visit to my grandmother's homeworld of Caeles had ultimately had numerous effects on my life. For instance — in addition to getting saddled with a fiancée — my escapades there had also involved me crossing a temporal rogue, who at one point stranded me in the planet's far past. I had managed to get back to the present, but not before encountering a future version of myself.

With respect to Earth, my time off-planet meant that I had necessarily missed time in school. Thus, when I came back, I was behind academically. However, rather than have me try to play catch-up, my mentor Mouse just decided to take over my schooling.

Likewise, Smokey missed significant class time during that same period (the full story of which I still hadn't gotten yet). As with me, Mouse decided to step in. Long story short, we were both essentially being home-schooled.

On the day of the costume party, we'd actually had a history paper due. Mouse, showing more leniency than normal, had extended the deadline until the following morning. Sadly, I had pretty much put it out of my mind until Smokey mentioned it. Now, of course, I had to scramble.

After teleporting from the kitchen, I popped up in my room in the penthouse. Noting that I only had about ten minutes left before my work was due, I dashed into the study at super speed, frantically searching until I came across what I was looking for: a notepad and pen.

I had, on at least one prior occasion, tried to bang out a paper at the last minute by typing at super speed. All I succeeded in doing was destroying a keyboard that wasn't meant to take the kind of abuse that comes from fingers pounding away at Mach speed. Mouse had offered to provide me with a specially designed keyboard that could withstand that kind of treatment, but I hadn't taken him up on it yet.

In short, I had to write the paper by hand. Unfortunately, it took longer than expected, for various reasons. (For example, I was actually writing faster than it took the ink to dry, which meant that I inadvertently smeared it a couple of times and had to start over.) Eventually, however, I got it done. Then, after switching back to normal speed, I tore the completed pages off the notepad and teleported to Alpha League HQ.

****

I popped up in Mouse's lab, a spacious room at HQ populated by numerous large worktables, incredibly sophisticated computer equipment, and monitors showing a continuous stream of data.

Mouse himself was nearby, fiddling with a piece of equipment on one of the worktables. Contrary to what his name implied, he was a big guy — roughly six-three in height and muscular, but not oversized like a lot of bodybuilders seem to be. Dressed in jeans and a dark thermal shirt, he merely glanced in my direction after I appeared.

"Well, this is a pleasant surprise," he remarked as he continued working.

Striding over quickly, I laid my disorderly sheaf of papers on the table next to him, saying, "There you go."

Mouse stopped what he was doing and picked up the pages. For a second, he ran his finger along the perforated top of the pages, where I had torn them out of the notepad. His disapproval was obvious, but he didn't make a comment. He then began flipping through what I'd written.

"This was supposed to be typed," he noted as he perused my work.

"Was it?" I asked with raised eyebrows. "I don't think I got that memo."

"Ten points off," Mouse said, tossing the pages back onto the table.

"Oh, come on," I groaned. "You're choosing form over substance. That's a great paper, written or typed."

"There are the seeds of some great thoughts in it, but from what I can tell they never get fully developed. Instead you just pile on a bunch of facts about the requisite time period, which results in you giving me a history lesson rather than any original thought, which is what I was after."

"Man, you are hardcore. Anywhere else, that's an 'A' paper."

"Done with 'B' effort," he added. "You wrote this, what — maybe five minutes ago?"

I just looked at him for a moment, then sighed. "More like two."

"That's sad coming from someone with your abilities," he noted. "And I'm not talking about your powers."

I simply nodded and looked down at the floor. I loved Mouse; he was like the big brother I'd never had, and his disapproval always stung.

"Fine," I finally muttered. "I'll do better."

"I know you will," Mouse stated. "Because next time, it'll be *twenty* points off."

We both laughed at that, and I found myself thankful, as always, that Mouse had a great sense of humor.

"So," he droned. "The party?"

"Lots of fun," I replied, without going into detail. "Thanks for suggesting I bring Smokey."

Mouse shrugged. "You needed a wingman; he needed to get out of HQ... Seemed like a good fit. I'm sure you would have thought of it yourself, but I understand you had other things on your mind."

His comment actually downplayed the facts. With my immediate family leaving Earth, my girlfriend breaking up with me, and a titular fiancée to look after, having "things on my mind" didn't seem an adequate description. I was so busy with my own issues that I tended to overlook the fact that, for reasons of his own, Smokey had moved into Alpha League HQ.

His presence there wasn't an imposition — all members of the League's teen affiliate had quarters at HQ — but it *was* uncommon. That alone should have made me more attuned to the fact that my best friend had some things he was dealing with. I knew some of what was on his mind, but we hadn't really talked in a while, and it had taken Mouse suggesting that Smokey accompany me to the West Coast to make me realize that I hadn't "been there" (in terms of being a friend) as much as I could have.

"So," Mouse continued, "does your presence here mean you guys are back?"

I shook my head. "No. We were planning to come back today, but got invited to a couple of social events, so we're prolonging the trip." Then I hastily added, "Unless you need me here for something."

"No," Mouse confirmed. "I mean, I've got some stuff going on, as always, but nothing you're needed for."

ISOLATION

"Okay, great," I said. "But there's one more thing before I head back: have you heard fr—"

"No, I haven't heard from Rune," Mouse declared, cutting me off. It was the question I always asked these days, so he was ready for it. "As usual, the minute he makes contact, I'll let you know."

I merely nodded, not saying anything. Rune was another member of the Alpha League and was generally considered to be some type of magician. In truth, he was one of an incredibly powerful, nigh-omnipotent group of beings known as Incarnates. I had recently helped them with a particularly difficult dilemma (which had required me traveling to a place beyond space and time), following which Rune had shocked me by stating that *I* was also an Incarnate. However, after we returned to Earth, Rune had performed some analyses and examinations that had caused him to reassess his original opinion.

"I don't know what you are," he'd ultimately admitted.

In brief, I apparently displayed *some* of the attributes of an Incarnate, but not others. In the end, Rune had left, saying that he needed to research a few more things and that he'd be in touch. That had been weeks earlier — before my family had left the planet — and I hadn't heard from him since.

"Anyway," Mouse continued, bringing me back to myself, "I wouldn't worry too much about it. If Rune needs to speak to you when he gets back, he'll find you."

"Of that, I have no doubt," I replied.

ISOLATION

Chapter 8

I stayed and chatted with Mouse for another fifteen minutes or so, then teleported back to my cousin's penthouse. I popped up in the kitchen; no one was there but Henrietta, who was busy cleaning up. Upon seeing me, she seemed startled for a moment. By this time, she knew that I was a teleporter, but — unsurprisingly — hadn't fully adjusted to my comings and goings in that regard. On my part, I had initially been nervous about displaying my powers around her, but Avis had vouched for her, saying that Henrietta would keep anything she saw or heard confidential.

Quickly recovering from her initial surprise, Henrietta stated that there was an omelet for me in the microwave. She also told me, without being asked, that Smokey had gone with Avis to work out.

Thanking her, I set the microwave for thirty seconds and then grabbed a fork from a nearby drawer. When the microwave finished, I told Henrietta that I was going to the roof to eat. Waiting until she acknowledged my statement with a nod, I then teleported.

Reappearing on the roof, I took a seat at the table where Avis and I had eaten donuts earlier. It was a beautiful morning, and I took a moment to simply bask in it. It seemed that I rarely got a moment to myself anymore, so simply having a little alone time was refreshing, in a sense. Glancing up, I thought it might even be a great day to go flying later.

Turning my attention to my omelet, I took a bite. Like everything Henrietta made, it was delicious — even reheated. I quickly wolfed it down. Then, trying to avoid surprising Henrietta again, I turned myself, the plate, and the fork invisible before teleporting back to the kitchen.

Henrietta was peering into the refrigerator when I popped up, probably trying to decide what to prepare for lunch or dinner. I quietly placed my plate and fork in the sink, then made them visible again. It felt a little like playing ding dong ditch — Henrietta had just cleaned the kitchen, after all, and here I was placing dirty dishes in the sink — but I got the feeling she'd prefer that to me simply appearing out of nowhere and giving her a mild heart attack.

Satisfied that I wasn't doing anything wrong, I phased and then flew up through the ceiling, past the rooftop deck, and out into the open sky.

****

I spent perhaps an hour just soaring through the air, albeit invisible and phased. There was something about flying that always lifted my spirits (not that I was depressed or anything before). Simply put, it just gave me the feeling of being completely unfettered, like I'd left all my problems, worries, and concerns on the ground.

Eventually, however, I had to head back. It was getting close to the time when Smokey and I would have to go to brunch, and I think we both preferred not to be late. With that in mind, I began flying back to the penthouse.

I was probably a few blocks away when my cell phone rang. Deciding against answering it in mid-flight, I teleported the remaining distance to my cousin's place, popping up on the roof. I immediately became visible and substantial, then pulled out my phone. Much to my surprise, it was Electra.

Remembering how our last conversation ended, I hesitated a moment, then answered.

"Hello?" I said, almost cautiously.

"Hey," she responded.

I was expecting more, since *she* had called *me*, but she didn't immediately say anything. It occurred to me then that she was working up to something, so I just held the phone, not saying anything.

Finally she let out a sigh and said, "I'm sorry about this morning. I wasn't being completely fair to you."

"It's okay," I replied. "I mean, it's a crazy situation that we're in. There aren't any rules for something like this."

"No kidding. I had a tough time explaining it to my dad."

"What?!" I exclaimed, not quite believing what I'd heard. "You told your dad? Why would you do that?"

"Because he's my dad," she said matter-of-factly. "I mean, he's never been a part of my life before, but now that he is, I want us to be close. That means sharing things."

"Yeah, but you don't tell him that your boyfriend has a fiancée. Nothing good can ever come of that."

"*Ex*-boyfriend," she clarified.

"Fine…*ex*-boyfriend," I grumbled. "So what — you guys had some kind of bonding session, and you just opened up and told him everything?"

"Okay, first of all, stop making it sound trite. It wasn't like that. He's actually been asking me for a while if I'm dating anyone, and I've been ducking the question."

"What do you mean, he's been asking for a while? He's only been out like a month."

There was dead silence on the other end of the line, and I immediately realized that I had hit a raw nerve. Electra's father — a former cape named Vir — had spent most of the last sixteen years in prison, albeit wrongfully. However, he had recently been paroled and was staying with Electra and her aunt. (One thing I had never told my ex, however, was that her father's release was my doing; I had used up a special favor to get him out.)

"Let me clarify," Electra finally stated. "He's been asking since he was released. Basically, I admitted that there was a guy I liked, but the situation was complicated."

"That sounds perfect," I stressed. "Why couldn't you leave it like that?"

"Because I don't want our relationship to start off with me keeping stuff from him."

"I get that, but you don't tell him that your boyfriend is engaged. That's 'Dating One-oh-One.'"

"You're not my boyfriend, and we're not dating," she shot back.

"In that case, it's '*Post*-Dating One-oh-One,'" I countered. "However you style it, it's not the kind of thing a girl tells her dad — not if she ever expects him to like the guy. Typically, fathers throttle guys over stuff like this."

"Well, thankfully, I don't have a typical dad."

"What's that mean — he's going to garrote me instead?"

"Stop it," she muttered, giggling. "Actually, he wants to meet you."

"Huh?" I muttered.

"He wants to meet you," she repeated. "It was actually the reason I was calling this morning, but the conversation kind of went off the rails, and you hung up before we could get back on track."

I frowned. "But your father's *already* met me."

"Well, he briefly met a guy named Jim, but didn't know that he was my boyfriend — at the time, that is."

"Lucky me," I mumbled.

"Anyway," she continued, "how'd you like to come to dinner tonight?"

"If you're talking about me and you, absolutely. If you're talking about a meal with your dad, absolutely *not*."

"What's the problem?"

"Have you not been a part of this conversation? It's a very bad idea."

"Come on, Jim. You can't be serious."

"I can and I am."

"Are you honestly saying that you don't want to have dinner with my father?"

"Pretty much."

"Why not?"

"Because it's going to be the most awkward and uncomfortable dinner ever. Why can't you see that?"

Electra didn't respond right away. There was just this stony silence coming from her end of the line that felt so complete that I had to check to make sure we hadn't been disconnected.

"Don't you want to get back together?" she finally asked in a soft voice.

My brow crinkled. "Is that an ultimatum?"

"Of course not," she spat out. "You know I'd never do that. What I'm trying to say is that, if we ever manage to become a couple again, you and my father will eventually have to become acquainted. But at that point, you'll forever be the guy who was afraid to have dinner with him. Do you really want that albatross around your neck?"

"I'm not afraid to have dinner," I insisted.

"Then what is it?"

I reflected for a moment, then let out a deep breath and said, "Basically, the last few weeks have been almost drama-free for me. More to the point, I've actually enjoyed it to a large extent. Somehow, though, I can't shake the feeling that dinner with your dad will be *major* drama."

"How about this then?" she countered. "If it starts getting awkward, you're free to leave. Just stand up and walk out, zip to the door, or just teleport. How does that sound?"

"'Step into my parlor, said the spider to the fly.'"

"Excuse me?" she said.

"Nothing," I griped. "Why is this such a big deal to you?"

There was silence for a second, then Electra seemed to come to a decision.

"Even though we broke up, I still care about you," she admitted. "A lot. I just want the two most important guys in my life to like each other. That's all."

Of course, she wasn't close enough for me to read emotionally, but there was a power and sentiment to her words and tone that almost anyone could have picked up on. And with that, I realized that I wasn't the only one thinking dinner would be uncomfortable; it would be awkward for Electra as well, but she was willing to deal with it, because ultimately, she was doing it for *us*. She was doing it so that — if and when we reconciled — a disapproving father wouldn't be an additional hurdle we'd have to clear.

ISOLATION

Suddenly I felt almost ashamed. I had only been thinking about her dad's request in terms of what it meant to me — not what it might mean to her or how it could possibly affect things down the road. Mentally, I'd had blinders on that kept me from seeing the big picture.

"Okay," I announced, decision finally made. "What time?"

ISOLATION

Chapter 9

Electra was practically euphoric when I finally agreed to dinner. We spent a few more minutes talking as she gave me the details, and for a brief span it was almost like we were a couple again: laughing, joking, excitedly discussing our plans for later... In short, I hated to get off the phone with her, but we both had other things we needed to do.

Afterwards, I teleported into the penthouse, appearing in the living room. Smokey was nearby, sitting on a couch and watching television.

"There you are," he said, grabbing the remote and muting the TV. "I'm guessing you had to scramble and write your paper at the last minute."

"Something like that," I confessed, not wanting to admit having to deliver it personally since it was handwritten.

Smokey laughed at that, easily reading between the lines. "What did Mouse say about it?"

"Ten points off. Twenty next time, although I wasn't sure if he was joking."

Smokey chuckled again. "See, if you had typed it on your laptop, like me, you could have just emailed it in."

"I'll keep that in mind for next time," I said. "So, how was the workout? I'm sure you got to ogle my cousin to your heart's delight."

Smokey shook his head emphatically. "First of all, your cousin can, like, bench press a building, so she and I are on way different levels in terms of routine. Basically, she gave me a few pointers, then dropped me off at some private gym where she got them to give me guest privileges, while she went somewhere else."

"Probably A-List HQ," I suggested. "Like the Alpha League, they have specialized workout equipment for people who can deadlift a battleship."

"That's probably right," Smokey concurred. "Anyway, she scooped me up a short time later and dropped me back off here. She then said she had some stuff to do and took off, and I took a quick shower to get ready for brunch."

I spent a moment debating whether I should shower again as well. However, I'd only been flying (and had been phased most of the time, only occasionally becoming substantial to feel the wind cascade over me), so I hadn't worked up a sweat. Bearing that in mind, I assumed I was passable with respect to brunch.

"That reminds me," I said. "I don't think either of us knows where we're going."

"Knowing the destination would be helpful," Smokey quipped as I pulled out my phone and called Vestibule.

I wasn't sure if she was expecting my call, but she answered on the first ring. Putting her on speakerphone, I explained that we lacked Cat's address, which caused her to snicker.

"Don't worry about it," she assured me. "We're coming to *you*, so be ready in ten. And pack your swimming trunks."

With that, she hung up.

"Well," Smokey droned. "Problem solved."

"Apparently," I agreed, then noticed something on an end table next to the sofa. Pointing, I asked, "What's that?"

"Oh," Smokey said, grabbing the item — a section of newspaper — from the table. "Check this out."

ISOLATION

He opened up the paper and I realized that it was some sort of gossip segment. There were pictures of celebrities on almost every page, including a few we'd spoken to the night before. And then I saw it: a full-color photo of Vestibule, me, Cat, and Smokey, all in our costumes.

Obviously, it had been taken the night before — most likely at one of the parties we attended. I'd known there were photographers at each event — it was par for the course with respect to those types of parties — but it hadn't really occurred to me that anyone would find us newsworthy.

"So what do you think?" Smokey asked.

"It looks like someone is doing a remake of *The Wizard of Oz*, but never read the book," I quipped.

Smokey laughed. "I thought something along those lines myself. At least whoever wrote the caption was more tactful."

He pointed to the passage below the picture, which read:

Superhero/model Vestibule and friends hitting the town.

"Where'd you get this?" I inquired.

"Someone left it at the gym," he answered. "The trainer working with me said it was okay to take it."

I raised an eyebrow. "Trainer?"

Smokey shrugged. "Avis told them I was a friend and to take good care of me. Almost everybody in that place had a personal trainer — probably included in the membership fee."

"Well, at least now I know what Electra was talking about," I said as I turned my attention back to the photo.

Presumably this was the pic she had been referring to during that first phone call. Looking at it now, with Vestibule and me in matching costumes, I could see how someone might get the idea that we were a couple.

"You spoke to Electra?" Smokey asked.

"Yeah," I confirmed, then recounted our initial conversation. When I was done, he looked at me slightly askance.

"Are you really saying you don't understand why she was upset?" he asked.

"She wasn't being fair," I insisted, "and even she admits that."

"All's fair in love and war," Smokey countered. "But just think about it from her point of view for a second. Vestibule made no secret of wanting to date you, and on at least two occasions she publicly shoved her tongue down your throat. Then, just a few weeks after Electra breaks up with you, you're painting the town red with her romantic rival. To the rest of the world, it looks like Vestibule stole you from her."

"Okay, that's ridiculous," I stated firmly. "Nobody stole anything, and Vestibule and I are just friends."

"Would it sound ridiculous to you if people started saying that Dynamo stole Electra from you?"

"What?" I almost screeched. "Is that what people are saying?"

"Well, it would be easy to see how they'd get that idea, right? He's big, strong, handsome…universally hailed as one of the top teen supers on the planet. He's known Electra longer, always thought she was pretty, and — now that she broke up with *you* — he's always on her arm."

"So people think he stole her from me?" I demanded.

"Would it bother you if they did?"

I shook my head in angry disbelief. What Smokey was suggesting was absurd, and deep down inside, I knew it. Still, I didn't like it, mostly because of what it implied about me — that I was a terrible boyfriend in some way. It had the potential to cast me, unfairly, in a bad light.

"Okay," I finally muttered in acquiescence. "You made your point. Even though she admits that she was being unfair, I can understand why she would feel the way she did."

"Cool," Smokey said, smiling. "You can thank me later for making you see reason and helping you understand women."

"Speaking of later," I intoned, "you'll be on your own tonight." I then enlightened him as to my second conversation with Electra and my upcoming dinner plans.

"Okay," he said when I'd finished, "awkward is a mild way of putting it."

"I could use a wingman," I stated hopefully.

Smokey looked at me with something akin to shock. "Not on your life."

"Fine," I muttered in faux disgust, making him snicker. "Anyway, you need to think about what you want to do after the yacht party. I can teleport you back home when I leave for dinner, or you can hang out here and I'll come back when we're done."

"To tell you the truth, I hadn't given it much thought," he admitted. "Things seem to happen pretty fast out here — like getting the invite from Alita. Is it okay if I just play it by ear?"

"No big deal to me," I declared.

"By the way," he said, "you were right about Vestibule. She's pretty cool."

ISOLATION

I raised an eyebrow. "Oh, so after she hooks you up with your childhood crush Alita, she earns enough brownie points for you to reassess your opinion."

"There's no hooking up," Smokey insisted. "Alita and I just had a friendly conversation and she turned out to be very personable. Plus, I still think Vestibule is somehow behind this invite."

"So does that mean you told Atalanta about it?" I asked, grinning.

Now it was Smokey's turn to frown, although he recovered quickly.

"If you must know," he said after a moment, "Atalanta isn't the jealous type. And yes, I did tell her that we were going to brunch and a yacht party."

I gave him a sly look. "Did you tell her it was me, you, and two girls?"

"I told her you and I were going with a couple of friends," Smokey stated.

"Sounds disingenuous," I remarked, shaking my head. "When Atalanta finds out, she's gonna rip your arms out of their sockets."

"She's welcome to try," Smokey said, chuckling, "but you can't tear apart smoke."

I laughed as well at that. Smokey's comment was a reference to his ability to become completely vaporous. We were still chortling when Vestibule called a few seconds later, saying that they were parked outside.

I told her that we'd be right down, and then we scrambled for a moment, getting together our swimming trunks and something to put them in. Ultimately, we ended up stuffing our swim gear into a small duffel bag I'd gotten during one of the earlier West Coast events I'd attended. It had originally been a gift bag, full of high-end swag. As it turned out, however, I'd mistakenly been given a goody bag meant for adults instead of one for minors, which had resulted in Avis going through it and removing various items, such as a gold-plated vaping kit, a bottle of expensive vodka, etcetera. By the time she was done, the bag was practically empty, and I'd left it in the closet until now.

Once Smokey and I were ready, I grabbed the duffel bag and teleported us to the lobby of the building, then we dashed outside.

ISOLATION

Chapter 10

The girls picked us up in a car whose make and model I'd never seen or heard of before. It was a sleek, black convertible, with a posh interior that included hand-stitched leather, wood trim, and a million other luxury features. It was obviously a high-end vehicle and came, I was certain, with a monstrous price tag.

Wearing a gray sundress, Cat was driving, and I found myself in the front passenger seat next to her while Smokey sat in back next to Vestibule, who wore a pair of navy blue gym shorts and a white tie-front shirt.

As we pulled away from my cousin's building, I couldn't stop myself from turning to Cat and saying, "Nice car."

"It's a gift from my dad," she explained. "My parents are divorced and he works a lot, so I don't get to see him much. This is his way of trying to buy my love." Then, placing the back of her hand up to her mouth, she leaned towards me and whispered conspiratorially, "It's working."

I laughed, as did Smokey and Vestibule, who had apparently overheard us speaking. I really enjoyed Cat's sense of humor, and was suddenly glad that she had invited us to brunch.

"So, is this like an exclusive model?" Smokey asked.

Cat nodded. "Yeah. It's European — from a special division within one of the big car manufacturers over there. They only make about a dozen or so every year, so it's rare."

Smokey was obviously impressed. "And it's *your* car?"

ISOLATION

"Yeah," Cat replied over her shoulder, "but it's just a car. I'd take time with my dad over this any day of the week." Then she seemed to reconsider and added, "Well, maybe not the *weekend...*"

We all laughed again.

****

The drive to Cat's house was fun. With the sun shining brightly and the top down on the convertible, the feel of the wind on my face was almost like flying. As natives of the West Coast, Cat and Vestibule were astute enough to be wearing sunglasses, but Smokey and I had failed to exhibit any foresight in that regard. Fortunately, Cat had an extra pair in a cubby at the front of the car; I passed them along to Smokey and then simply rotated my vision through the light spectrum until I could see without being bothered by any type of glare.

Smokey had brought the newspaper section with us, and the four of us spent the bulk of the drive laughing and talking about the various photos (including our own). In short, it was a bit of a continuation of our time at the diner.

Getting caught up in the conversation, I didn't pay close attention to where we were going. Eventually, however, I noticed that the road we were on started to slope up.

"So where exactly are we going?" I asked Cat.

"The Hills," she responded. "It's where my mom and I live."

Eyebrows raised in surprise, I subtly glanced back at Smokey and noted that his expression mirrored mine. "The Hills" was a colloquial term for an area of the city where many of the rich and famous resided. Bearing in mind the kind of car Cat drove, the fact that she lived in an exclusive zip code really shouldn't have been a news flash. Plainly speaking, she was so down-to-earth that I simply had trouble envisioning her as a blue blood. (Of course, now that I'd gotten to know her, the same could be said of Vestibule.)

A short time later, after driving up a few winding roads, we came to a stop in front of the gated entrance to an expansive residence. I didn't see Cat do anything, but without warning the gate began to swing open. A minute later, we were pulling into a circular driveway in front of a mansion that I guessed was about seven thousand square feet in size.

"Come on," said Cat as she put the car in park and got out.

The rest of us exited as instructed (with me carrying the duffel bag), then followed as she stepped lithely up a set of stone stairs to a magnificent pair of double doors; she tried the handle of one and then slipped inside as the door swung open.

Turning towards us, Cat gestured for us to enter, saying, "Welcome to my humble abode."

As we went inside, we found ourselves in a two-story foyer that opened up into a majestic great room which contained, among other things, a two-sided fireplace, posh furnishings, and a regal winding staircase that led up to the second floor.

"Follow me," Cat said as she began walking towards what appeared to be the rear of the house. "Brunch should be set up out back by the pool."

We quickly fell into step behind her, striding down a hallway that was obviously floored with expensive hardwood. As we sauntered through the house, Cat played the role of tour guide.

"That's the library over there," she said, pointing to a doorless room full of built-in shelves crammed with hardback books. "This is the music room, where I'm forced at gunpoint to practice piano for thirty minutes a day. And over here…"

Although I didn't do it intentionally, I found myself tuning Cat out. In essence, walking through her house reminded me of the mansion of Alpha Prime — the world's greatest superhero (and my father). Of course, my father's place was absolutely palatial, and dwarfed almost any house that didn't have a footprint that could be measured in acres.

Reflecting on my father's house, of course, brought my father himself to mind, and I suddenly became cognizant of the fact that I hadn't spoken to him lately. However, ours was a complicated relationship — in fact, until fairly recently, there had been no relationship to speak of — but it was something we both continued to work on. Recalling that my mother had made me promise to keep in regular contact with Alpha Prime before she left, I made a mental note to call him later.

"And here we are," Cat announced, bringing me back to myself.

We had just come through a sliding glass door and were now on a covered patio that contained an eye-catching outdoor living room, as well as an elongated dining table currently covered with what I was assumed was brunch: Belgian waffles, breakfast sausages, croissants, an assortment of cheeses, strawberries, and more.

Just off the patio was a good-sized pool with an adjoining, oversized hot tub. Lining one side of the pool were a number of outdoor chaise lounge chairs, as well as a canopied daybed; on the far side of the pool was a small structure that I took to be a pool house.

"Well, it looks like the food's here," Cat noted, waving a hand towards the dining table. "Feel free to help yourselves."

"Thanks," said Smokey. "I think I…"

He trailed off as the sound of water splashing drew everyone's attention. It appeared to be coming from the pool, and I — along with everyone else — automatically turned in that direction.

There was a woman in the pool. Apparently she'd been there since we'd stepped onto the patio, quietly swimming beneath the surface and had only just come up for air. At present, she was turned to the side so that only her profile was visible, but it was enough for me to see that she was blonde, well-tanned, and had flawless skin.

Unexpectedly, the woman snapped her head back, flipping her long blonde hair behind her and at the same time sending water cascading out in an arc. Then, eyes closed, she casually ran a hand from her hairline to the back of her head, essentially squeezing any excess water from her hair. She brought her hand to rest on the back of her neck and gently massaged the area for a few seconds, letting her head loll to the side in a way that was almost self-indulgent. Then, opening her eyes, she seemed to notice us for the first time. She turned in our direction, and that's when I got my first real look at her, and found myself staring.

She was breathtakingly beautiful, with a face that could have graced any magazine cover. Truth be told, the same could probably be said of innumerable women on the West Coast. (In fact, I had seen quite a few of them at the parties we'd attended the night before.) However, there was something about the woman in the pool, a girl-with-something-extra quality that I couldn't quite put my finger on. Moreover, without even reaching out empathically, I could sense that Smokey felt the same.

Giving us a gorgeous smile, the woman began heading our way, gracefully exiting the pool via a set of stone steps that led down into the water. The effect as she left the pool, however, was more like the mythological Venus rising from the ocean. (Adding to that impression was the bikini she wore, the top of which was designed to look like two seashells.) As she came clear of the water, I couldn't help but notice that her figure was as flawless as her face.

"Hi, baby," the woman said as she grabbed a sarong with a floral print from one of the lounge chairs and wrapped it around her waist. "Vestibule."

Cat and Vestibule greeted the woman with "Hey, Mom" and "Hi, Aunt Capri," respectively. Cat then gestured towards me and Smokey and introduced us to the woman, whom we already understood to be her mother.

"Nice to meet you, ma'am," Smokey said, and I expressed a similar sentiment.

"Call me Capri," she insisted. "Not 'Mrs.,' not 'Miss,' not 'ma'am,' — just Capri. Got it?"

"Yes, ma—" I began, then caught myself as Capri gave me a sideways look. "I mean, yes, Capri."

Smokey made a similar capitulation, and Capri seemed satisfied. She then looked the two of us up and down before turning to Cat and saying, "Well, which one is the boy you like?"

ISOLATION

The bluntness of her question took me completely by surprise, and I picked up on similar emotions from Smokey. To her credit, Cat never missed a beat.

"I didn't say I liked him," Cat immediately replied. "I said he was cute. There's a difference. A cute guy can be a jerk, in which case I probably *wouldn't* like him. But to answer your question, it's Jim."

Capri looked at me again as if weighing some decision, then turned back to her daughter. "So, is he a nice guy or not?"

"Yes, he's nice, Mom," Cat admitted, "but he's on the rebound, so there's a question mark as to whether he's worth pursuing anything with."

I fought to keep my face impassive, but telepathically I reached out to Vestibule.

<Are you kidding me?!> I mentally roared. <Is there anything you *didn't* tell her about me? Social Security number, perhaps? Mother's maiden name?>

<How do you know it was me?> she retorted. <It could have been Smokey.>

<Except I know Smokey, and he'd never do anything like that.>

<So what — is that like some kind of guy code?>

<Don't try to change the subject.>

<All right, I admit it,> she muttered in exasperation. <I told her. But you have to understand, she's my cousin. If she's interested in a guy and I know something about him, I have to speak up.>

Mentally, I shook my head in despondence and then broke the connection.

"Anyway, we'll just be over here," Capri stated, heading for the outdoor living room.

"Wonderful," Cat said flatly. "When do the rest of the gay divorcees arrive?"

"Any minute," her mother noted with a smile.

Cat looked as though she had additional commentary, but before she could say anything, a woman wearing a maid's uniform stepped onto the patio, gesturing to get Capri's attention.

"Please excuse me," Capri said before heading towards the maid, who began whispering something in her ear as soon as she was close enough. A moment later, the two of them hurried back into the house.

I waited a few seconds until I was certain Capri was out of earshot, then turned to Cat and said, "So, do you and your mother always speak like that?"

Cat frowned. "Like what?"

"Talk about people who are right in front of you as if they aren't in the room."

"Unfortunately, they do," Vestibule interjected, laughing.

"She's right to an extent," Cat admitted. "Mom lacks subtlety and has no filter. I've learned to respond bluntly as a coping mechanism. It was either that, or be perpetually embarrassed by the things she says."

"I can't imagine what that must be like," Smokey commented.

"You get used to it," Cat said with a shrug. "Come on."

She then began walking towards the pool, with the rest of us following her. A few seconds later, she stopped in front of a couple of the lounge chairs.

"Okay, you guys can go change in the pool house," she said, pointing to the building I'd noticed earlier.

"What about you two?" Smokey asked.

ISOLATION

In response, Cat reached down with both hands and began lifting the sundress over her head. At the same time, Vestibule began untying the front of her shirt.

Eyes wide in surprise, I shared a glance with Smokey and realized that he — like me — was wondering if we'd somehow wandered into a scenario we'd only heard about in movies. A moment later, I found myself relaxing as I realized that Cat had a bikini on under her dress. Likewise, Vestibule was wearing swim gear under her clothes.

"Why are you two just standing there?" Cat asked as she tossed her dress on the lounge chair. "Go change — unless you want to be pushed into the pool with your clothes and shoes on."

"Hmmm," Smokey droned. "Seems your mother isn't the only one lacking subtlety."

We all laughed at that, and then Smokey and I headed to the pool house.

ISOLATION

Chapter 11

The pool house was actually more like a guest suite, with a kitchen, bedroom, bathroom, etcetera. Smokey and I quickly changed into our swimming trunks, and then hurried back out to the pool.

We spent roughly the next hour engaged in various forms of horseplay with the girls: doing belly flops into the pool, splashing one another with water, playing Marco Polo… It was incredibly fun, and it felt great to just goof off to a certain extent, and for all intents and purposes just be a kid.

We had just started batting an inflated beach ball around when a cell phone began to ring. Almost comically, we all scrambled out of the water and rushed toward the quartet of lounge chairs where, respectively, we'd left our phones.

"I win," I crowed when it came to light that it was my phone that was ringing. I pumped my fist in victory for a moment as the others went back to the pool. Then I noticed who was calling.

My father.

Suddenly wanting privacy, I began walking towards the pool house as I answered the phone with a brief, "Hey."

"Hey, Jim," Alpha Prime said in return. "What are you up to?"

"Just hanging out with Smokey and some friends," I answered as I went into the pool house and made sure the door was shut. "And for the record, I was going to call you later today."

My father laughed. "I'm sure you were, but it's not a big deal. I was off on a mission anyway."

"Oh?" I muttered in surprise. "I didn't realize that."

"It was kind of last-minute and very hush-hush. That said, it should wrap up shortly, and that's why I was calling."

My brow furrowed. "Do you need my help with something?"

"Thanks for offering, son, but no. We're good. I really just wanted to ask if you wanted to get dinner tonight."

"Uh…" I droned momentarily. "Unfortunately, I can't. I've got plans."

"Oh," my father intoned softly. "I see."

I could hear the disappointment in his voice. We'd never really had a relationship until fairly recently, and even then I'd kept him at arm's length for a while. We seemed to be in a good place at the moment — one with a foundation we could build on — and now it probably looked like I was pushing him away again.

"It's not like that," I assured him. "I'm supposed to go to dinner tonight with Electra and—"

"Electra?" my father repeated, almost excitedly. "Well, why didn't you say so?"

"It's complicated," I answered. "But why don't we shoot for having dinner tomorrow instead? Smokey and I should be back for good by then, even if he stays over tonight."

"Stays over?" he echoed. "Where exactly are you?"

"West Coast. We're at brunch with some friends."

"Hmmm," he muttered. "Not a *champagne* brunch, I hope."

"No," I replied, chuckling. "No champagne."

"So who's with you?"

"Like I said before, Smokey's with me, along with Vestibule — whom you know — and her cousin, Cat."

"Any adults around?"

"What's with all these questions?" I finally asked. "Why are you talking like I'm a little kid who needs a chaperone?"

"Look," my father started to explain, "I trust you, okay? But your mother felt I was too hands-off as a parent. So, before she left, she made me promise to take a more active interest in what you're doing on a daily basis. When she gets back, I need to be able to tell her that I stayed on top of where you were, who you were hanging out with, that you went to bed on time, yada, yada, yada... So just humor me, okay?"

"Fine," I muttered in acquiescence. "Cat's mother Capri is here. Satisfied?"

My father didn't immediately respond. In fact, the silence stretched on for what felt like a lengthy period of time (but was probably no more than ten seconds), prompting me to say, "Hello? Are you there?"

"Ah, yeah," he murmured. "I'm still here. What was the name of your friend's mom again?"

"Capri," I answered. "And before you say anything about it being disrespectful for me to address her by her name, that's what she told us to call her."

"No, I wasn't going to say anything about that," he assured me. "But tell me, what does she look like?"

My mouth almost fell open. "You're kidding, right? Are you seriously asking me to play matchmaker for you? For all you know, she's married."

"No, son — that's not it," he insisted. "I just..." He trailed off and then took a deep breath. "You know

79

what? I'm sorry. Honestly, I thought maybe she was someone I knew. I wasn't trying to put you on the spot."

"It's okay," I said. "I apologize for misinterpreting things. Do you want me to find out if she's the person you know?"

"No, don't worry about it," he answered. "It's not important."

"Are you sure?"

"Yeah," he stressed. "Anyway, I have to go, but we're on for tomorrow night, right?"

"Definitely," I promised, then uttered a hasty goodbye and got off the phone.

I spent a moment dwelling on my relationship with Alpha Prime. A year earlier, you couldn't have paid me to be in the same room with him. Now, I was looking forward to dinner with him. Shaking my head at how strange it all seemed, I went back outside.

The first thing I noticed was that no one was in the pool any more. Instead, my three compatriots were seated on some circular patio furniture that was situated around a fire pit table (which, unsurprisingly, was not currently lit). More to the point, they were all eating.

Hastily plopping a strawberry into his mouth and swallowing, Smokey said, "Sorry, man, but we decided to go ahead and grab some food while you were on the phone."

"You might want to hurry if you want something," Cat added. "My mother's 'Cougar Club' is here, so there may not be anything but scraps left soon."

"Cougar Club?" I repeated in confusion.

Chewing on a piece of waffle, Cat gestured towards the area where brunch was set up, and I noticed then that

Capri — sitting on a sofa there — had been joined by a group of five more women.

"They may be thin," Cat remarked, having apparently swallowed the waffle bit she was eating, "but those chicks can pack away some food."

"You know we can hear you," declared one of the women — an attractive brunette.

"I just wanted you to know that it's okay to eat your fill," Cat shot back. "So go on and pig out. It's okay — nobody here will judge you."

The brunette suddenly looked unsure of herself, as if she actually *did* feel like she was being judged by others.

"There's that famous subtlety," I joked, winking at Cat. I then hurried over to get some food.

Chapter 12

Getting something to eat turned out to be like swimming in shark-infested waters. Although all of them were attractive, Capri's friends were as blunt and straightforward as she was in terms of speech.

"Wow," one of them said as I grabbed a plate and started getting food. "He's really cute."

"He's a little young — even for *you*, Amanda," said another.

Keeping my back to them, I continued piling food onto my plate, acting as if I couldn't hear them.

"I'm not thinking about him for *me*, dingbat," Amanda retorted. "I'm thinking he'd like to meet my daughter, Kayla."

"Sorry, ladies," I heard Capri announce. "He's not on the market."

"What does that mean?" asked someone whom I'm sure was the brunette from earlier. "Has Cat staked her claim?"

"Not exactly," Capri said.

"Then he's fair game," Amanda declared.

"He's not interested," Capri insisted.

"Why don't we let *him* decide that?" Amanda suggested. "Once he sees Kayla, I think his interest will be piqued, and I just happen to have a pic—"

"Huh?" I suddenly yelled in the direction of my friends. "Okay, I'll be there in a sec."

I then made a beeline for Cat and the others, practically leaving a dust trail behind me. However, something on my face must have shown what occurred, because Smokey took one look at me and started laughing.

"You looked flustered," he noted. "Did something happen?"

"Yeah," I responded as I took a seat. "Apparently there's some kind of male auction going on here, but nobody told me about it."

The others laughed heartily at that.

"If it's any consolation," Smokey said a few moments later, still grinning, "the same thing happened to me."

"It's not," I assured him, causing another round of laughter (which I joined in). Then, without further ado, I began eating.

****

The food was delicious. Assuming that Cat knew what was best, I had followed her lead and gotten the waffles (among other things), and found them to be fantastic. In fact, I ended up going back for seconds, as did Smokey.

Afterwards, we all just sat around and talked. As at the diner, it was great to just hang out with other people and engage in lighthearted chitchat. Plainly speaking, too many of my conversations involved weighty matters, whether it be forced engagements, interstellar empires, or nefarious supervillains.

Also, despite everyone's best efforts, we all somehow got suckered into another bet by Vestibule. In essence, after she herself and then Smokey received almost back-to-back phone calls, Vestibule proposed that we see how long we could go with our cell phones completely off.

The bet was only for bragging rights, but it added a comedic element to the conversation, because — without fail — someone would invariably reach for their phone every few minutes, if only to check for text messages. Fortunately, a person was only out of the running if they actually turned their phone *on*. Still, it was hilarious watching someone reach for and look at a device simply out of habit when they empirically knew it was turned off.

Ultimately, the phone game came to a premature end when Capri yelled in our direction, telling Cat that her father had been trying to reach her and kept getting shunted to voicemail. Calling off the bet seemed the only fair thing to do as Cat grabbed her phone and stepped away for some privacy. It was apparently a quick call, however, as she returned maybe a minute later.

"Everything okay?" Vestibule asked.

Cat nodded. "Yeah. He was just confirming that I still wanted to go with him for 'Take Your Daughter to Work Day.'"

"Do you?" inquired Smokey.

"Of course," Cat shot back immediately. "I love my dad, and we always have a great time together. I get my sense of humor from him."

She looked as though she wanted to say more, but was interrupted by her mother shouting at us once again.

"Hey!" Capri yelled, getting our attention. "Come join us."

I could see that she and her friends were now moving as a group towards the pool. Was she asking us to get into the water with them?

Trying to get clarity, I stood and shouted back, "What was that?"

"We're getting in the hot tub," she explained. "You guys should come join us."

ISOLATION

Caught flatfooted by her statement, my mind wasn't even capable of forming an answer. Even though I knew empathically that none of the women had any romantic interest in me or Smokey, I was suddenly both enticed and a little intimidated by the idea of being in a hot tub with a bunch of beautiful women. Thus, I simply stood there watching as Capri and her friends all slipped into the bubbling water, laughing.

"Come on," one of them shouted in our direction. "We don't bite...*much*."

This caused a round of raucous laughter to erupt from all the women. I spent a moment trying to come up with a witty reply, but apparently Cat interpreted my silence as me considering the offer.

Reaching out, she latched onto my wrist and hissed, "Don't you dare."

Her tone was both playful and forceful at the same time. She tugged slightly on my arm, and — taking the suggested hint — I sat back down. Cat then released her grip on me, but I now found myself staring at her.

Noting my attention, she said, "I'm sorry. I didn't mean to come off as bossy or anything. It's just that the last time I had friends over and they got in the hot tub, Mom embarrassed them so badly that they never came back. Don't read too much into this, but I like you guys, and I don't want her to run you off."

"That's not likely," I uttered in a monotone, then finally tore my eyes away from her.

Apparently, Cat had thought I'd been staring because she'd been a little high-handed. The truth was far different.

ISOLATION

When she had touched me, I had felt a surge of some sort — an unexpected flux of energy. A force. A power.

Cat was a super.

ISOLATION

Chapter 13

It was easy to be around people and not know that they had any special powers or abilities. There are many kinds of talents that simply don't manifest themselves in ways that can be seen. (Telepathy, for instance.)

That said, there are certain individuals with a unique gift for sniffing out supers. I certainly don't claim to be one of them, but my empathic abilities did give me a leg up in that department. Basically, there's a certain quality to their emotions that many supers have, an aspect of their character which hints in an I-have-a-secret sort of way that they have a gift.

I had gotten nothing like that from Cat. I had picked up no hint that she was anything other than a normal person. More to the point, I had never before sensed another person's power in quite the same way that I had picked up on hers.

Of course, it was entirely possible that I had developed a new ability. According to Mouse, my power set wouldn't be completely defined for some time to come — if ever. That said, I have a specific tell that surfaces whenever I manifest a new power: an odd buzzing in my head. Needless to say, that hadn't happened this time, which implied that Cat was the source of the power I'd felt. Surprisingly, she didn't even seem to be aware that she had let the cat out of the bag, so to speak.

It was an unusual development, to say the least, and put me on my guard to a certain extent. Unable to stop thinking about what had happened, I spent the rest of brunch being somewhat withdrawn — a fact that was noticed by the others. It put something of a damper on what had, up until then, been a lively and enjoyable day.

ISOLATION

Eventually, we had to start getting ready for the yacht party. Cat told me I could use the pool house to shower and get ready, then showed Smokey to a guest room in the mansion where he could do the same. Fifteen minutes later, we all met up at the table where brunch had been served. Thankfully, by that time, Capri's Cougar Club had adjourned their meeting, and Capri herself had disappeared somewhere inside the house.

Absentmindedly, I noted that — like me and Smokey — the girls had put on the clothes they were wearing earlier. It suggested that they were just looking forward to a fun outing (as opposed to trying to impress anybody), and reinforced the notion that they really were down-to-earth.

After confirming that Smokey and I had everything we'd come with, we headed towards the car. We were just getting in when I picked up on a familiar — but completely unexpected — emotional vibe. I recognized it immediately, but felt I had to be wrong.

Wanting to investigate, I looked at Cat and said, "I think I need to run to the restroom before we go."

"Oh, um, okay," she murmured. "If you go back inside, it'll be on—"

"It's okay — I'll find it," I interjected, already halfway up the steps. A second later, I slipped inside and closed the door behind me, then immediately phased and became invisible. Floating up into the air, I began empathically following the trail of the emotions I'd detected.

Being phased, I was able to travel in a direct line, without regard for walls, furniture, or anything else. A few moments later, I found myself in a back hallway of the mansion, where two people were currently walking towards me.

One of them was Capri. She had changed out of the seashell-top bikini, but was currently dressed no less provocatively. Looking like she'd just come off the runway, she sported a form-fitting black minidress with a plunging V-neck that practically went to her navel.

Behind her was the person whose emotions I had detected: my father, Alpha Prime.

Although I'd picked up on him empathically, actually laying eyes on him was a bit of a shock. He must have flown at Mach speed to get here so fast. Of course, when I'd spoken with him earlier, he hadn't said exactly where he was. For all I knew, he could already have been on the West Coast (or somewhere nearby), but I hadn't gotten that impression.

Rather than the trademark black-and-gold uniform of the Alpha League, he was dressed in civilian attire at the moment: a pair of khakis, a T-shirt, and a dark blazer. It wasn't a look that everyone could pull off, but at six-seven, with a chiseled physique and movie-star looks, one would be hard-pressed to find clothes that looked bad on him.

Suddenly, Capri veered into a side room, with my father right on her heels. Curious as to what was going on, I followed them, phasing through the wall and then floating up into a corner.

"Okay," Capri said as my father closed the door. "You wanted to talk, so talk."

"I'm sure you know why I'm here," Alpha Prime stated.

"Well, I know why most men come through my door," Capri said with an inviting smile. "But you used up all your vouchers in that regard a long time ago, so I assume it's about the boy."

"The *boy* is my son."

"Oh, trust me — I know. The fruit doesn't fall far from the tree."

Alpha Prime shook his head. "No, he's not like me. Not in that way."

Capri cocked her head to the side. "Oh, really? That's not the way *I* heard it. Word on the street is that he's juggling a fiancée, a girlfriend, supermodel groupies... If he's not you all over again, it's only because he's raised the bar."

"That's not fair. Whatever you've heard, there's no way you got the real story, but believe me when I say that he's not the kind of guy I was when it comes to women."

"Oh? And what kind of guy was that? I've never really heard you say it out loud."

"Did I ever mistreat you?" Alpha Prime angrily blurted out. "Misuse you in some way? Put pressure on you to do anything you didn't want to do?"

Capri crossed her arms and gave him a smoldering look. Rather than answer, she said, "We were talking about the boy. Go on."

My father let out a deep breath. "The way I understand it, he's been spending a bit of time with your daughter."

He didn't explain anything further, but he seemed to be implying something that Capri took offense to.

"And?" she asked.

"Well, isn't she...?" He looked down, unable to go on.

I wasn't sure what he was suggesting, but several things came to mind that left a bad taste in my mouth.

ISOLATION

"Isn't she what? Yours?" Capri barked, then laughed in a way that was almost a cackle. "Can you even count? My daughter came along way after you and I were done."

"I realize that," my father said in annoyance. "I can do the math. What I was trying to ask is if she's like *you.*"

Capri gave him a knowing smile and declared, "One hundred percent." She then placed a hand on her hip and thrust it out to the side tantalizingly. "With genes like these, the arrow don't miss the mark."

Alpha Prime frowned. "Don't you think that's a problem?"

"I don't recall *you* voicing many complaints," Capri retorted.

A little red-faced, my father said, "Again, Jim's not me. He's still a kid. He's—"

"Do not tell me you're about to play the he's-too-young card!" Capri forcefully interjected. "To hell with being the world's greatest superhero — that would make you the biggest hypocrite on the planet! How many parents, siblings, friends, etcetera made that argument to you about some girl you were dating, and how many times did you listen?"

"Can you stop making this about me for two seconds?" my father asked in irritation. "This is about our kids — my son and your daughter — and right now, he doesn't know what she is."

"Oh, yeah," she said sarcastically, "because it made all the difference in the world when *you* found out about *me.* I mean, you stepped off — stopped calling, stopped asking me out, stopped sending me flowers. Oh, wait" — she put a finger to her chin and stared off into space, as if reflecting on something of deep import — "you didn't stop doing *any* of that."

Alpha Prime didn't say anything, just stared at her expectantly.

After a moment, she sighed and said, "Look, let's not blow this out of proportion. They're just friends. Maybe that's news to you, but people of the opposite sex can have platonic relationships. If it starts looking like it's more than that, somebody may have to say something, but until then let's not make things awkward with a conversation that may never need to happen."

My father seemed to contemplate for a second, then nodded. "All right, that seems fair."

"Great," Capri said. "Now that that's out of the way, tell me the truth. Did you really only come here to talk about your son, or is there something else you wanted to do?"

She asked her question in a husky, alluring tone and raised an eyebrow teasingly. A knowing glance passed between them and they both smiled. Sensing an unexpected, but similar, flurry of emotions arising simultaneously in the two of them, I practically fled the room, going through walls and hallways as fast as I could without making my presence known.

Once at the front door, I became visible and solid again before stepping outside. Ignoring the comments and questions as to whether I had "fallen in," I slipped into the front passenger seat. A moment later, we were on our way.

ISOLATION

Chapter 14

The yacht party took place on a one-hundred-foot vessel that was docked at a local marina. We had to get past security to get on board (fortunately, we were on the list), but after that, it was pretty much what you'd expect on a floating mansion: lots of opulence in terms of layout, design, and so forth.

We weren't the first to arrive and were far from the last, so in that regard we had good timing. I didn't have a lot of experience with boats, but it didn't take much expertise to recognize that this was a craft built for leisure and pleasure, and therefore perfectly suited for the day's activities.

At some point, we pulled away from the dock and headed out to the ocean. At that juncture, there were at least a hundred people on board — probably more. At a glance, I would have pegged most of the guests as being in their early twenties. Dressed mostly in bikinis and swimming trunks, they all seemed to be in full party mode. Helping add to that mood was the fact that there was a healthy spread in terms of food, a live DJ, and an open bar. (That last had a bartender who seemed less than thorough in carding those who might be underage.) All in all, the scene on the yacht was reminiscent of images I'd seen in a hundred music videos.

Unfortunately, the change in venue did nothing to alter my disposition. I still couldn't stop thinking about what had happened with Cat and trying to figure out what it meant. (Not helping matters was the conversation I'd eavesdropped on between my father and Capri, which only seemed to highlight the fact that whatever I'd sensed when Cat touched me was important in some way.)

ISOLATION

Recognizing that I was raining on their parade to a certain extent, I pretended to take a call and told Smokey and the girls I'd find them when I was done. Instead, I simply meandered until I came across a quiet spot near the railing at the back of the boat and sort of camped out there, alone with my thoughts. I was still there when Vestibule found me around an hour later.

She didn't say anything initially, just stood next to me and stared out at the ocean for a minute or two.

Finally, she turned to me and asked, "You want to talk about it?"

"About what?" I asked.

"Whatever's fouled your mood. We were all having a great time, and then it was like some part of you shut down. Actually, you didn't just shut down — you started draining energy from the rest of us."

"I know," I said with a soft chuckle. "That's why I let you guys go off on your own. There's no way you'd enjoy the party with me hanging around in my current state of mind."

"So what — are you like bipolar or something?"

"Really?" I muttered incredulously. "Bipolar? That's the first place you go?"

She shrugged. "Well, it's not like you're sharing." When I didn't immediately respond, she added, "Come on. You know you can tell me anything."

I simply looked at her for a moment, weighing what she'd said. Maybe the way to deal with this issue was to tackle it head-on. I certainly wasn't getting anywhere wrestling with it on my own.

"All right," I said after a few seconds. "Your cousin Cat — what's her power?"

ISOLATION

A slightly shocked expression came over Vestibule's face, although she quickly recovered.

"I, uh, I don't know what you mean," she answered. She did a good job of keeping her tone even, but emotionally I could sense that she was alarmed in some way.

"Sure you do," I retorted. "Your cousin has some kind of talent or ability. What is it?"

Vestibule shook her head emphatically. "No, you're wrong. Cat's normal."

Reading her emotions, I got the sense that she was being disingenuous. With nothing to lose, I decided to press forward.

"We both know that's not true," I countered. "So I'm asking you again, what's her power?"

Vestibule initially looked as though she wanted to continue denying it. Suddenly, however, she just threw in the towel.

Taking a deep breath and looking down, she simply declared, "I can't. She's my cousin. It's not my place to say."

"Okay, I can understand that," I declared. "So should I just ask Cat directly?"

Vestibule's eyes went wide in concern. "Please don't. She doesn't want anyone to know." Then she frowned, giving me an odd look. "So how did you find out? Did something happen?"

"You could say that."

"And it's bothering you," she surmised.

"Honestly, I'm bothered by the fact that what happened was new to me," I admitted. "Knowing what Cat's power is might help me figure things out."

"It won't. It'll just complicate things."

"How?"

Rather than respond, she simply shook her head. "Can't you just let this go?"

"That depends," I replied. "Should I be worried?"

Vestibule gave me a confused look. "Worried?"

"Yeah," I said with a nod. "I mean, is she likely to go nuclear or something?"

"What?!" Vestibule screeched. "No! It's nothing like that."

"Then what is it? The more cryptic you are about it, the more it seems like it's something I need to know."

Sighing, Vestibule raised a hand to her forehead and massaged her temples for a moment, then gave me a frank stare. "Okay, let me talk to her and see what she says. I'll try to convince her to tell you, but I can't make any promises in that department."

I gave her a curt nod. "Fair enough."

ISOLATION

Chapter 15

I held my post at the railing for maybe another hour. The party was in full swing for most of that time, and I had to admit that it did look like fun. However, I just didn't feel like participating. The thing with Cat had me fully preoccupied for some reason, and had kind of sapped my desire to do anything else.

Like a good friend, Smokey checked up on me, showing up shortly after Vestibule left to go speak to her cousin.

"Hey, man," he droned as he approached. "You okay?"

"Yeah," I assured him. "Why do you ask?"

"Because we're at a freakin' yacht party being hosted by a celeb, with a fair number of famous people present — as well as a few starlets — and you're moping around like somebody stole your bike."

"Sorry," I intoned with a momentary grin. "Guess I've just got some stuff on my mind."

"Apparently you're not the only one."

"Huh?" I blurted out, giving him a confused look.

"The girls," he stated in explanation. "They huddled up a little while ago and have been in deep conversation ever since — like they're plotting to take over the world. I tried to engage with them, but it was pretty clear that they intended it to be a one-on-one chat."

"Guess it seems like everyone's deserted you," I surmised.

Smokey shrugged. "Don't worry about it. I know you're probably fretting over this dinner you have coming up."

"Yes — a meal with my ex and her father," I said, shaking my head in dismay. "Sounds like the title of a bad rom-com."

Smiling, Smokey nodded in agreement. "Speaking of exes, I talked to Sarah."

My eyes widened in surprise. "Really?"

"Yeah — a few days ago."

I stayed silent for a moment, absorbing this. I had always liked Sarah, who was Smokey's ex-girlfriend. More importantly, they had always seemed like a rock-solid couple, but there had been aspects of their relationship that even I, his best friend, hadn't known. The facts were complicated, but ultimately they had broken up around the time I returned from Caeles, with Smokey refusing to even speak to Sarah. (In fact, it was her continually dropping by his house in an effort to talk to him that had made Smokey take up permanent residence at Alpha League HQ.)

"It was a good talk," he continued, bringing me back to myself. "We cleared the air about a lot of things."

"So does that mean…?"

"No," he answered, shaking his head as I trailed off. "We're not getting back together. I mean, I'm with Atalanta now, and I really care about her."

I simply nodded, not saying anything.

"Anyway," Smokey droned, changing the subject, "even with all my compadres deserting me, I've actually been having a blast on this yacht, just talking and getting to know people."

"Does that include our hostess?" I asked, raising an eyebrow.

Smokey grinned. "Somewhat. I got to chat with Alita, but only for a few minutes. This is her event, so she's got a lot of demands on her time — guests, the crew, servers, and so on. Still, it was nice of her to make a little time for me, and I really enjoyed talking to her."

"A word of advice: I'd avoid sounding so chipper when Atalanta asks you how the party was."

Smokey outright laughed at that. "I already sent her a few pics. If she thought I was having too much fun, she'd have let me know."

"Or flown here at light speed and punched a hole in the boat."

We both chuckled at that. I occasionally needled Smokey about how powerful Atalanta was, but I honestly thought he'd had it right earlier when he mentioned that she wasn't the jealous type. It just didn't seem to be her style. If she ever felt that Smokey had done something inappropriate as a boyfriend, my impression was that she'd simply end the relationship.

"Well, I think I'm going to leave you to your moping," Smokey said after a few moments. He then gave me a clap on the shoulder before preparing to go back to the party.

"Hey," I said as he started to walk away. "Any thoughts yet on when you want to go home?"

He turned to me but continued to walk backwards, saying, "Honestly, I'm leaning towards giving it another night."

I gave him a smile and a nod, essentially conveying that his decision was fine with me. He really seemed to be enjoying himself, and for the umpteenth time I was happy Mouse had suggested bringing him with me. I had been having a lot of fun going to various events the past few weeks, but having my best friend with me made those experiences transcendent in a way that was difficult to explain.

ISOLATION

After he left, my mind quickly turned back to thoughts of Cat and her unspecified power. Somewhere in the back of my mind, I realized that my focus on this was bordering on obsession, but I couldn't help myself. I simply had to know.

I might have stood there at the railing indefinitely, simply replaying in my head what had happened and trying to determine what it meant. At some juncture, however, I noticed someone approaching me.

It was Cat.

As she walked towards me, I picked up feelings of nervousness, trepidation, and anxiety. No — it was actually more like dread.

Once she reached me, she just stood there for a moment, plainly uncomfortable. But then I sensed something resolve in her.

Plainly nervous, she said in an unexpectedly soft voice, "So you know about me."

"Not really," I admitted. "I mean, I know that you have some sort of power or ability, but that's about it. I have no idea what it is you can do."

"But you *want* to know."

I nodded. "Yeah."

Her brow crinkled for a second and she asked, "How'd you even find out about me? Did someone tell you?"

"No," I assured her. "Nobody betrayed your confidence, if that's what you're asking — certainly not Vestibule."

Cat smiled. "Yeah, I know she'd never tell. We're tight, and even if we weren't, she adheres to the motto that blood is thicker than water."

"And I respect that," I said. "So, your power —
what is it?"

Cat stared at me for a moment, then looked down
at the ground.

"I thought I'd be able to do this," she muttered,
almost to herself. "Thought I could just walk over here and
tell you." Then, looking up at me, she added, "But I can't."

"I don't understand," I stated with a frown. "Why
is this such a secret? Why can't you just blurt it out?"

Cat's eyes suddenly looked watery, and I could tell
that she was on the verge of tears.

"I like you," she finally said. "Not in a boyfriend-
girlfriend kind of way, just as a friend. And I got the
impression that you liked me, too."

"I do," I admitted. "You're smart, witty, and just a
lot of fun to hang out with. But what does that have to do
with your power?"

"Because if I tell you," she said flatly, "you aren't
going to like me anymore."

"Huh?" I muttered, perplexed.

"You aren't going to want to be my friend. You
won't want anything to do with me."

I simply stood there for a moment, trying to
process what she was saying, then exclaimed, "That's
absurd! What could be so bad that I would stop being your
friend or wanting to hang out with you?"

"Please," she said. "Just let it go. I really want us to
be friends."

"As far as I'm concerned, we *are*," I assured her.
"But the thing about friends is, they trust each other. Part
of what makes a friendship is letting people in as opposed
to keeping them at arm's length. So the real question here
is, are you going to let me in?"

ISOLATION

She didn't say anything at first, just looked at me, and I could sense her wavering.

"I'm sorry, I just can't," she finally said, before turning and walking away.

ISOLATION

Chapter 16

I gave it maybe fifteen minutes so that it wouldn't appear that I was storming off mad (especially since I wasn't), then I chased down the others to tell them I had to go. I found them on the dance floor near the DJ, clearly enjoying themselves. Even Cat appeared to have shrugged off the doldrums that had plagued her during our brief chat and was showcasing her dance moves.

Rather than approach them directly, I reached out telepathically to let Smokey know I was taking off and got a mental "Good luck" from him with respect to my upcoming dinner plans. I also opened a channel to Vestibule, putting her in charge of getting Smokey back to my cousin's place if I didn't make it back in time.

<No problem,> she assured me, <but where are you off to?>

It hit me then that I hadn't shared with Vestibule or Cat that I would be leaving.

<There's something I need to take care of,> I said. <I told Smokey but forgot to mention it to you or Cat.>

<Okay, but you will try to make it back, right?>

<I'll try, but no promises. Tell Cat goodbye for me, okay?>

Mentally, Vestibule bristled slightly. <You don't want to tell her yourself?>

<I'm not sure she wants to talk to me right now.>

<Of course she does. And if you don't say anything to her, you'll be doing exactly what she was afraid of: acting like you don't want anything to do with her.>

Mentally I sighed. <Look, just tell her and let her know I'll chat with her later.>

I then broke the connection and teleported.

ISOLATION

I popped up at home — a three-story mansion that was technically the ambassadorial residence of the Caelesian envoy to Earth. My alien grandmother had been the original ambassador, but now I somehow found myself stuck with the title. I didn't care for the position, but it was hard to complain since it came with practically no duties and some nice perks (like diplomatic immunity).

Since my family's departure, the place was now home to only me and Myshtal. Frankly speaking, it had felt big when my mother and grandparents had been living here as well. Now that they were gone, it felt absolutely humongous. However, it was the only place where my family had all lived together (albeit for only a short time), so it had essentially become "home" to me.

With the time change, I only had a small window in which to get ready before dinner. My plan had been to take a quick shower and change clothes, but first I needed to turn off the alarm system, which had started beeping the moment I appeared.

Stepping to a numbered panel situated on a nearby wall, I quickly punched in the security code. A moment later, the beeping stopped. The next order of business was to visually give the mansion a once-over to make sure everything was fine. With that in mind, I shifted into super speed and checked the place out from top to bottom.

A minute later, I was able to confirm that there were no issues — nothing untoward had happened during the time Myshtal and I had been gone. No kid had accidentally hit a baseball through any of the windows. No storm had come along and torn off the roof. No skillful cat burglar had picked the lock on any of the doors.

The only thing of note was that the diode on the answering machine was flashing, indicating a message. After checking on everything else, I went back to it and hit *Play*.

Frankly speaking, I expected any messages to be the telephonic equivalent of junk mail. With the prevalence of cell phones, almost anybody who needed to reach me could — and would — call me on that device. For many people, the home phone number was now reserved for individuals, organizations, and events they really didn't feel a need to talk to: pushy salesmen, sweepstakes entries, the guy who bullied you in high school but now acts like you were friends... And that's before you even got to the unsolicited ones, like robocallers and telemarketers.

In this instance, there turned out to be two messages. One was a political ad, encouraging me to vote for a particular candidate in an upcoming primary (which I might have done if I were of the age of majority). The other was a message from Kenyon, the former caretaker of the embassy, who had been custodian of the place for decades.

Under the formal definition of the word, "caretaker" refers to someone who looks after a residence during the owner's absence. However, once my family moved in, there wasn't much for Kenyon to do. Thus, he had recently retired (and been given a healthy pension by my grandparents). That said, he generally checked in once a week to see if we needed anything, and my grandfather — recognizing the man's desire to stay active — usually found something for him to do.

Kenyon had kept up the practice of reaching out during my family's absence, but I had been less capable than my grandfather in terms of identifying issues that could utilize his knowledge and skills. On this occasion, the message, as expected, just consisted of him checking in. I mentally made a note to find something this week that would require his attention.

Hearing the messages on the answering machine, however, brought to mind something else: my cell phone was still off. Pulling it out, I hit the power button and quickly saw that I had missed about a half-dozen calls and texts. For a moment, I worried that one of them — or several — were from Gray.

Mister Gray, as he preferred I call him, was the head of a secret organization that had been granted almost limitless authority by governments worldwide. Ergo, although he had no superpowers to speak of, he was one of the most powerful men on the planet. Moreover, events had recently unfolded that required me to go to work for him. Bearing in mind that Gray had often treated me like I was a threat to humanity, it was a situation that I found distasteful in the extreme, but there was nothing I could do about it. However, as a result of some shrewd negotiating by Mouse, being in Gray's employ did not mean I had to leave the Alpha League. In addition, much to my surprise, Gray had been fairly accommodating, telling me to take some time after my family left and that he'd call me when he needed me. Still, just knowing that I was part of his organization rankled.

Thankfully, none of my calls were from him; all but one were from Mouse, and the first also indicated a voicemail had been left. I almost snickered at the thought of Gray leaving a voicemail, as it simply wasn't his style. If he had been trying to reach me and been unsuccessful in doing so, I had no doubt that I would have quickly been approached by several Men in Black telling me to turn my phone on.

Putting Gray out of my mind, I played back Mouse's message.

"Jim," I heard Mouse say, "call me when you get this. It's not a big deal, but — if you have a little capacity — I have a project I could use your help with."

Noting the time, I saw that the call had come in while I'd been having brunch. The other calls from Mouse came sporadically after that, but with no accompanying voicemail. As with the calls, all but one of the texts were from him as well, and essentially repeated the same message: he could use some help with a project, but my presence wasn't mandatory.

The remaining call and text were both from Electra, along with a voicemail. In short, she was simply confirming that dinner was still on. Like Mouse, her messages had come hours earlier, so it probably looked like I was ignoring her (or had changed my mind).

Still hoping there was a chance of getting out of dinner, I called Mouse back first. I didn't get an answer, but left a voicemail stating that I was completely at his disposal and to call me back asap. I then sent him a text stating basically the same thing.

Next, realizing that I was cutting it close, I texted Electra back a "thumbs-up" emoji. A response came back almost immediately: the word "Hoo-ray!" accompanied by fireworks. Apparently, she had been awaiting my response, and I suddenly felt bad for keeping her in suspense for what had probably been hours.

Fighting guilt, I took a shower and got ready at super speed. As a result, I still had a few minutes to kill before dinner.

ISOLATION

Considering how uncomfortable the evening was likely to be, there was no way I was showing up even a nanosecond early. That being the case, I went to the living room and plopped down in an easy chair. Closing my eyes for a second, I tried to relax, telling myself that it was only dinner. At the same time, I put some effort into trying to avoid the subject that had preoccupied my thoughts for the past few hours: Cat and her mysterious power.

Apparently I was a bit more tired than I realized, because before I knew it, I had dozed off.

Chapter 17

I woke up with a start, nudged awake by something like a soft fluttering. I realized immediately what it was: my phone vibrating, indicating an incoming call. I pulled it out, but by that time the caller — whom I noted was Electra — had hung up. Noting the time, I saw that I was five minutes late for dinner. A moment later, a text popped up:

Just arrived. Are you here yet?

I didn't have to look at the name to know that it was from Electra. I immediately wrote back, stating:

I'm here.

Pocketing my phone, I then teleported, popping up in the rear parking lot of the restaurant where Electra had made dinner reservations. Much to my surprise, Electra herself was standing near a corner of the building, and was just turning in my direction. I waved and began walking towards her.

It was cooler here than on the West Coast, and she was dressed for the weather. Outfitted in a form-fitting black sweater, blue jeans, and black boots, she didn't show as much skin as I'd grown accustomed to seeing lately, but it didn't detract from her beauty or allure. In short, despite my misgivings about the evening, I couldn't help smiling when I saw her.

As I drew close, I heard a familiar musical note ring out — the sound Electra had set to indicate an incoming text. She glanced down at her phone, then gave me a skeptical look.

"Just saw your message," she stated, then held up her phone so I could see it. "You sent this before you left, didn't you?"

"Yeah," I admitted. "So?"

"So you lied."

"No, I actually beat the message here — which I knew would happen — so it's true."

"You know, there are so many ways I could tear that apart, that it isn't even funny," she said. "But I'm just so glad you came that I'm going to give you a pass."

"Thanks," I said. "What are you doing back here anyway?"

"I know you," she said. "This is your *modus operandi* — teleporting into the back parking lot, the roof of a building, etcetera."

"Hmmm," I droned. "I didn't realize I was so predictable."

"Only to the people who know you," she replied with a wink. "Come on, let's go eat."

Looping her arm into mine — a move which caught me by surprise — she began leading me to the front of the restaurant.

ISOLATION

Chapter 18

The restaurant where we were having dinner was a hibachi grill — a place Electra and I had visited several times while dating and really enjoyed. Upon entering, we found her father Vir waiting to be seated, along with Esper — another member of the Alpha League, who also happened to be Electra's maternal aunt (as well as the most powerful telepath on the planet).

"Dad, you remember Jim," Electra said.

"Of course," said Vir, smiling as he extended a hand in my direction. "Nice to see you again."

"You, too, sir," I stated in response as I shook his hand.

He was maybe an inch shorter than me (which put him at about five-eleven), with wavy brown hair and handsome features. Knowing that he shared the same power as my girlfriend, I had imagined getting some kind of mild shock when we shook hands — perhaps as a warning regarding his daughter. Nothing like that happened. In fact, from what I could sense, Vir was sincerely glad to meet me. Still, there was a mild sense of relief when he released my hand.

"Jim," Esper said, stepping forward to give me a hug. "It feels like it's been forever."

"For me, too," I remarked, then regretted it as I saw Electra look away with my peripheral vision. "But, as they say, absence makes the heart grow fonder."

"So it does," Esper noted, sharing a glance with Vir.

A moment later, the hostess appeared, telling us that our table was ready.

ISOLATION

****

Dinner turned out to be way more fun than I ever would have imagined. First of all, having a hibachi chef prepare your meal is like getting dinner and a show in one. On this particular occasion, our chef first regaled us by twirling and juggling his cooking utensils, agilely tossing his knife, fork, and spatula in the air, catching them behind his back, and so on.

The entertainment continued as he began placing food on the grill. From stacking onion rings into a small volcano that blew smoke to repeatedly tossing an egg into the air with his cooking implements (and catching it with the same), it was an enjoyable spectacle. Last but not least, as he began cooking some shrimp, the chef tossed pieces at us, daring us to catch them in our mouths.

All in all, dinner preparation alone was worth the price of admission, so to speak. The fact that the meal itself turned out to be delicious was just icing on the cake, and I found myself grateful that Electra had strong-armed me into coming.

As to Vir, he turned out to be a really fun guy. Although I was wary at first, he had an easy-going manner that quickly put me at ease. Frankly speaking, he didn't seem like a man who had spent the better part of two decades locked up. He had a bright outlook and an animated personality that was rather unexpected, to be honest. More importantly, although I had been expecting it, he never once brought up anything about me and Electra (or more specifically, our relationship issues).

With respect to my ex, things couldn't have gone better if I'd planned them. In almost no time at all, we both seemingly fell back into our old roles as boyfriend and girlfriend — in word and deed, if not name. We tasted each other's food, shared knowing glances, whispered silly comments to each other... Electra even reached over at one point and held my hand for a second; it was plainly out of habit, because she hastily let go when she realized what she'd done and looked away in embarrassment for a moment. (Mentally, I gave myself a high five and did a fist-pump, because it was evidence that there was hope for us yet.)

In short, the night was going far better than I ever could have hoped. Vir and I not only seemed to be getting along, but — from what I could read of his emotions — he genuinely liked me. That alone made the evening a monumental success in my book. And then, things came to a rather abrupt end.

Basically, we were just about to order dessert when a familiar tone sounded from Esper's purse.

"The office," she muttered as she pulled out her phone and pressed a button. The tone stopped and she merely stared at the screen for a second before putting it away. "Something's up. I have to go in."

"Emergency?" Vir asked.

Esper shrugged. "Don't know yet, but a car's on the way."

"Ahem," I muttered, clearing my throat. "If it's helpful, I could...?"

I trailed off, but raise my eyebrows questioningly.

"Would you mind?" Esper asked.

I shook my head. "Not at all."

"Okay, great," Esper said, coming to her feet, which prompted us all to rise. She then turned to Vir and gave him a quick peck on the lips. "See you at home later."

"You hope," Vir added, a subtle indication that — depending on whether there was a crisis and how extensive it was — Esper could be gone for days.

Rather than reply, Esper simply gave Electra a hug goodbye and then said, "Come on, Jim."

With that, she began heading for the door; moments later, we were behind the restaurant. At that juncture, I teleported her, sending her to the main conference room at Alpha League HQ.

A second later, I felt her open a telepathic channel to me and announce, <Made it.> I gave her a mental nod in reply and then went back inside as she broke the connection.

When I got back to the table, I noticed Vir handing a credit card to our waitress, a sure sign that dinner was over.

"I hope you don't mind," Vir began, "but Amp said there's a specialty ice cream shop a few blocks away, and she'd rather have dessert there."

I stared at him for a moment, trying to figure out who he was talking about, and then I remembered: "Amp" was his nickname for Electra.

"No problem," I assured him. "I think I know the place she's talking about."

"Great," he said. A few minutes later, the bill was paid and we were heading outside.

Not knowing where they had parked, I let them take the lead. As I walked behind them, I found myself wishing that Esper hadn't had to go. With her present, there had been a sort of balance to our group: two couples. Two males, two females. Two adults, two teens. One man and one woman, one boy and one girl. Without her, things felt askew and off-kilter.

ISOLATION

For instance, we were apparently about to take their car to the ice cream shop for dessert. Had Esper been with us, it would presumably have been either her and Vir in the front seat with me and Electra in the back, or vice versa. Thinking about what the drive would be like now, I imagined Vir behind the wheel, with me and Electra seated behind him. Somehow, however, I didn't think that would fly (plus, I didn't want him envisioning me and his daughter in the backseat of *any*thing.) I thought of me sitting in the front passenger seat while Vir drove, and didn't really care for that. Even less palatable was the notion of Electra driving and me next to her, while Vir sat in the backseat — probably directly behind me.

It turned out, however, that I was worrying for nothing. As if he had been reading my mind, Vir had a solution to my problem.

Turning unexpectedly to his daughter as we reached their car, he said, "You know, sweetheart, the ice cream shop's only a few blocks away. Why don't you drive on over and grab us a booth? Jim and I will walk. I need the exercise, and it'll give us a chance to talk."

Electra looked nervously from her father to me and then back again. "Uh, I don't know, Dad. Maybe we should just skip—"

"No, Amp," he stressed, shaking his head. "My baby wants ice cream, so we're getting ice cream. Plus, I'm sure Jim doesn't mind, do you, Jim?"

He looked at me as he asked his question, plainly putting me on the spot. With my brain screaming at me to say that I absolutely, positively, categorically, and unconditionally *did* mind, my mouth said something else.

"No, I don't mind at all," I uttered woodenly.

"See?" Vir intoned. "We're all good."

"Okay," Electra mumbled, sounding unsure. "I guess I'll see you in a few minutes."

With a look of concern on her face, she leaned forward and gave her father a hug. Then she stepped in my direction and shocked me by giving me a kiss.

It only lasted a second or two, and then she suddenly pulled back. I realized then that she was as shocked by her actions as I was. Reading her emotions, it was clear that she had never intended to kiss me, but — apparently distracted by what her father had said — she had unwittingly reverted to what had been customary for us when parting ways.

Shaking her head in disgust at her own actions, she got into the car and drove away without another word.

At that juncture, Vir turned to me, asking, "You ready?"

ISOLATION

Chapter 19

We walked in silence for about a minute, both of us wrapped in our own thoughts, it seemed.

"Thanks for dinner," I finally said. "I really enjoyed it."

"It's Esper you should be thanking," Vir replied flatly. "It was her credit card I used. I'm kind of a kept man at the moment."

"Oh," I muttered softly, not sure what else to say.

Vir laughed. "You don't approve, I take it?"

I shrugged. "It's not my place to comment."

"But you do have an opinion."

"In my opinion, Esper and Electra are overjoyed to have you home. That's what's important."

"Well," he droned with a smile, "you're a lot more tactful than I was at your age. Given what I just told you, I would have called myself a bum."

I snickered at that, enjoying his ability to poke fun at himself.

"But it's not quite what it seems," he went on. "Basically, when I went away, I signed all of my assets away to be held in trust for Amp. I didn't know if I'd ever get out, but I wanted her to be taken care of."

I simply nodded at first, not saying anything. I was well aware of the fact that Electra had a trust fund, but had no idea what was in it or how much it was worth — wasn't sure that I *wanted* to know.

"So you're broke because you gave everything to your daughter," I summed up after a few moments. "Not because you're careless or irresponsible."

"That's how I hope people see it — especially Amp," he said. "Plus, I've got some things in the works so

117

that hopefully I'll start pulling my weight in the area of family finances."

"That's great," I said matter-of-factly, then looked at him askance. "Anything you can talk about?"

"Yeah," he declared with a laugh. "Trust me, this isn't like in the movies, where an ex-con fresh out of prison lines up the score of a lifetime. This is completely legit. In fact, your mentor Mouse is helping me with it."

"Really?" I blurted out, not bothering to hide my surprise.

Vir nodded. "I wasn't completely idle during those years I was locked up. I always had ideas about things, and since I got out, I've been putting them down on paper. Your buddy Mouse has some friends in corporate America who he feels may be interested in some stuff I've come up with, and if we can work out the details…"

He trailed off, but I understood where he was going. "You'll sell your ideas for a mint."

"Not *sell*," he corrected, smiling. "*License* — ownership is everything. But there will be a hefty licensing fee."

"That's impressive," I said sincerely. If Mouse was involved — and I hadn't gotten the impression that Vir was lying — then this was all completely aboveboard.

"Anyway," Vir droned, changing the subject, "I'm sure you're wondering why I wanted to meet you."

"I suppose because of my relationship with your daughter," I guessed, "among other things."

"Not per se. You'll understand better when you have kids of your own, but the first thing you think when your teenage daughter says she likes some guy is, 'I need to meet him.' That's per the Dad Handbook."

I laughed. "So there's a guide for all this stuff that dads do?"

"In all honesty, you mostly play it by ear, but wanting to meet any guy she likes is pretty standard."

"Well, I don't feel so bad now, if that's the only reason you wanted us to have dinner."

"And if I'm being completely honest, there *is* another reason that piqued my interest."

He didn't say anything else, but I suddenly felt the wind going out of my sails. I had thought we were getting along well, but I should have known this was coming.

Letting out a sigh, I softly said her name. "Myshtal. The princess."

Vir shook his head. "Jim, I like you, but I have to say I'm disappointed. You just cost me ten bucks."

I looked at him in confusion. "Huh?"

"I bet Amp a sawbuck that you wouldn't bring up the subject of your fiancée if I didn't ask you about it directly. I expected you to dance around the subject until I shoved it in your face."

"Sorry to disappoint," I muttered, still feeling uncomfortable about this conversation.

"Lighten up," Vir practically commanded, clapping me on the shoulder. "I'm not here to judge. Hell, I'm the poster boy for getting involved in situations beyond your control, and from all I've heard, you're not in this situation by choice."

"That's putting it lightly."

Suddenly, Vir came to a stop. Looking me in the eye, he said, "My point is that sometimes doing the right thing doesn't always give us a fair result. But that doesn't mean you should have done anything differently."

I looked at him, absorbing what he said and empathically feeling that he was being frank and sincere.

"Thanks," I intoned. "I really appreciate…"

I trailed off as, for the second time that day, I picked up a familiar emotional vibe, this time rapidly heading in our direction. A moment later, I heard something swish through the air directly above us, and then my father swiftly descended to the ground next to us.

Looking at who was with me, Alpha Prime greeted him with a curt nod and a solemn, "Vir."

"AP," Vir stated in return.

My father turned to me. "I thought you were having dinner with Electra tonight."

"It was actually all of us," I clarified, then explained that it had been a double date, of sorts.

"Esper left," Vir added, "but Electra's waiting for us at an ice cream shop about a block over."

"I'm sorry," Alpha Prime said, "but we urgently need Jim for something back at HQ. He'll have to finish his date another time."

"Is it the same thing Esper was called in for?" Vir asked.

"That's classified," my father replied, then looked at me. "Whenever you're ready, Jim. Main conference room."

Speaking to Vir, I said, "Tell Electra I had a great time, and I'll catch up with her later."

Vir acknowledged this with a nod, and then I teleported myself and Alpha Prime.

ISOLATION

Chapter 20

We popped up in the main conference room, as my father had requested.

"Hang tight for a second," he said. Tapping a communicator that sat unobtrusively in his ear, he then announced, "We're here."

Still unsure of what was going on, I took a seat at the conference table and, out of habit, started swiveling from side to side in the chair. A moment later, I began feeling an odd tingle at the back of my mind — like something I was supposed to remember but couldn't quite get a handle on. At the same time, I noticed my father giving me an odd look. Empathically, he was giving off a weird emotion — an unusual combination of agitation and expectation.

"Something wrong?" I asked.

"Uh, no," he said, shaking his head. "Stay here for a second."

"Will do," I replied as my father headed to the door and strode from the room.

Still wondering what was happening, I leaned back in the chair and kicked my feet up onto the desk. For Alpha Prime to seek me out the way he had — presumably locating me via my cell phone, which has a tracker — I had assumed I was needed for something important. Yet, here I was, basically just cooling my heels.

A minute or so later, Alpha Prime came back into the room, still giving me an odd look.

"Okay," I blurted out. "What is it?"

"What's what?" my father asked.

"You keep looking at me like you expect me to turn into an eggplant or something, so what's going on?"

ISOLATION

"Nothing," he insisted. "Well, actually, there is something, but I'm not sure how to break it to you."

"Just tell me," I stated.

"All right," my father said, then took a deep breath. "Mouse has gone rogue."

ISOLATION

Chapter 21

"I don't believe it," I declared flatly.

"I'm sorry, but it's true," Alpha Prime said.

"No," I stressed, shaking my head emphatically. "No way."

"Are you kidding?" asked Buzz, the official speedster of the League. "You don't believe what your own eyes are telling you?"

"No, I don't," I said defiantly. "There has to be some kind of explanation."

"There is, and you've seen it," Buzz shot back. "Or would you like to see the footage again?"

"Sure," I said. "Why not?"

Everyone else exchanged glances, apparently not caring for my skepticism.

We were still in the main conference room at Alpha League HQ, but we had been joined by several other League members. After making his stunning statement, Alpha Prime had called together a number of his colleagues, and then — with us all seated around a conference table — proceeded to tell a story that I found incredulous, if not completely preposterous. However, he had visual aids in the form of video footage to back him up. But even after viewing it twice, I still couldn't believe it.

"Maybe the third time's the charm," Buzz muttered as my father picked up a remote from the table and pressed a button. On a wall at the far end of the table, a white screen began to display a video clip.

The footage began by showing a location that I recognized immediately: Mouse's lab. In addition to Mouse himself, my father was present, along with two other members of the League: Luna and Solar Surge. Mouse was dressed as I'd seen him that morning, while the other three wore their Alpha League uniforms, with Luna also sporting twin swords that she wore on her back. There was no audio, but from the angle shown, the camera that had filmed this scene must have been placed up high in a corner, because it gave an expansive view of the room.

In the middle of the lab was something I'd never seen before — a large object about the size of two caskets stuck together and standing upright. It appeared to be made of some sort of dark metal, but it was hard to tell on the video. It was also difficult to really describe the actual shape of the object because the outer edges of it seemed blurry.

"Okay," I said, "what's that thing called again?"

"The Tristan Construct," said Luna as Alpha Prime paused the video. "It's named for the remote volcanic island where it was found."

"And what's wrong with the footage?" I asked. "Why is it all fuzzy around the edges?"

"Because that's the way it actually looks," noted Alpha Prime. "Mouse said something before about it possibly not being fully embedded in this reality."

I frowned. "What exactly does that mean?"

My father shrugged. "Different dimension, different timeline... Who knows?"

My brow furrowed as I considered what he said. Despite watching the video two times before, this was the first time I'd really asked any questions. Plainly speaking, I think I was just in shock over what I'd seen — and was about to witness again as the footage resumed.

In the video, Mouse walked around the Construct a couple of times, appearing to scan it with a device that he

124

held while the other League members stood off to the side. Next, my mentor went to a keyboard and monitor situated atop one of the worktables and began typing.

All of a sudden, the screen went dark for maybe two seconds. The first time I saw the video, this was the only part of the footage where I had asked anything. Seeing it again prompted me to voice my concerns once more.

"So explain to me again what happened here," I essentially demanded.

Pausing the video once more, my father said, "All indications are that the Construct sent out some kind of energy burst that apparently caused the camera to power down for a few seconds. And when it came back on…"

He started the video again as he trailed off. The screen went back to an image of Mouse's lab, only now, the Construct appeared to be glowing with an emerald light.

Without warning, Mouse suddenly pointed his right arm in the direction of Alpha Prime. At that juncture, I noticed that he appeared to be wearing some sort of metallic brace on the hand and wrist in question. It was a device I'd seen on him once before — when he thought we were being attacked in his lab — and it gave the impression of being a weapon. A moment later, that theory was proved correct when my father suddenly went flying backwards like he'd been rammed by a jet.

Solar Surge and Luna immediately sprang into action, with the former using his hands to fire a blast of dark energy (his namesake "surge") at Mouse while the latter leaped at him, swords drawn and her mouth open in what I assumed was a battle cry. Holding up his right hand, Mouse appeared to deflect the blast coming at him, presumably through use of the brace. The redirected energy struck the attacking Luna directly in the face and sent her tumbling to the side, limbs flailing.

Solar Surge prepared to fire at Mouse again, then seemed to jump as Mouse suddenly appeared on his left. And on his right. And in front of him. In fact, the entire lab was suddenly filled with a million copies of Mouse, all dressed and looking exactly alike, as well as rushing madly about. However, in addition to the jeans and thermal shirt, each "Mouse" was also wearing a backpack — an item I recognized as Mouse's bug-out bag.

Solar Surge reached for one of the "Mouses" near him. Although he should have been close enough to touch the "Mouse" in question, his hand appeared to close on empty air. The multiple copies of Mouse were holograms of some sort. Surge suddenly began to grab randomly at the Mouse versions moving around him, obviously convinced that the original was somewhere in the crowd.

He was joined moments later by Alpha Prime and Luna, both of whom had re-entered the fray. However, they fared no better than Surge at locating the real Mouse. And then, just as quickly as they had appeared, all of the holograms vanished.

At that point, Alpha Prime stopped the video.

"As you can see," he said to me, "Mouse went on the offensive and attacked us."

"But why would he do that?" I asked. "Just attack you out of the blue?"

"We think the Construct caused it," Surge said. "When it released the energy that knocked out the camera, we believe it affected him in some way — maybe caused some type of mental imbalance."

I pointed angrily at the screen. "Did that look like an attack by a mentally unbalanced person?"

"Just because he wasn't wild-eyed and foaming at the mouth doesn't mean he was playing with all his marbles," my father said.

I shook my head in dismay, then glanced around the table at the other League members present.

"Are you honestly telling me that all of you are buying this?" I demanded. "That you honestly believe Mouse went off the reservation?"

There was no immediate response, then Surge said, "Hey, no one wants to believe this, but I was there — plus, we have it on tape."

"Do we have any other footage?" I asked.

"No," Buzz shot back. "But if what you saw didn't convince you, I don't know what good another video would do."

"Mouse has multiple cameras in his lab," I explained. "Another angle might provide more insight on what exactly happened."

"Unfortunately, this is the only footage we have," Alpha Prime noted. "For some reason, we weren't able to extract anything from the other cameras in the lab."

"We should probably work on that," I suggested. "It might help get a better understanding of the facts."

"The facts speak for themselves," Luna chided. "You're just refusing to see reason because you and Mouse are close."

"You're right on that point," I said. "I love Mouse — he's like my brother. And I know he wouldn't do what I saw without a pretty good reason."

Silence filled the room for a moment. Empathically, I could feel anger and frustration from some regarding my steadfast refusal to admit that Mouse had gone rogue.

"Look," Alpha Prime finally said, "why don't we table the issue of why Mouse did what he did and simply focus on finding him and stopping him."

"Stopping him?" I echoed, nonplussed. "Stop him from doing what?"

No one immediately spoke, then Buzz offered, "From hurting anybody."

I stared at Buzz angrily for a second, then simply asked, "So why am *I* here?"

"I thought it was obvious," Alpha Prime stated. "We need your help figuring out where Mouse has gone to ground."

"Why in the world would I help you hunt him down when I'm not sure he did anything wrong?" I demanded.

"Because if we find him and he attacks again, someone might get hurt," Buzz stated.

"But if *you're* there," my father quickly interjected, "it's a lot more likely that we can avoid any conflict. Mouse trusts you — he'll listen to you."

I chewed on this for a moment, then let out a sigh. "What makes you think *I* can find him?"

"Because you know him better than almost anybody," Alpha Prime said.

"What about Vixen?" I countered. "I'm sure Mouse's girlfriend will have a better idea of where he's hanging his hat."

"Can't find her," Luna explained. "She's disappeared."

"So track her," I suggested. "Her cell phone, her communicator… You can use those and other stuff to pin down her location."

"We tried," Solar Surge noted. "No luck. Wherever she is, she's off the grid."

"Well, did anybody reach out to Braintrust?" I asked.

There was no immediate response to my question, which made me wonder if they had understood me. Braintrust (also known as "BT") was a cluster of clones sharing a single hive mind. Smart and knowledgeable (and with a wealth of resources), BT often worked closely with Mouse.

"To be perfectly frank," my father finally said, "we were hoping to keep this in the family, if you catch my drift. And since BT isn't officially a member of the League…"

He trailed off, but I understood where he'd been going: he didn't want BT involved.

"So I guess that means I'm 'it,'" I concluded.

"I'm afraid so," Alpha Prime said. "But we'll keep the option of going to BT open, as well as anyone else who might be able to help."

"Okay, then," I droned, coming to my feet. "Let's get started."

ISOLATION

Chapter 22

We started off in Mouse's lab — me, Alpha Prime, Buzz, and Luna. It looked pretty much as it had on the footage (which wasn't surprising since all of the action had happened just a few hours earlier). The place was a little unkempt, with some papers strewn about and a few computer components littering the floor in some areas — the result of having three League members running around trying to wrangle holograms. Otherwise, aside from all the equipment and monitors being off, the room looked as it generally did. There was one thing I noticed, however.

"What happened to the Construct?" I asked.

"It's been moved to a safe location," Alpha Prime said. "Can't risk whatever happened to Mouse happening to anyone else."

"That raises an interesting point," I noted. "Why weren't you, Luna, or Surge affected?"

"Presumably it had to do with proximity," Luna chimed in. "Mouse was closer to the Construct, so he was influenced by whatever it did. The rest of us were seemingly out of range."

"Hmmm," I droned. "What was that thing doing here anyway?"

"It was found by a research team in some volcanic rock on a remote island," Alpha Prime said. "It then passed through the hands of a few government scientists, who really didn't know what it was or what to do with it. Ultimately, they ended up asking Mouse for help."

I nodded as he spoke, understanding that it was not an unusual pattern. Top scientists in a dozen fields were known to consult with Mouse on occasion. The man was absolutely brilliant, with a level of genius that couldn't even be defined or categorized.

He was also incredibly organized, I thought, looking around again at the clutter. There wasn't much of it, but still...

Switching into super speed, I zipped around the lab, picking up papers and other stuff from the floor and placing them on one of the worktables. It took almost no effort on my part and kept the place looking presentable, which was what I knew Mouse would want. Plus, I spent a decent amount of time in the lab, so I felt a certain obligation to keep it tidy.

Satisfied, I switched back to normal speed. Without warning, Luna suddenly advanced on me, looking angry.

"What did you do?" she demanded.

I found myself dumbfounded by her reaction. Luna had a reputation for being a little bit crazy, but I didn't have a clue what might have set her off in this instance.

Turning on his own super speed, Buzz dashed over and came to a halt in front of her.

"Easy," Buzz said, holding his palms toward her. "Just slow down." He gave Luna a moment to take a breath, then continued. "Jim didn't do anything. I was watching him, and all he did was clean the place up."

Her face still stamped with an intense expression, Luna casually glanced around for a few seconds. Seemingly satisfied with the explanation (and her own visual confirmation), she gave a short nod.

"I apologize," she said, although her tone didn't convey the necessary sentiment. "This situation has me on edge."

"It has all of us a little wound up," Alpha Prime added, then focused his attention on me. "Well, Jim, you wanted to see the lab. Thoughts?"

"None so far," I admitted. "There's an old adage about criminals always returning to the scene of the crime. Going with the wild assumption that Mouse did something wrong, I was just curious as to what he might come back here for."

"And?"

I shrugged. "Just eyeballing the place, nothing jumps out at me. I mean, I was here this morning — I'm here practically every day, in fact — and there's nothing that strikes me as being out of place."

As I spoke, however, a new thought occurred to me, and I realized I was overlooking something.

"Hmmm," I droned. "Hang on a sec."

Without waiting for a response, I teleported, popping up in a huge, cavernous chamber. It was a secret room that connected to Mouse's lab, although I had only been in it a few times before. It was primarily used for storage, as evidenced by a nigh-endless number of boxes and bins. Empathically, I sensed that Mouse wasn't anywhere around, and it only took a few seconds to go through the place at super speed to determine that it contained no clues to his whereabouts.

Next, I teleported to the sleeping quarters that Mouse maintained at the lab. It was basically the equivalent of a one-bedroom apartment connected via a door to the main workspace. As with the secret chamber, it contained nothing which indicated where Mouse might be. Somewhat disappointed, I teleported back to the lab.

The second I appeared, I got an evil look from Luna. However, she held her tongue.

Ignoring her, I said, "Just checked out a couple of places, including the adjoining sleeping quarters. Nothing hints to where Mouse might be."

"Would you tell us if it did?" asked Luna snarkily.

I frowned at her, then looked at my father. "Does she *have* to be here?"

"I thought it might be helpful since she was on hand when things went sideways," he said.

I turned my attention back to Luna. "Why were you here anyway? This happened during the day. Don't you get your powers from the moon?"

"My powers *grow* under the light of the moon," she corrected.

"So you get crazier as the day goes on," I concluded.

Luna looked like she wanted to slug me, but before she said or did anything, my father interjected.

"Enough," he almost bellowed. "Let's try to remember that we're on the same team."

"I'm not the human powder keg," I protested defensively, "about to blow up every time someone blinks."

"I get that," my father said. "But whatever happened to Mouse happened right here in this lab, under our very noses. If it was the Construct that did it, there might be a lingering effect, even if the device itself is gone. That means it could happen to somebody else. With that in mind, it might help, Jim, if you give us a heads-up about what you're about to do before you do it."

Still smoldering over Luna's attitude, I merely crossed my arms and stated, "I'll try."

"Good enough," Alpha Prime announced with a nod. "So, if we're done here, what's next?"

I shrugged. "I don't know. Most of the time when I'm around Mouse, it's *here*. This is where he spends, like, ninety-nine percent of his time, so I don't know much about where he hangs out when he leaves. I mean, he's got an apartment — I know that much — as well as official quarters here at HQ, like everybody else. He only mentions them in passing, but he's also got family, so maybe they're worth talking to. Beyond that, I'm not sure."

"Well, we've already scoped out his apartment and his formal League quarters," Buzz said. "We turned up nothing."

"There are a few other places we can check," Alpha Prime said. "If everyone's ready, we can head out and—"

"Timeout," I said, forming the letter "T" with my hands. "I can't speak for anyone else, but I've had a long day, and I'm still mentally digesting everything I've heard tonight. I'm going home to catch some sleep, and we can pick this up in the morning when I can look at everything with fresh eyes. Or you guys can push through and just brief me tomorrow."

The other three exchanged glances. Even without my empathic abilities, I could tell that they weren't ready to call it quits, even temporarily. Of course, I wasn't being completely honest with them. It *had* been a long day, but I could easily tweak my internal systems and go on indefinitely. In truth, however, things had been moving at a fast clip, and I simply wanted some time to think about everything that had happened — in particular, my role in helping to hunt down my mentor.

"All right," my father said. "That makes sense. We'll call it a night and pick things up bright and early."

With that, he dismissed Buzz and Luna, who seemed reluctant to leave but did as told.

"So," my father droned once we were alone, "care to crash with your old man?"

"I appreciate it," I said sincerely, "but I think I want to stay home tonight."

"I know I've said it before, but I really do want you to think of my place as your home, too."

"Sorry," I muttered in apology. "I didn't mean it like that. It's just that I've been jetting all over the place lately, so maybe staying in a familiar environment will help me wrap my head around all this."

"I think I understand," Alpha Prime stated. "Anyway, if you want to take off, I'll turn off the lights and lock up."

I was about to say it wasn't necessary — that I had planned to do all that — when his words struck a chord with me.

I spent a quick moment eyeballing the lab, then asked, "After Mouse took off, who shut everything down in here?"

"What do you mean?" Alpha Prime asked.

"Well, the monitors are all off, as well as the computers — everything except the lights, in fact. Who shut it all down?"

My father shrugged. "I thought everything in here typically shut down on its own when no one was around, like a computer when you step away from it for too long."

I nodded. "Yeah, that's the sleep mode, but the computer comes out of it when you come back and move the mouse or start typing. Likewise, this place is supposed to wake up when people come in. That didn't happen, so everything in here is shut down rather than asleep. So who did it?"

ISOLATION

"I don't know," Alpha Prime admitted. "As far as I know, it just powered down on its own."

"Unless Mouse did it," I suggested.

"That's the most likely explanation, and it's not beyond his ability to do it remotely."

"I guess," I mumbled softly, not fully convinced. However, before I could comment further, a shrill buzzing started sounding from my phone.

"I gotta go," I blurted out, and then — after phasing and becoming invisible — teleported.

ISOLATION

Chapter 23

I popped up at the embassy, where my ears were immediately assaulted by the sound of the alarm going off. Staying invisible and phased, I dashed through the place at super speed — twice — and found nothing. Frowning in confusion, I turned the alarm off after becoming visible and substantial.

It was the alarm, of course, that I'd received notice of via my phone. The funny thing was, I didn't recall setting it before leaving for dinner. However, that didn't mean that I hadn't done it. Much like a person may unplug an iron out of habit but not have a specific memory of the act, it was entirely possible that I'd set the alarm as a matter of routine without consciously thinking about it. (There was even an app on my phone that let me activate it remotely, so I might have even done it by accident.)

Regardless of how the alarm had come on, I had popped up expecting to find an intruder to deal with, but such had not been the case. The only person whom I could tell had been inside recently was me. In fact, I only discovered one thing that might be construed as out of order: the door to Myshtal's room was open, although I was certain I had closed it when I checked the embassy previously.

Just to make sure I was covering all the bases, I reached out both empathically and telepathically. I didn't encounter any other minds or emotional vibes, so I felt confident that I wasn't dealing with an invisible burglar or anything along those lines. Basically, it just appeared that there was a glitch in the system — something I'd have to get looked at.

ISOLATION

At least now I have something for Kenyon to do, I thought. In fact, I spent a moment debating on whether to call him while the subject was fresh in my mind, but decided against it. I wasn't sure if he was up, and it was almost as easy to text him. That being the case, I quickly tapped out a message outlining the issue and sent it.

Next, I pulled my empathic and telepathic abilities back to their normal range. Once that was done, I teleported up to my bedroom. The plan was to take a quick shower and go to bed, but I'd only just appeared when my phone rang. It was Myshtal. I let out a soft groan. With everything that had been going on regarding Mouse, I had completely forgotten about her.

"Hey," I said upon answering, hopefully sounding more enthusiastic than I felt. "What are you up to?"

"On my way to a gala with Monique," she answered. "Apparently there's some kind of 'no cell phone' rule tonight, so I figured I'd call you now. Were you busy?"

"Not at all," I said. "As a matter of fact…"

I trailed off as I suddenly heard a distinct sound echoing through the embassy — one that I knew, but had seldom heard: the doorbell.

Basically, the embassy sits on a walled estate, and the only official way in is through a gated entrance. (There are some secret entrances, but the number of people familiar with those is limited.) Typically, visitors drive up to the gate and either call or use an intercom located at the entry to reach someone inside the embassy. At that point, if they're expected, they get buzzed in (and usually whoever they're coming to see will meet them at the door).

In this instance, no one had called. No one had reached out via the intercom. Most importantly, I hadn't buzzed anyone in. (Sure, people occasionally climbed over the wall — usually kids with too much time on their hands — but in those cases, they never rang the bell.) In short, hearing the doorbell was a little bit of a shock.

Once again reaching out empathically, I found myself surprised at who was at the door.

"I'm going to have to call you back," I said to Myshtal, then barely waited for her acknowledgment before hanging up. As I did so, however, I noticed that Kenyon had responded to my message. I swiftly read the text from him, noting that he'd agreed to tackle the issue of the alarm first thing in the morning. I replied with a brief "Thanks," before hastily putting my phone away.

Teleporting to the front door, I yanked it open and — even though I already knew who it was — found myself staring at who was outside.

Electra.

ISOLATION

Chapter 24

She was dressed as she had been at dinner and was holding two large styrofoam cups with a straw in each.

"Here," she said, thrusting one of the cups at me as she marched inside.

"What's this?" I asked as I closed the door.

"Chocolate shake. Dad told me you had to take off, but I figured you shouldn't have to miss dessert."

"Uh, thanks," I mumbled. "You didn't have to do that."

"I know, but I wanted to," she declared with a smile. Then, without waiting for an invitation, she sauntered into the living room and took a seat on the sofa.

"How'd you get in?" I asked.

"You opened the door for me," she answered with a wink, then patted the seat next to her, indicating I should sit.

"Funny," I muttered as I plopped down next to her. "I meant the gate."

"Oh, come on," Electra cooed. "You've seen me in action."

As she spoke, she held up a hand and I saw an arc of electricity dance across her fingertips.

"So you overrode the code," I surmised. "Or disrupted the power supply, or something to make the lock disengage."

"Something like that," she stated with a smile. Then she gestured towards my shake, saying, "Hey, drink that before it melts. I raced like the dickens to get that to you, so you'd better not let it go to waste."

Snickering at her playful demand, I took a big sip.

"How is it?" she asked.

"Good," I replied. "It's got a little bit of an unusual flavor, but still tastes good."

"Great. I'm glad you like it."

Taking another sip, I declared, "I do, but like I said, you didn't have to make a special trip for this."

"Well, it wasn't just for that," she admitted. "I wanted to talk to you about what happened at the restaurant."

"You mean Vir completely sandbagging me in the way he asked me to take a walk with him?"

"Hey!" she cried out, giggling as I continued to drink my shake. "Don't talk about my dad like that! And for the record, he sandbagged me, too."

"Except you didn't have to get grilled by him."

"Vir didn't grill you," Electra declared with a laugh. "That's not his style."

"Trust me, coming from the father of a girl you like, even 'Good morning' can feel like you're being raked over the coals."

As I finished speaking, I raised a hand to my mouth, stifling a yawn. I was obviously more exhausted than I realized.

"Nice to know that you still like me," she said slyly, "but you getting sandbagged by my dad isn't what I wanted to talk about. It was the kiss."

I nodded as I began to yawn a second time. "Yeah, I figured that was it, but don't worry — I didn't read anything into it."

"You didn't?" she queried in surprise.

"No," I sort of moaned as I drowsily stretched my arms out. "It's like what you said on the phone: if we hang out, we'll fall back into the habit of being a couple. That includes doing all the things that couples do, like when you

141

held my hand for a second at dinner, or kissing each other goodbye."

"So you're saying I kissed you out of habit, not because I wanted to."

"Well, I'm hoping you wanted to a little bit," I said.

"Maybe I did," she admitted sheepishly, "but I need you to understand that…"

ISOLATION

Chapter 25

I woke to the feeling of an unexpected (but not uncomfortable) pressure on my side. Opening my eyes, I saw Electra snuggled up next to me, with her arms wrapped around my torso. We had apparently fallen asleep on the couch. (In fact, reflecting back on it, I had actually dozed off while she had been talking.)

Placing my hand on her wrist, I tried to gently disengage myself, but came across some unexpected resistance.

"No," Electra firmly announced, tightening her arms around me without looking up. "I want you to stay right here."

"But I can't," I said, finally breaking her grip and moving her hand away. "And neither can you. Your father's probably going bananas by now."

"No, he's not. I told him I was crashing here last night."

"You did what?!" I screeched, coming to my feet.

"Will you relax?" she murmured nonchalantly. "Dad trusts you. And more importantly, he trusts *me*."

"No, no, no, no, no," I blurted out, shaking my head. "That's just something fathers say to find out what guy will be stupid enough to take the bait. I'm not that guy."

"You're making a big deal out of nothing," she declared as she stood and stretched.

"Well, you can tell me all about how I overreacted later, but right now I'm teleporting you home."

Electra gave me an odd look. "You sure you want to do that?"

Her question made me pause for a moment, but if she had a point, it wasn't immediately evident to me.

"I don't see what the problem is," I said.

"Well, you're trying to send me home, unkempt and ungroomed, the second I wake up," she noted. "It's tantamount to kicking me out in the morning after I spent the night here. Now that *is* the kind of thing that would set a father off."

I simply stared at her for a moment, not believing what I was hearing. Obviously, she was just yanking my chain, but over-protective fathers wasn't a subject I found humorous at the moment.

"Nothing happened," I said, "so there's nothing to report that would set *anybody* off."

"Still doesn't mean you get to kick me out."

"Nobody's kicking you out," I insisted. "I'm taking you home."

"No, you're trying to *send* me home — and looking a mess, at that."

Groaning, I wiped my face with my hand.

"Look," she continued, "I'm not asking for much — just a toothbrush, a washcloth, and a bathroom I can use."

I was on the verge of telling her she had all that at home, but was interrupted by my phone ringing.

I held up a finger to Electra, indicating she needed to give me a moment, while at the same time pulling out my phone. It was Alpha Prime calling me.

"Yeah," I muttered as I answered the phone — not an ideal greeting, but all I could muster at the moment. If he was put off by it, my father's tone didn't convey it.

"Hey," he said in greeting. "Glad you're awake. You ready to get started?"

"I suppose," I replied without much enthusiasm. "Want me to meet you at HQ?"

"No, I'm on my way to you now."

"Okay. How long before you get here?"

A second later, I heard the doorbell ring for the second time in the last twelve hours, while my father, chuckling, said, "Not long."

"Great," I mumbled, hanging up the phone. I looked at Electra and then gestured in the direction of the door. "Can you get that for me, please?"

"Uh, sure," she replied with a nod. "But—"

"Great," I stated, cutting her off. "I'll be back in a minute." Then I teleported.

Chapter 26

Popping up in my bedroom, I shifted into super speed and raced through my morning routine (including a quick shower). When I was done, I swiftly got dressed and teleported back to the living room. I'd been gone less than a minute.

When I appeared, Electra had apparently opened the door and let Alpha Prime in. At the moment, the two of them were looking at each other like they were having a staring contest. In fact, for a second, it seemed as though they didn't even know I was in the room. There was an intense look on Electra's face, and it occurred to me that maybe Alpha Prime, upon finding her here so early in the morning, had made a comment that reflected a misunderstanding of the situation.

Such a remark wouldn't have been completely out of place. From the time she was an infant, Electra had been raised as an orphan by the Alpha League. Although she had recently found out about her real family (including her dad, Vir), Alpha Prime had been her primary father figure for most of her life. If he thought she had done something inappropriate, he'd probably comment on it.

I took a moment to clear my throat. "Ahem."

The sound seemed to break whatever spell my two guests were under, causing them both to look in my direction.

"Oh, hey son," Alpha Prime said.

"Hey," I replied almost absentmindedly to him. My attention was focused on Electra, to whom I simply said, "Come with me."

I turned immediately and began walking away. As expected, she fell into step behind me. Less than a minute later, we reached our destination: one of the embassy's guest bedrooms.

"You can freshen up in here," I told her. "There should be new toothbrushes in the bathroom medicine cabinet and fresh towels in the linen closet."

"Thanks," she said. "I should only be a few minutes."

"Take your time," I replied, then teleported back to the living room, where my father just seemed to be idling.

I stood there for a moment, waiting for him to speak, but he just stayed silent.

"Well," I began, "aren't you going to say something?"

"About what?" he asked.

"Electra."

"What about her?"

I looked at him askance. "You've got no comment on the fact that she's here early in the morning, looking like she just rolled out of bed?"

"Last time I checked, son, you were grown and capable of making your own decisions."

"No, I'm *not* grown," I countered. "I'm not even an emancipated minor. I'm just legally entitled to enter into contracts and make decisions for myself that would normally be left up to parents. But I still can't vote, buy alcohol, or do other 'adult' things."

As I spoke, I reflected on the fact that my semi-emancipation was one of the things my mother and grandparents had arranged before they left. It sounded cool on paper, but it meant that I now had to deal with things like paying for utilities, taxes, and so on. In short, their absence meant I had to grow up quickly in terms of certain responsibilities.

"However you style it," Alpha Prime shot back, "you're still entitled to make adult decisions in a lot of areas. In my opinion, who you let come over for a slumber party falls under that heading."

I spent a moment absorbing this, then noted, "You have a distinct parenting style, that's for sure."

My father laughed. "Come on — you sound like you *want* me to yell at you. The truth is that I've known Electra her entire life, and you're my son. There aren't two teens I trust more on the planet."

"Well, given the way you and Electra were eyeballing each other, I was under the impression that maybe you had said something."

"No, I think you just caught us during a lull in the conversation."

"If you say so," I remarked with a shrug. "Anyway, what's first on the agenda?"

"Honestly, I thought we'd grab some breakfast," he answered, and for the first time I took real note of the fact that he was in civilian clothes.

"Um, okay," I droned. "But I can just grab a power bar or something."

"Nonsense," my father shot back. "It's still the most important meal of the day, you know."

"Okay, fine," I muttered, wondering why I was getting pushback this morning from everybody on everything. "So what's after that?"

"There's a spot where Mouse used to spend his time before joining the League. I thought we'd check that out."

"Sounds good," I said with a nod.

"Ooh!" I heard Electra interject from the other side of the room. "I want to go!"

ISOLATION

I turned in the direction of her voice and saw, as expected, that she had rejoined us.

"Sure," Alpha Prime remarked, causing me to give him a smoldering look. In return, he simply said, "It's fine, Jim. There's unlikely to be any danger, and another set of eyes wouldn't hurt."

"If we need extra eyes, we can get Li," I replied. "He was supposed to be back yesterday."

My father seemed to mentally chew on this for a second. Li was another member of the League's teen affiliate. Unlike the rest of us, however, he wasn't human. He was an AI — Artificial Intelligence — with an android body. He had been gone the past few weeks on an assignment, but should be done with that by now.

"Unfortunately," my father finally said, "Li's mission got extended. He's out of pocket for the foreseeable future."

Taking the news in stride, I looked back at Electra. "Don't you need to go home, freshen up, and all that?"

"Well, if you teleport me there," she noted, "you guys can go get breakfast and scoop me up afterwards. By that time, I'll be ready."

"Oh, so now you want me to teleport you home," I groused, realizing in the back of my mind that she must have heard more than just the last part of the conversation between me and Alpha Prime.

"Quit being a grump," she demanded teasingly. "Yesterday you're complaining about wanting to spend time with me as a friend, now you're acting like you don't want me around."

"What I don't want is you getting hurt," I corrected.

ISOLATION

She suddenly gave me a serious look. "You're not always going to be able to protect me, Jim — just like you can't protect Li if he's in trouble right now, or Smokey if he's got his back against the wall someplace. This is the gig — walking headfirst into potential danger — and we all signed up for it."

It was a good speech, probably one that every super has to make to friends, loved ones, and colleagues at some point. I'd probably given a variation of it myself on several occasions.

"She's right, you know," my father asserted, adding his two cents.

I let out a sigh and then asked Electra, "Are you ready?"

She nodded, and I teleported her home.

ISOLATION

Chapter 27

My father had actually driven to the embassy, his vehicle of choice being a large black SUV. It was actually parked inside the gate when we left, and for a moment I pondered how he'd gotten it inside since I hadn't buzzed him in. Maybe Electra hadn't closed the gate when she came in, or maybe he had just picked the vehicle up and flown it over the wall.

In the end, curious as to whether the gate had been left open all night (especially in light of the alarm going off), I asked him about it as we were leaving.

"Basically, I just picked it up once I got to the entrance and jumped over the gate with it," he stated. It wasn't quite the same as flying the vehicle over, but close enough that I mentally gave myself a pat on the back for guessing correctly.

Of course, Electra's car was still outside as well. When I teleported her home, I had completely forgotten about it, and I spent a moment mentally chastising myself for the oversight. Then again, if her own car hadn't been top-of-mind for Electra herself, then I could be forgiven for overlooking it.

We ended up getting breakfast from the drive-through of a fast-food place that opened early. I hadn't wanted to let on about it, but I was actually famished. Using super speed shifts my metabolism into high gear, so I usually follow up any use of that ability with some hearty eating. However, after zipping through the embassy looking for burglars, all I'd had the previous night was the shake Electra had brought me, and I'd eaten nothing since waking up. The end result was that I ordered at least one of just about everything on the menu: pancakes, eggs, bacon, toast, and more.

In contrast, my father only ordered a sausage biscuit sandwich, which he ate as he drove. That said, I wolfed my food down in short order, using the sacks it had come in as trash bags when I was done and tossing them on the floor in the back, behind the driver's seat.

"You know," I began, "I could have just teleported us to the restaurant."

"We spend little enough time together as it is," my father replied. "If a meal here and there is all I can get, I'd like to make it last."

"You can get more than a meal," I assured him, "especially with everyone else off-planet. I only mentioned teleporting in relation to using as much time as possible to find Mouse."

"The mission's important, but you can't put everything else on hold because of it — especially necessities, like eating."

"Well, I eat fast, as you just saw."

"Okay, I get it," Alpha Prime asserted. "You're ready to get back on task."

"It's Mouse," I reminded him. "If the situation was reversed, he'd be pulling out all the stops to find me and figure out what was going on."

"Don't worry. We'll find him."

"And that raises another issue: what happens when we actually locate him?"

"We take him into custody, of course."

"And after that?"

My father looked at me with a queer expression on his face. "What do you mean?"

ISOLATION

"Well, you guys are insisting something's wrong with him. What's the plan after we actually get our hands on him? Do we just hold him and hope that whatever might be wrong simply wears off? Are we taking him to a hospital? What?"

Alpha Prime appeared to mull on the question for a second, then said, "We're still debating that issue."

I looked at him askance, not liking his plans for Mouse (or the lack thereof), but decided it wasn't worth arguing about at the moment. The first order of business was finding my mentor; any other issues could be dealt with after that.

ISOLATION

Chapter 28

After our discussion about Mouse, Alpha Prime and I engaged in mostly small talk for the remainder of the drive to Electra's house. She was apparently chomping at the bit, because she came walking out the door the moment we pulled into her driveway. She quickly waved goodbye to her father (who had come to the door to see her off), before opening the rear passenger door and getting in behind me. I saw Vir glance in my direction, but I judiciously avoided eye contact by turning to look at Electra in the backseat.

"You got enough room back there?" I asked as my father began to back out of the driveway.

"Oh, yeah," Electra effused as she settled in. "I could probably fit a dining room set back here. Maybe a couple of couches, too. An ottoman…"

I laughed and reflected for a moment on how much I missed her. Missed being around her. Missed seeing her every day. Even though she had really irritated me earlier, I was actually happy she had joined us. Perhaps sensing my mood, Electra gave me a wink before I returned to facing forward (which I shrewdly timed so as to avoid any additional scrutiny from Vir).

"So," I droned, looking at my father, "where are we headed?"

"Mouse's shop," he replied.

Frowning in confusion, I glanced back at Electra, who merely shrugged in a don't-ask-me fashion.

"Mouse's shop?" I echoed a few seconds later.

Alpha Prime just looked at me and smiled.

****

"So Mouse worked here?" I asked.

"Sort of," my father said.

We were currently in what appeared to be a small electronics repair shop, located in what Mouse had once described as a Bohemian part of town. In addition to me, my father, and Electra, Solar Surge was also present. In fact, he had already been on the premises when we arrived and had opened the door for us.

Taking stock of our surroundings, I noticed that the front of the store appeared to serve as a sort of showroom, and I saw a couple of appliances on display, including an old microwave with mechanical dial controls and an ancient picture-tube television. The shop was clean and tidy, but I didn't get the impression that anyone came here often. If it were a house, I would have said it lacked a lived-in feel. I supposed I could say that, as a purported place of business, it lacked a "worked-in" feel — no coffee rings on the work counter, no trash in the wastebasket, and so on. Plainly speaking, the place was devoid of warmth.

"Basically," Alpha Prime continued, "this shop was just a front — a cover for Mouse's superhero activities before he joined the League."

"You're kidding," muttered Electra.

"Not at all," my father said.

"So," I droned, "you're saying Mouse was a humble shop repairman by day, and a bold vigilante by night."

"Something along those lines, but that's a story for another day," my father stated, then looked at Solar Surge. "Anything?"

"Not that I could see," Surge answered. "Doesn't look like anyone's been here."

Alpha Prime nodded, then turned in my direction.

"Jim, you want to give the shop a once-over?" he inquired. "See if anything catches your eye?"

Rather than reply directly, I shifted into super speed and zipped through the store. It turned out to be more sizeable than I had imagined, with a workspace in the back, an expansive basement, and living quarters above the shop.

Dashing back to the showroom, I returned to normal speed and declared, "I'm going to second Surge's report. There's nothing to suggest that Mouse was here."

"That's disappointing," my father confessed. "All right, we'll post a guard or something to keep an eye on the place in case he shows up. For now, though, let's move on."

ISOLATION

Chapter 29

"Moving on" essentially meant spending the remainder of the day going to various places that Mouse — either presently or at some point in the past — used as a base of operations, safe house, or something in-between. This included a modest house in the suburbs, a stylish condo near downtown, and a large warehouse with a secret underground lab.

Our pattern was typically the same at each location: I would dash around at super speed, seeing if anything struck me as being indicative of where we might be able to find Mouse. (Needless to say, I never saw a single clue that could help in the search for my mentor.) During transit between locations, we normally made at least one stop for me to get food.

Going from place to place in the SUV was both a blessing and a curse. It was, naturally, far slower than teleportation or super speed. However, it gave me time not only with Alpha Prime, but also with Electra. Of course, having my father along was kind of like having a chaperone, but it was the most time I'd had with her since we broke up, so I was happy with the trade-off. That said, it wasn't quite enough to pin down my mounting frustration as each site visit failed to help in our quest to find Mouse.

Ultimately, the end of the day saw us at a local marina, poking around a spacious liveaboard that apparently belonged to my mentor. I had heard him mention his boat a couple of times, but hadn't given it much thought beyond that. It wasn't quite the yacht that I'd been on the day before, but it was still rather nice.

I went through what was now my usual routine of checking out the place at super speed. Unsurprisingly, the boat offered no more assistance in locating Mouse than any of the other places we'd been.

"Well," Alpha Prime began after I reported back, "at this point I can't say it's surprising. However, we still have other places we can check out."

"Hold up," I said, trying not to sound as crabby as I felt. "Can we just take a break for a second?"

My father gave me a thoughtful look. "Something on your mind, son?"

"Yeah," I said with a nod. "All this running around that we're doing is a colossal waste of time. If Mouse has gone rogue as you suggest or on the run, he's not going to go to any of the places you guys know about. He's simply too smart for that."

"But remember — he's been exposed to something," Electra reminded me. "It's got him unbalanced, so there's no telling what he'll do."

"Even unbalanced, Mouse isn't dumb enough to visit any place other people know about," I countered. "Not if he knows we're looking for him."

"So what are you saying?" Alpha Prime inquired. "That this has just been some kind of snipe hunt?"

"Snipe hunt, head fake — call it what you want," I remarked. "I just know that instead of scouring all of his stomping grounds that you're familiar with, we should have been looking for all of his hangouts that you know nothing about."

"Well, what do you suggest?" my father asked.

"I don't know," I confessed. "I just know that conventional thinking isn't going to cut it with Mouse. If he's really gone off the reservation, we're going to have to think outside the box just to get a handle on where he is. I mean, he's not going to leave his calling card lying around."

"Hold that thought," Alpha Prime said. At the same time, he tapped the communicator in his ear and, speaking to whoever was on the other end, tersely stated, "Go."

Electra and I waited silently as my father listened to the incoming message.

"Mm-hmm," he muttered. "Okay…yeah…got it. We'll be there shortly."

Sensing his message had something to do with our current mission, I barely waited for him to turn the communicator off before blurting out, "What did they say?"

"Mouse just left his calling card," Alpha Prime answered.

Frowning, Electra asked, "What do you mean?"

"He just attacked HQ," my father explained.

ISOLATION

Chapter 30

Per my father's instructions, I teleported the three of us to Alpha League HQ immediately. We popped up in the Combat Arena — a scopious chamber used for training exercises and practicing threat scenarios.

Off to one side, I noticed a couple of League members, including Luna, looking somewhat the worse for wear. Not far from them, I noticed that the floor of the chamber was blackened and scorched, like some kind of explosive had gone off.

Taking charge, Alpha Prime stepped forward and stated, "Okay, tell me what happened."

The statement wasn't directed at anyone in particular, but Luna took the lead, saying, "Mouse showed up, that's what happened. We were incorporating some new weaponry into the training arsenal when he kicked open the door and came striding in with something like a grenade launcher. Next thing you know, he was firing it at us."

"That's crazy," I insisted. "Why would he do that?"

"Because — just like in his lab — whatever the Construct did has unhinged him somehow," Luna declared. "You seem to have trouble accepting that."

"Did he say anything?" I asked, ignoring her disdainful commentary.

Luna nodded. "Yeah — he said he would destroy us all. Does that count?"

There was silence for a moment as Luna's words (*sans* sarcastic remarks) sank in. Of course, I still had trouble with what I was hearing. That said, maybe the Construct *had* done something to Mouse — infected him in some way so that, like a person delirious with fever, he was acting in a manner that was inconsistent with his personality.

"So what happened after he shot at you?" Electra asked.

"You mean aside from me ending up in the blast radius of a grenade?" Luna quipped. "I suppose I was knocked off my feet."

"I believe she was asking what happened to Mouse," my father explained.

"He took off," Luna said. "By the time I got back up and went after him, he was gone."

"There are cameras all through this part of the building," I noted. "They film us during training exercises and show the video to us later so we can see what we did wrong."

"What's your point?" Luna inquired.

"I think Jim's trying to suggest that the cameras might tell where Mouse went," Alpha Prime chimed in.

Luna was silent for a second, then declared, "We already thought of that. The cameras apparently shut down when Mouse came after us, so there's no footage."

"Presumably that was Mouse's doing," Electra said.

Luna nodded in agreement. "That was our thought as well."

"So why here?" I asked. "Out of all the places at HQ, why would he stage an attack *here*?"

"I'm not sure anyone can answer that," Electra replied. "If Mouse really is unstable, there may not be any logic behind what he does or why."

"No," I shot back, shaking my head. "Even half-crazed, I can't imagine Mouse taking action like this without a reason, no matter how far-fetched."

Luna gave me a harsh look. "Maybe you should–"

ISOLATION

Her words were cut off as the entire chamber shook momentarily with tremors, accompanied by a hollow booming sound. Almost immediately thereafter, klaxons began sounding in alarm, along with flashing lights.

Despite the room shaking, everyone present managed to stay on their feet, but we all knew exactly what we'd experienced: an explosion.

ISOLATION

Chapter 31

Alpha Prime tapped his communicator and shouted over the sound of the alarm, "Talk to me!"

His face grew stern as he listened to whatever report he was receiving. On my part, I instinctively reflected on the explosion.

The blast wave from an explosion travels faster than the accompanying sound wave. However, the tremors and sound of the explosion had practically been simultaneous. In addition, I noted that the building wasn't falling down around us. Taking those facts together, I came to the immediate conclusion that the explosion was nearby, but hadn't been large.

"Mouse just attacked us!" my father yelled after a few seconds.

"He's back?" I exclaimed.

"Yeah, back," Alpha Prime confirmed in a wavering tone as the alarms suddenly cut off. Obviously a second assault so close to the first wasn't anything he'd contemplated.

"Where?" asked Luna.

"The Vault," Alpha Prime stated.

However, the words were barely out of his mouth before Luna and the League members who'd been with her took off — apparently headed to the area in question. Electra and I didn't move; instead, we simply looked to Alpha Prime for direction.

As the name implied, the Vault was a secure area (one of several, in fact) on the premises of Alpha League Headquarters. It was used to store numerous items of value, but also housed a diverse collection of paraphernalia seized from supervillains over the years: doomsday devices, weapons of mass destruction, and so on. Bearing that in mind, the Vault was generally off-limits to members of the League's teen affiliate. Thus, I had never been inside the place. That said, I had been *outside* it before.

"Jim," my father said, getting my attention.

Knowing what he wanted without asking, I teleported us.

The three of us popped up outside a massive blast door that was about ten-by-ten feet in size. In fact, the door formed the wall at the end of a short corridor that was about thirty feet long. There were normally a couple of guards on duty outside, but at present they weren't at their post and the blast door — which was the entry to the Vault — was currently open.

My father literally flew into action, leaving his feet and flying forward at what was probably just under Mach speed. I shifted into super speed in order to keep up with him and followed. (Electra, of course, didn't have the ability to move faster than normal, but them's the breaks.)

We dashed inside, and I noted in passing that, just like an old-fashioned bank vault, the blast door appeared to be more than a foot thick and made of some sort of hardened steel. Once on the other side, however, I experienced a momentary sense of *déjà vu*: the inside of the Vault was almost a duplicate of the exterior, with a short hallway that terminated in a wall-sized blast door that was currently ajar. It took me a second to realize and understand that we were not in the Vault proper yet, and there were apparently two doors (at a minimum) that one had to get past in order to get there.

While I was processing this information, my father had never stopped moving; I stayed right on his heels, noting in the back of my mind that it was a little weird to see him flying in civvies. Past the second blast door, we found ourselves in an oversized room that was perhaps two thousand square feet in size.

As before, Alpha Prime didn't stop and neither did I, but I was able to take in the room as we moved through it. Basically, it was filled with what looked like display cases, each of which was geometrically spaced throughout the place. In all honesty, it gave the room a museum-quality feel, like there was some kind of exhibit on display.

My father headed towards what appeared to be a narrow corridor in a side wall, and I followed him into it. After about ten feet, it opened up into a room that was even larger than the first, and upon entering it, Alpha Prime came to a halt. A moment later, I came to a stop next to him, and saw myself gazing upon a strange sight.

Like the first room, this one was full of display cases. Looking past them, I saw Mouse standing near the back wall. He was sporting his Alpha League uniform, which was clothing I'd rarely seen him wear. (Most times, he dressed casually in his lab.)

On the floor around Mouse were maybe half a dozen guards, all seemingly unconscious. Perhaps five feet behind him was Buzz, appearing to run at my mentor at top speed. In fact, even though I was at super speed myself, Buzz's arms and legs were a blur, plainly indicating the mind-boggling amount of effort he was exuding. Truth be told, it was a lot like one of those cartoons, where a character's legs start swiftly whirring around before they take off in a burst of speed. The only difference was that here, Buzz wasn't going anywhere. He was literally running in place.

On his part, Mouse completely ignored the speedster behind him. Instead, his attention seemed focused on a tall, rectangular section of wall that extended out into the room directly in front of him.

I didn't have time to observe anything else as movement from my father drew my attention. Looking in his direction, I saw him flying backwards — like someone had grabbed him by the scruff of the neck and yanked him off his feet. Behind him, near a side wall, I noticed a circular node of dark energy about eight feet in diameter, which seemed to be the area Alpha Prime was headed towards.

I'd barely taken note of all this before I got a taste of what my father was experiencing. One moment, everything was fine; the next, it was as though a giant vacuum cleaner had gotten turned on and pointed in my direction.

Months earlier, I'd had the sublime experience of almost getting sucked into a black hole. That was exactly what this felt like, and I found myself being inexorably pulled in the same direction as my father.

I became insubstantial, and the suction immediately ceased. Looking at Alpha Prime, I saw that he had righted himself and was attempting to fly away. However, much like Buzz, he wasn't going anywhere. In fact, he was slowly being pulled backwards.

Reaching out telepathically, I said, <Hey! I can get you free by turning you insubstantial.>

<Great,> he replied. <What are you waiting for?>

<You have to go back to normal speed,> I explained. <Otherwise, you're going to slingshot through the wall and end up ten miles away.>

<And if I dial it down for even a second, I'm getting sucked into whatever that is behind me.>

<Then we do it all at the same time — on three,> I declared, and my father gave a brief nod of agreement. <One…two…three!>

Our timing wasn't quite perfect — Alpha Prime did zoom forward for a few feet before coming to a halt — but it worked. Like me, he was now free of the mini-black hole (or whatever it was).

So that I wouldn't be zipping around my father like an annoying fly, I shifted back to normal speed as well. As soon as I did, I heard the screech of torn metal along with the sound of glass shattering as a number of the nearby display cases were forcefully and powerfully wrenched in the direction of the dark circle, slamming into the wall where it was located. There they stayed, pinned to the wall as if they'd been glued there.

Seeing that, I understood that the dark node wasn't a black hole, per se, as nothing actually got sucked *into* it. It was, however, some sort of gravity well — and a powerful one at that. Alpha Prime and I had apparently been the closest things to it, as it had seemingly affected us before anything else. In practically no time, however, I saw everything within its sphere of influence swiftly getting drawn in. Fortunately, it seemed to have a very limited range — otherwise, everything in the room would have been pulled towards it.

As with me, the sound of the display cases being ripped away had drawn Alpha Prime's attention momentarily. Almost in unison, we both turned back to Mouse, who spared us a quick glance but otherwise ignored us.

<Hang tight,> I told Alpha Prime. <I'll teleport him.>

ISOLATION

<No,> my father urged. <Just make me solid again.>

<Not a good idea,> I replied, then reached out with my teleportation power, intending to send Mouse to one of the holding cells we maintain at HQ. To my surprise, my power closed on nothing. It was as if Mouse wasn't there.

I tried again, without success, and then a third time with the same result. Obviously, Mouse was somehow negating my ability to teleport him. A moment later, he looked at me, raised his hand in a quick salute, and then vanished.

ISOLATION

Chapter 32

It took about an hour before any type of debrief occurred. Electra and I spent the bulk of that time waiting in the conference room, with her playfully admonishing me for leaving her behind once we got to the Vault.

"You could have carried me," she said on more than one occasion. "Scooped me up in your arms and such."

My reply was always along the lines of, "Be serious. We both know you're not the type of girl who likes being scooped up in that scenario. Plus, you were right behind us, and only missed Mouse by, like, fifteen seconds."

In short, we basically engaged in an hour of playful banter, with Electra — who was sitting next to me — occasionally taking my hand. I was initially surprised by her doing so, but decided to just enjoy the moment rather than quiz her about her actions and what she was thinking.

Eventually, Alpha Prime came in — accompanied by Luna and Buzz — and the serious look on his face immediately set the tone for the discussion that followed.

"Okay, here's what we've got," my father began, as he, Luna, and Buzz took seats across from us. "The initial attack in the Combat Arena was probably a diversion — something to draw our attention. Then, while we were preoccupied with the aftermath of that, Mouse slipped into the Vault."

"Makes sense," Electra said. "We wouldn't be expecting him back after he'd just put in an appearance."

"No, it only makes *half*-sense," I argued. "I agree that we wouldn't be expecting him again so soon, but the Vault and Combat Arena are in close proximity. If he wanted a diversion so that he could sneak into the former, he'd have done it at the other end of HQ. Instead, he did it practically next door. I mean, Luna and the others only got there about a minute after the rest of us."

"You're right," Alpha Prime conceded, "but as Electra noted before, Mouse isn't himself right now. It may not be possible to rationalize his actions."

"Or maybe we just can't see the rationale," I countered.

"Are you kidding?" Luna interjected. "Your buddy attacked us two times today in succession, and you even had a ringside seat for one of them. What's it going to take for you to pull your head out and accept what the rest of us already know? Mouse has gone off the rails."

"What I can't accept is how quickly all of you turn on one of your own," I shot back. "But not just any other colleague — your leader."

"*Ex*-leader," Buzz corrected. "Especially after what he pulled today in the Vault."

"That makes for a nice segue," Alpha Prime chimed in. "Let's talk about what happened in the Vault."

"So what do we know?" asked Electra.

"On the surface, it's pretty straightforward," my father stated. "Mouse broke in, the guards tried to detain him, and he knocked them out with some kind of concussion grenade."

"But that's not the explosion *we* heard," I offered, making it more of a statement than a question.

"No," Alpha Prime agreed. "That was Mouse trying to blow up Buzz."

We all looked at the speedster, who stated, "I was first on the scene — happened to be nearby and heard the concussion grenade go off. Acoustics aren't great in some parts of HQ, so it took a minute of running around and checking out various areas before I got to the place where it had detonated."

"The rear room of the Vault," Electra surmised.

Buzz nodded. "Yeah, and Mouse was at the back wall when I got there. I went straight at him, then noticed some kind of explosion starting to go off ahead of me. I was able to avoid it, but the place was apparently booby-trapped."

I took in Buzz's statement without comment. As a speedster, he wouldn't have had any problem sidestepping a bomb that was going off. From his perspective, the explosion would have occurred in slow motion and would have been easy to dodge.

"I could tell the explosion wasn't going to be massive," Buzz continued, "so I just went around it. That said, it did make a lot of noise and shook the place, although it didn't do much damage. Anyway, in trying to bypass it, I hit some liquid that was on the floor and lost my footing — ended up banging into the wall. Whatever it was, it was super-slippery. I had trouble just getting back on my feet, and then I couldn't get any traction. I ended up just running in place. I wasn't able to get to Mouse no matter how hard I tried, even though he was just a few feet away."

"So how'd you get unstuck, so to speak?" inquired Electra.

"A few minutes after Mouse left, the liquid just evaporated," Buzz answered. "I wish I knew what it was, because I'd definitely like to avoid it from now on."

"Frictionless grease," I said. Everyone turned to me with expectant looks, so I went on. "Buzz stepped in frictionless grease."

Luna gave me a confused look. "What's that?"

"I won't explain it as well as Mouse," I confessed, "but friction is the force between two objects that keeps them from slipping and sliding away from each other when they're in contact. It's friction between your feet and the ground that allows you to walk or run — or even stand up."

"And frictionless grease, as the name implies, removes friction," my father concluded. "That explains what happened to Buzz."

"So that's something that Mouse invented?" asked Electra.

"I don't know," I admitted with a shrug. "The concept has been around for a while and Mouse discussed it during one of my physics lessons, but I wasn't aware he'd done anything with it."

"What about this other thing that you guys had to deal with?" asked Luna. "The localized black hole."

"It was a gravity well, created by *this*," remarked Alpha Prime as he placed a small silver ball on the table. "It has a limited range, but it's very powerful. I'm not even sure *I* would have been able to break away from it, if not for Jim."

"Wow," muttered Electra. "How'd you deactivate it?"

"We didn't," my father admitted. "Just like the frictionless grease evaporated, it just sort of turned off after Mouse left."

"Or Mouse turned them off," I added, "since he didn't need them anymore."

Alpha Prime's eyes narrowed as he looked at me. "After we got away from the gravity well, I told you to make me solid again, but you said it was a bad idea. In fact, you didn't make me substantial until after Mouse was gone. What was that about?"

"The gravity well seemed to trigger after we came into the room," I answered.

"A booby trap," Electra concluded. "Similar to what Buzz experienced."

"Yeah," I stated with a nod, "and I figured there'd be more of them."

"Well, it turns out you were right," Alpha Prime stated. "We did a sweep of the Vault after Mouse left and found two more of the gravity-balls. They didn't turn on when we located them, so presumably they only trigger when Mouse is present."

"So once he departed, all his snares went dormant," Luna noted.

"Apparently," Alpha Prime concurred, then looked at me. "But I think this really highlights how important it is to have you be part of this search effort, Jim. You know how Mouse thinks, what he's likely to do, and so on. I'm not sure anyone else would have considered Mouse setting that many traps in the Vault."

"That brings up another question," I said. "What was he doing in there?"

There was a quick exchange of glances between my father, Buzz, and Luna. Obviously my question touched on something of import.

"As you know," Alpha Prime finally said, "the Vault houses a lot of weapons that we've collected over the years."

Electra nodded. "Yeah, we saw the display cases that hold some of them."

"Well, yes and no," my father said, waffling a hand from side to side. "The stuff in the display cases is, for one reason or another, completely defective. They'll never work again. They pose no risk, and we really just keep them out for those occasions when we have distinguished visitors."

"So they're just conversation pieces," I summed up. "Things you can show off when some bigwig — say, a government bureaucrat — drops by. You make him feel important by showing him an area that's off-limits to almost everyone, but they really don't get to see anything that's worth the price of admission."

"Now you get it," Luna chimed in.

"Okay," said Electra, nodding her head. "So where do you keep the good liquor?"

"The walls," I interjected, reflecting back on what I'd seen Mouse doing in the Vault. "They serve as some kind of additional storage system, like rolling stacks in a library."

"Very good," my father said with a smile. "The walls, the floor, the ceiling…everything. That's where we keep the stuff that's still worrisome."

"Behind walls and stuff?" Electra intoned skeptically. "Sounds kind of flimsy, even if they are inside a vault."

"You probably didn't get a good look at it," Buzz commented, "but the walls, floor, and ceiling are even thicker than the blast doors at the Vault's entrance. Trust me, anything we put there is safe."

"And we also have a few offsite storage facilities," Luna added, giving Alpha Prime a knowing look.

I understood without asking that she was referring to my father's hidden retreat, which was where a number of destructive devices were stored. I had never been there

— didn't even know where it was — but it didn't seem relevant at the moment.

"So now we get to the nitty-gritty," I remarked. "Mouse was at one of the wall storage sections. So the question is, what did he take?"

Once again, the three adults in the room spent a moment looking at each other. It gave the impression that the answer wasn't going to be palatable, and it wasn't.

"We're not sure," Alpha Prime finally confessed.

I gave him an incredulous stare. "What do you mean, you're not sure? Don't you guys keep an inventory list or something along those lines?"

"Of course we do," my father replied. "We've got a state-of-the-art system to keep track of stuff like that. But I'll give you three guesses who designed it, and you won't need two of them."

"Mouse," I said flatly.

"Yes," Luna confirmed. "Our index, catalog, and itemization process for weapons and such is his baby."

"So what's the problem?" Electra asked.

"Apparently during his little house call, Mouse scrambled the inventory system," Buzz answered.

"In essence, you don't know what you have anymore," I concluded.

"That's true to some extent," Alpha Prime concurred. "But the real issue is that we don't know what he took."

"Well, what can the stuff in there do?" I asked.

"Everything up to and including destroying the world," Buzz said. "Not to mention just taking it over."

"Well, good thing that's not on Mouse's list," Electra said.

Once again, the adult League members were silent, as if they weren't sure how to respond.

"Oh, come on," I droned. "You can't believe that Mouse is planning to take over the world."

Buzz shrugged. "He's joked once or twice about how much easier things would be if he just took charge. It's something all of us occasionally kid each other about. But now that he's off his rocker, who knows?"

"More importantly," Luna added, "why take something that can only be used for global domination if that's not your intent?"

"But nobody knows what he took," I reminded them. "Or if he took anything at all."

"We've got people working on it," my father assured me. "They'll figure it out. And there's also a little bit of a silver lining."

"Which is what?" I asked dubiously.

"The devices in the Vault that can actually do harm are all disassembled," Alpha Prime stated. "They're in pieces that aren't kept together. So, at best, Mouse got one component of some device, but it won't do him any good without the rest."

"Mouse is a genius," I reminded them. "If he's got a device that's missing a component, he can just build it."

"If he's got the resources," Luna chimed it. "But I don't think that's the case. I think he's alone and isolated, without a lot of assets."

"Other than hacking skills, gravity wells, and frictionless grease," I noted. "Not to mention anything else he might have up his sleeve."

Luna looked as though she had something to add, but Alpha Prime cut her off.

"That's enough, you two," he declared. "I think you're both right to an extent. Mouse obviously isn't to be taken lightly, but — at the same time — if he could just build anything he needed, he wouldn't be stealing from the League."

"So basically," Electra said, "we need to get our arms around what he took so we can figure out what else he might need."

"And once we know that," Alpha Prime added, "we might be able to catch him."

ISOLATION

Chapter 33

Alpha Prime, Buzz, and Luna left shortly thereafter, with my father promising to reach out to me regarding next steps. That left me and Electra in the conference room by ourselves.

"You want me to teleport you home?" I asked her once we were alone.

She seemed to mull it over for a moment, then asked, "What are *you* going to do?"

"Honestly, I don't know. I mean, none of this makes sense to me. I know what I saw earlier, with Mouse in the Vault, but I still can't wrap my head around it."

"You mean him going on the attack and wanting to destroy the League?"

"Not just that — this whole idea of him maybe taking over the world." That part in particular was troubling to me — mostly because I had been scanning my father and his colleagues empathically during our conversation, and had picked up on feelings of sincerity in that regard.

"Well, as you so plainly noted," Electra said, "we don't know what he took. So maybe we don't need to cross that bridge yet."

"But why would he take *any*thing?" I asked. "I can't imagine that there's something in that Vault that's better than…"

I trailed off as the thought that was in my mind finished forming.

"Better than what?" Electra asked, bringing me back to myself.

"I need to go check something out," I replied.

"What? Where?"

"Mouse's lab."

"Then I'm going, too," she insisted.

"Suit yourself," I said with a shrug, then teleported the two of us.

ISOLATION

Chapter 34

We reappeared in Mouse's lab. The room was completely dark, and I was about to switch my vision over to the infrared when the lights began to come on — seemingly as a result of our presence.

"So what are we doing here?" Electra asked.

"Frankly speaking, I'm not sure," I replied as I started to walk around. "It just occurred to me that, if he wanted to take over the world — or just destroy the League — Mouse would probably have something ten times better than anything a supervillain could come up with."

Following me, Electra said, "And you think he'd keep it in his lab?"

I shrugged as I continued scanning the room. "I'm not sure about *that*, but he did everything *from* his lab. That being the case, there might be something here he'd want or need."

"So what's your theory — that he'd come back here?"

"That was my initial thought, but it didn't pan out before." I then explained to her how a group of us had come to the lab the previous day. "If he does need something from here, it's possible he's simply *accessing* it in some way."

"You mean like logging in remotely to a computer or something?"

"Yeah," I agreed with a nod. "But from what I can see, nothing is on in here except the lights. None of the gadgets or devices on his worktables, none of the PCs. In fact, I can't even see how to power these computers up."

ISOLATION

It was a true statement. There were a number of computers around the lab, but I hadn't seen a power button on any of them as I walked around.

Electra appeared to mull this over for a moment, then asked, "But would he need specific computers on if he just wanted to access the network?"

"Good point," I admitted. "But it assumes that any info Mouse would want would actually *be* on the League network."

Electra frowned. "So what are you saying — that Mouse had his own *private* network?"

"I'd be shocked if he didn't," I stated. "But look, here's the main thing: I'm in this lab with Mouse almost on a daily basis. Every idea he has, every notion, every inspiration, it goes from cradle to grave inside these walls. So whatever he's doing right now, whatever he's thinking, wherever he's holed up — there's some clue to it in *here*. I'm just not seeing it."

"That makes sense," Electra agreed, "but maybe you're too close to the problem. It might help if you step back for a moment and take a mental break. After all, we've been at this all day."

"Yeah, but it's Mouse," I said. "He wouldn't be taking a break if the situation was reversed."

"Maybe not, but even he'd agree that it's still important to eat, sleep, and so on," she argued, mimicking words I'd heard earlier. "So how about this: why don't we go grab some dinner, try to talk about something else, and then give it another whack?"

I looked at her with a raised eyebrow. "Why Electra, are you asking me on a date?"

She laughed. "No, it is most definitely *not* a date. But if you play your cards right…"

She gave me a coy look as she trailed off, and I sensed an unexpected amalgam of emotions from her — flirtatiousness mixed with excitement and affection. However, before I could offer any type of comment, my attention was drawn by an odd beeping sound.

"What was that?" Electra inquired as the noise sounded again.

"I'm not sure," I responded, shaking my head, "but it sounds like…"

I trailed off and the beeping sounded once more, coming from the far side of the room. I began walking in that direction, accompanied by Electra. By the time the beep sounded a fourth time, I had figured out the source of the noise: a computer monitor on one of the worktables. Looking at it, I was surprised to see a cursor blinking in the upper left corner of the screen.

"It's on," whispered Electra, almost in awe.

"Yeah," I muttered, nodding.

"But how?"

"I'm assuming, like the lights, it was somehow triggered by us being in the room. Maybe it just took it a minute to power up."

Electra opened her mouth to say something, but became silent as the cursor suddenly moved, spelling out a query:

Name?

"It's asking for a name," Electra noted, pointing to a keyboard that was connected to the monitor.

"Really?" I uttered sarcastically. "I had no idea."

ISOLATION

I received a playful punch on the arm in response to my commentary. Ignoring Electra's antics, I continued staring at the screen, thinking.

"What are you waiting for?" Electra finally asked.

"I'm trying to figure out how to respond," I answered.

"Just type Mouse's name," she stated in an impatient tone.

"There's no way it's that easy. Mouse doesn't operate like that, and no computer in here is going to offer unfettered access to its systems solely because you typed in his name."

"So what do you suggest?"

"I don't know," I confessed, rubbing my chin. "But there's an old saying about honesty being the best policy, so…"

Pulling the keyboard in front of me, I hastily typed out my name:

Jim Carrow

I hit the *Enter* button and waited. The cursor blinked for a few times and then vanished. A moment later, the screen went blank.

"Idiot," Electra muttered, only slightly tongue-in-cheek. "I told you to enter Mouse's name."

I was about to make a smart-aleck response when the screen came back to life, saying:

Please answer the security question.

A confused look came across Electra's face. "What security question?"

"Give it a minute," I advised.

As if in response to my comment, additional verbiage suddenly appeared on the screen:

If you have me, you want to share me. But if you share me, you won't have me.

Electra frowned. "What kind of security question is *that*?"

"The Mouse kind," I replied. "It's a riddle."

She gave me an incredulous look. "You're kidding, right?"

"Does it look like I'm kidding?" I asked, gesturing towards the screen.

"So what are you going to do?"

"Answer it, of course."

"So wait — you know the answer?"

"Naturally," I stated in a playfully smug tone.

"So what is it?"

"It's a 'secret.'"

"A secret?" Electra repeated. "So what does that mean — you can't tell anyone?"

"It's 'secret,'" I stated again.

"I heard you the first time. What I haven't heard yet is the answer."

Frustrated, I wiped my face with my hand. "The answer is 'secret.'"

Electra crossed her arms in anger. "So you really aren't going to tell me?"

Shaking my head in exasperation, I turned back to the monitor and began typing the answer:

Secret

ISOLATION

"Ooooh," Electra droned as I finished and hit the *Enter* button. "Now I get it. If you have a secret, you want to share it. But if you share it, it's not a secret anymore."

Ignoring her, I kept my eyes on the screen. It went blank for a moment, then briefly flashed the phrase, *Access Granted.* A second later, the word *Files* appeared in the top left corner of the screen. Below that heading, a long list of what I presumed to be file names began to appear.

"Nice!" Electra exclaimed. "You got access to Mouse's system."

"Yeah," I remarked with a smile. "Pretty cool, huh?"

"Cool? It's freakin' awesome!" she announced with a grin that I eagerly returned.

Our euphoria, however, was short-lived. Looking at the screen, I began to notice a phrase appearing in parenthesis behind a number of file names:

(File corrupted. Unable to retrieve.)

"That's not good," Electra noted.

"You think?" I muttered caustically as the corrupted tag began attaching to more and more of the file names. Within seconds, almost all of the files had received that label.

"So everything on here is corrupt?" Electra uttered in surprise. "How weird is that?"

"Not weird at all if you know Mouse," I stated.

"You think *he* did this — corrupted all the data."

"It would definitely make it harder to find him or figure out what he's up to," I declared. "But, if it *was* him, it looks like he didn't manage to corrupt *every* file."

185

I pointed at the screen as I spoke, singling out what appeared to be the lone uncorrupted item on the screen.

"What is that?" Electra asked.

"Based on the file extension, it looks like some kind of video," I noted as I double-clicked on the file name.

Almost immediately, a window opened on the screen. Right away, I recognized what I was seeing as the same footage I'd viewed the day before of the scene in Mouse's lab. I let it play for a few seconds and then paused it.

Electra looked at me curiously. "Why'd you do that?"

"Because I've seen it before," I answered, then explained how I'd already watched the video. "I should have realized that's what it was, since it was the only thing they recovered from the cameras in here. But long story short, there's nothing new here."

"So what now?"

I shrugged. "I guess now I accept your invitation to go on a date."

"Again," she reminded me laughingly, "not a date."

I waved a hand at her dismissively. "So you say."

Still smiling, she said, "Actually, I—"

The sound of my phone ringing cut her off. I pulled it out and saw that it was Alpha Prime calling.

Taking a few steps away, I answered with a quick, "Hello."

"Hey," my father said. "I think we're standing down for the night."

"Sounds reasonable," I acknowledged. "It's not like we have a bunch of clues to follow up on."

"True," Alpha Prime agreed. "Anyway, I was wondering if we were still on for dinner."

ISOLATION

"Oh," I muttered softly, caught flatfooted. I had completely forgotten about our dinner plans. I looked at Electra, who was busy staring at something on the computer monitor. "Well, uh, actually, Electra just asked me out."

"Did not," she shouted over her shoulder.

"But hey," I continued, "you have any objection to joining us?"

"That's okay, son," he insisted. "I know you two have things to discuss. We'll do it another time."

"No, no, no," I blurted out. "I don't want to keep putting this off. Plus, Electra and I need a chaperone anyway — to make sure she keeps her hands to herself."

Electra gave me an evil look for a second, then turned back to the monitor.

Laughing, my father said, "Well, it has been a while since I spent a decent amount of time with either of you. I tell you what: I'll grab some pizzas and meet you guys at your place. We'll hang out for a bit and just chat."

"Sounds great," I said. "See you soon."

Alpha Prime then muttered a quick goodbye, and I hung up the phone. Turning my attention back to Electra, I saw her still watching the computer monitor. Walking towards her, I soon realized — as I suspected — that she was watching the footage of the previous day's altercation in the lab.

She shot me a glance and then paused the video before turning towards me.

"How do you feel about pizza for dinner?" I asked. "At my place."

"Fine by me," she replied.

"Also, Alpha Prime's joining us — if that's okay."

"Again, I'm fine with it," she declared. "Are we leaving now?"

"Unless you can think of a reason to stay," I remarked, then glanced at the monitor. A moment later, Electra followed my gaze.

"I never got a chance to see it," she explained. "So I was curious."

"Did you want to finish it?" I asked.

She shook her head. "No, that's okay. Like you said, there's nothing there. I mean, the part I saw was interesting, but I didn't get the impression anything on there would help us find Mouse."

"Are you sure you don't want to see it all?"

"Yeah," she assured me. "But if I change my mind, we can always come back."

"Hmmm," I droned, thinking. "Hang on for a sec."

I then did a quick survey of the area around us, but only had to go as far as the next worktable to find what I was looking for: a memory stick.

"What are you doing?" Electra asked as I came back to the keyboard.

"Making a copy," I responded. "You relying on my word that there's nothing on the video bothers me — makes me feel like I'm being too cocky. Now I want to go back and look at it again to make sure."

It took me a second to locate an appropriate port to insert the memory stick into (surprisingly, it was located on the side of the monitor), but after that, the system seemed to understand what I was trying to do. It asked a question about downloading the current file to the inserted medium, and a few moments later the video file — or rather, a copy of it — had found a new home on the memory stick.

"You know, you could have just watched it again right here," Electra noted as I removed the memory stick and put it in my back pocket.

"Yeah, but I might want to look at it more than once," I explained. "And I prefer being able to do it at my leisure. Also, once we leave, I'm pretty sure everything in here will power down again. Since I'm not sure how this machine even turned on, I'm not banking on that happening every time I come back here."

"Okay," she intoned after mulling over my comments for a second. "I can get on board with that. So, if you have everything, can we go now?"

Giving her a nod, I teleported us.

ISOLATION

Chapter 35

We popped up in the living room of the embassy. Electra immediately flopped down on the couch.

"Ahh, it feels good to finally relax," she announced, kicking off her shoes. "I feel like I've been on my feet all day."

"I know what you mean," I said as I sat down next to her.

"Puh-leeze," she droned. "You can just turn off pain receptors and nerve endings if things start to hurt or get uncomfortable. The rest of us have to suffer through."

"Doesn't mean I can't sympathize."

"Oh, you sympathize?" she mocked. "That's so sweet."

I came to my feet. "You know what? I'm just going to sit somewhere else."

I moved to step away, but she grabbed my hand.

"Come on — you know I'm just teasing," she insisted, at the same time tugging on my hand until I sat back down. "Now, how long before Alpha Prime shows up with the food?"

I shrugged. "Don't know. However long it takes him to grab some pizzas and drive over here."

"So he's driving?"

"I suppose. I mean, we left his SUV at the marina, so I assumed he'd go back and get it. And speaking of driving, in case you forgot, your car's still parked out front."

"I actually thought about that after you teleported me home this morning. And that reminds me: I should probably call my dad and let him know where I am."

ISOLATION

"And be sure to tell him I'll have you home before curfew," I demanded as Electra stood up and took her phone out of her pocket.

"We'll see," she remarked with a coy smile as she stepped away to make her call.

Left on my own for the first time all day, I spent a few moments reflecting on everything that had happened. Needless to say, I still had trouble with the notion of Mouse attacking his League teammates (not to mention possibly wanting to take over the world). It just didn't make sense. And sadly, my second sojourn to the lab had been less than fruitful. (Well, there *was* the video, but the more I thought about it, the less I felt it would pay dividends in any significant way.)

I was still mentally reviewing the day's events when Electra came back a few minutes later.

"Everything good?" I asked.

She nodded. "Of course. I told him we were in the middle of an assignment, and he understood."

"Wow," I murmured. "He's a lot more reasonable than I would have guessed."

"Well, if you'd stop prejudging him, you'd see that my dad is pretty great," Electra declared. "Anyway, my phone's almost dead. Do you have a charger I can borrow?"

"Uhhh," I droned. "Not really."

She stared at me for a second. "Seriously? You're not going to let me borrow a charger?"

"It's not that," I assured her. "I'm just not sure that I have one."

"Don't have one?" Electra echoed, giving me a strange look.

"Let me rephrase: I'm sure I have one. I just don't know where it is."

"Then how do you keep your phone charged?"

"I don't. Or rather, I don't have to charge it."

Electra continued looking at me oddly. "You're going to have to explain that."

I sighed. "A while back, Mouse took my phone and made some upgrades to the architecture. One of the things he did was install an advanced battery that really doesn't have to be recharged."

I didn't bother talking about any of the other improvements, like the enhanced casing that made the phone nigh unbreakable. The issue of the battery alone was apparently surprising enough.

"Well," Electra droned, "that's impressive. Mouse didn't do that for *me* — or any of the other teens that I'm aware of. All we got installed was a tracker so the League can find us whenever they like."

"Come on — he's my mentor," I stressed. "Of course there are going to be some perks that go along with that. But on the downside, I think Mouse said this battery thing isn't perfected yet, so I'm really just a guinea pig. Once it becomes clear that it's not going to explode in someone's pocket, I'm sure everybody will get one."

"I wouldn't be so sure," she demurred. "But why don't we put that conversation on pause and discuss something else until Alpha Prime gets here."

"Works for me," I said.

ISOLATION

Chapter 36

Instead of chatting, we ended up watching television in the theater room — a soundproof chamber with a one-hundred-twenty-inch projector screen and rows of seating that consisted of powered recliners. It was a room that had seen limited use since my family's departure, so I was happy to have a reason to put it in service.

The show we watched was one of Electra's choosing: a prerecorded horror anthology comprised of thirty-minute segments. However, rather than sit in her own chair, Electra chose to squeeze in next to me. Although oversized, the recliner wasn't really designed to accommodate two, but after a little shapeshifting on my part — basically, altering some of the contours of my body — we were able to sit comfortably. (And even if we'd remained uncomfortable, I wasn't going to complain.)

We were perhaps five minutes into the second show segment when the doorbell rang, sounding on a device built especially for the theater room.

"That's Alpha Prime," I announced, after reaching out and confirming that fact empathically.

Electra stood up as I grabbed the remote and turned the television off. A moment later, I was on my feet as well, and then — after shifting my body back to its normal shape — teleported us to the front door. I immediately opened it to let my father in.

"Hey," Alpha Prime said as he walked inside.

"Whoa!" exclaimed Electra, noting (as did I) that my father was holding five pizza boxes in each hand. "Did you get a second job delivering fast food or something?"

"Hardly," my father replied with a laugh. "But I've been watching Jim stuff his face all day, so after our last escapade in the Vault, I figured he'd be hungry enough to eat a horse."

Electra and I both laughed at that, but his statement wasn't far from the truth. I had tweaked my internal systems after our run-in with Mouse so that I wouldn't get hungry. However, given my druthers, I probably would have eaten much earlier (and in copious quantities).

"Let me give you a hand," I said, taking a stack of the pizza boxes from my father. "All right, let's go eat."

****

We wound up eating in the breakfast nook — a cozy area near the kitchen that was dominated by a counter-height table that could seat eight. It was the place where I'd normally taken meals with my family, so it was second nature for me to eat there on this occasion.

Apparently Alpha Prime was of the same mind as Electra in terms of taking a step back from our Mouse hunt, so to speak. He didn't mention it at all during the meal, instead choosing to regale me and Electra with some humorous anecdotes from his past adventures. I had to admit that he was a good storyteller, and I enjoyed listening to him.

After eating, the three of us played a couple of board games, at my father's suggestion. In all honesty, it felt weird to me to be doing so when the issue of Mouse was still so prevalent, but Alpha Prime had insisted.

"Listen," he'd said, "I've been where you are — in the middle of a mission that not only has high stakes but personal relevance. If you don't do something to keep your spirits up, you'll get into a funk so overwhelming that it will be impossible to be fully effective."

Thus, I had reluctantly given in, but ultimately had a great time. I didn't win any games, but it was lots of fun playing with my father and Electra. (And it did feel good to take my mind off my problems.)

"Okay, it's obviously not my night," I declared after losing the fourth game. I then pushed my chair back from the table and stood up.

"You're quitting?" Electra asked in a surprised tone.

"Just going to grab some more pizza," I replied. At the same time, I hooked a thumb over my shoulder towards the kitchen, where we'd placed the food.

"I'll get it for you," Electra stated, coming to her feet. "Just stay here and chat with AP."

I simply stared at her as she walked to the kitchen. Frankly speaking, I was a little surprised; typically Electra despised stereotypical roles, like a woman fetching a man's food.

"Well," my father intoned, getting my attention, "I think I'm going to head out."

"Oh, okay," I responded as Alpha Prime stood up. "I'm sorry it wasn't the dinner you probably had planned, but I really enjoyed this."

"Me, too," he conceded with a nod. "This was great. I mean, I still want us to have some father-son time, but I wouldn't mind doing this again."

"Same here," I remarked, "on both counts."

"Anyway, let's talk about tomorrow for a sec," my father proposed, turning serious. "There's someone I think we should talk to, so be ready bright and early."

I nodded. "Sounds good. Who are we going to see?"

"Let me hold that in reserve for tomorrow," he said. "I don't want you dwelling on it too much."

"Ha!" I chortled. "And you think I won't dwell on it now that you've mentioned it?"

"Yeah, it is kind of a catch-22," he admitted as Electra came back with a couple of slices of pizza on a plate.

"Hey," she said to him as she placed the pizza in front of me, "you're not leaving, are you?"

"Yeah, I have to take off," he declared. "Me and Jim have an early start tomorrow."

"You mean *we* have an early start tomorrow," she corrected.

Alpha Prime looked at me, and I just shrugged, saying, "You're the one who dragged her into this."

My father threw up his hands in capitulation. "All right, I'll see the two of you in the morning."

With that, he gave Electra a hug and a kiss on the forehead, and then I walked him to the door and saw him off.

Returning to the breakfast nook, I saw that Electra had put away the board games.

"You heading home, too?" I asked before taking a bite of the pizza she'd brought me.

"Do you want me to?" she asked coquettishly.

"What I want is to stay on your father's good side."

"Why is everything with you always about my dad?" she pouted.

"It's not," I countered. "Occasionally, it's about Esper."

She laughed at that. "Okay then, why is it always about the adults I live with?"

I sighed. "Look, I want us to get back to the point where we were before, but — everything else aside — it's going to be difficult if those two don't like me."

"Wouldn't your time be better spent on making *me* like you?"

"Nah, because if Vir and Esper like me, I can get you on board," I quipped. "Speaking of Esper, have you heard from her?"

"Nope," Electra answered, shaking her head. "But she's off on assignment, so we may not hear from her until she gets back."

I simply nodded in understanding. Whatever mission Esper got sent on, she was probably operating under radio silence until it was completed.

"Anyway," Electra continued, "why don't we continue this back in the theater room?"

As she spoke, she picked up the plate of pizza she'd given me and began walking away.

"So, you want to continue our date night?" I quizzed, following her.

She giggled. "It's not a date, and what I really want is to finish the show we started before Alpha Prime showed up."

"So you *do* want to continue our date," I teased.

I kept needling her about our "date" as we headed back to the theater room, occasionally taking a bite of pizza as we walked. On her part, Electra laughingly denied each time that it was a date.

Once in the theater room, Electra took control of the remote and squeezed in next to me again on the recliner, while I finished off the pizza. It was only at that point that I began paying any real attention to the show. Electra appeared to find it engrossing, but to me it was incredibly boring. In fact, I started to doze almost immediately, and within minutes I was fast asleep.

ISOLATION

Chapter 37

I woke up alone in the recliner. Looking around, I noted that I was still in the theater room, although the screen was now off. I frowned, trying to recall the previous night; the last thing I remembered was sitting in the recliner with Electra, watching some awful horror show.

Now that she had come to mind, I reached out for my ex empathically, and picked up her vibe almost immediately. I frowned. From what I could sense, she seemed to be in a room that had been designated as my mother's office. (My mom had been a midlist author of superhero romances.) Curious as to what she was doing in there, I was about to teleport to her when my cell phone chirped to let me know I'd received a voicemail message.

I pulled the phone out and saw that I actually had two missed calls: one from Myshtal the night before, and one from my father just a minute or so earlier. (In fact, it was probably Alpha Prime's call that had woken me up.) I also saw that they had both left me voicemails.

Myshtal's message was fairly straightforward: she was just calling to check in and would chat with me later. My father's message was similarly direct: he was on his way and would be at my door within thirty minutes.

Yawning, I stood up and stretched. I'd had to shapeshift again when Electra sat next to me, so I quickly morphed back to my normal frame. I then did a repeat of the previous day, teleporting to my room and racing through my morning routine and shower at super speed. I then dressed and teleported to my mother's office.

Although her back was to me when I popped up, Electra — without turning around — gave me a hearty,

"Good morning." She had obviously sensed my bioelectric field — an ability that let her know when others were near.

"Hey," I said in response. "What are you doing in here?"

Electra, who had been standing at my mother's desk and leaning over, stepped to the side, revealing a laptop. Her body had previously been blocking it, so I hadn't even known it was there.

"I hope you don't mind," she began, "but I woke up kind of early and was looking for something to do."

"So you spent the night here again," I noted.

"Yeah, but I already talked to my dad, so try not to make a thing of it."

I barely avoided letting out a groan of exasperation, but managed to simply say, "Okay, fine. Now, how'd you find your way in here?"

"After I freshened up in the guest room again, I was looking for something to do and remembered the video from Mouse's lab."

As she spoke, I instinctively reached towards my back pocket. Of course, the memory stick wasn't there — it had been in my other pants. But, upon reflection, I suddenly realized that it hadn't been there either, because I'd checked my pockets before showering. (Truth be told, I had practically forgotten about it.)

"I got the memory stick from your pocket," she went on, "and then pecked around until I found a laptop. I hope that was okay."

"How'd you get it out without waking me?" I asked.

"The memory stick?" Electra queried with a laugh. "You were practically in a coma. I could have had a brass band playing in here and you wouldn't have woken up. I guess you were dead tired."

Rather than respond, I turned my attention to the laptop screen, noting that Electra had paused the video.

"So, did anything leap out at you?" I asked.

"Not really," she admitted. "But you can take a look and see what you think, since you were going to watch it again anyway."

"Might as well," I said, stepping towards the laptop. "But I need to get you home soon so you can change and do whatever, because Alpha Prime will be here shortly."

"In case you didn't notice, I've already changed, genius."

I blinked, then looked her up and down. I suddenly realized that she was indeed wearing different clothes.

"What...?" I muttered. "How...?"

"Your mom," she stated, giggling.

I had trouble hiding my incredulity. "Excuse me?"

"You remember that charity auction I went to with your mom about a month ago?"

I nodded. My mom and Electra had actually had a great relationship — which seemingly continued even after she broke up with me. It wasn't unusual for them to go to lunch together, go shopping, etcetera.

"Anyway," she went on, "if you remember, I actually came over here to change and we left together. However, I never came back and got the clothes I originally wore. Your mom told me that she'd washed them and put them in a bag for me, but I never actually got around to picking them up."

"So you just poked around this morning until you found them."

"Guess that was providence, huh?" she stated with a smile.

"I suppose," I muttered, then turned my attention to the laptop. I hit *Play* and the video resumed. I watched for about ten seconds, and then my eyes went wide and I drew in a sharp breath.

"What is it?" Electra asked in sudden alarm.

"This isn't the same video," I said woodenly.

ISOLATION

Chapter 38

It turned out that the video wasn't just a single clip; it was multiple clips combined back-to-back into a single file. More specifically, it appeared to be the footage from Mouse's lab, but from various camera angles.

When I had first played it on the monitor in the lab, the segment of footage I'd seen was the same thing Alpha Prime and the others had shown me. Thus, I had — wrongfully — assumed that the entire file was something I'd seen before. However, what Electra was watching when I found her in my mother's office was footage of the same scene, but from a different perspective. Luckily, it only took a few seconds of viewing for me to realize that.

After I understood what I was looking at, I watched the entire video file from beginning to end. Thankfully, it was relatively short — maybe two minutes altogether — but unfortunately, nothing in any of the footage stood out to me. I watched it a second time (with Electra looking over my shoulder), eyes peeled for anything out of the ordinary. However, it wasn't until I watched it a third time, at the juncture when the myriad holograms were running around Mouse's lab, that I noticed something unusual.

"There!" I said excitedly, pausing the footage and pointing.

Electra narrowed her eyes and leaned forward. "I'm not sure what you're seeing."

"Right *there*," I reiterated, tapping the screen. "That guy doesn't have a backpack on."

"Okay," Electra muttered without a lot of conviction. "One out of a billion holograms isn't wearing a backpack. So what?"

"It's not just a backpack," I explained. "It's his bug-out bag."

"Again, so what?"

I debated trying to explain the significance of it in greater detail, but didn't want to waste time.

"Just hang out here for a second," I said. "I need to go check something out."

"Not without me," Electra stated fiercely.

From the look on her face, it was clear that she was serious. Rather than argue, I simply teleported us.

ISOLATION

Chapter 39

Our destination was Mouse's lab. As before, it was dark when we appeared. I switched my vision over to the infrared and made a beeline for one of the nearby worktables. There was a cabinet underneath it, which I opened. A moment later, the lights in the lab started coming on, and I switched my vision back to normal as I pulled out the contents of the cabinet: Mouse's bug-out bag.

Electra began walking towards me as I set the bag on top of the worktable.

"It's still here," I muttered, more to myself than Electra. I hadn't even thought to check for it previously; after viewing all the holograms in the video wearing it, I had just assumed it was gone.

"What's the big deal about this thing?" she asked.

"Don't you get it?" I asked. "It's his bug-out bag. This is the bag Mouse takes when he has to go on the run."

To emphasize my point, I opened up the bag and pulled out a couple of its contents: a computer tablet, a sat phone, and a small wad of cash.

"I guess he didn't have time to take it," Electra surmised. "He did leave in a bit of a rush."

I shook my head as I began putting everything back in the backpack. "That just doesn't sound like Mouse. The whole point of the bag is to provide him with resources he'll need. He wouldn't just leave it."

"Maybe the Mouse you knew wouldn't," she countered. "But this seems to be the all-new, screw-loose version."

"Nice," I said acerbically, trying not to get angry.

"I'm sorry," she apologized, "but you know what I mean. The person we're dealing with doesn't seem to be the same Mouse who led the League — not if he's attacking us and breaking into the Vault."

"And I still say he wouldn't do that without a reason."

"You're also saying he wouldn't leave without his bug-out bag, and yet…"

She trailed off, gesturing towards the backpack.

"There is another possible explanation," I stated.

Electra gave me an inquisitive look. "Like what?"

"Maybe he didn't go anywhere," I said.

ISOLATION

Chapter 40

Comically, we spent a few minutes shouting for Mouse to come out. Of course, he never responded or appeared.

"Do you honestly think he's hiding somewhere nearby?" Electra finally asked.

"Anything's possible," I confessed with a shrug. "That said, 'nearby' doesn't necessarily mean within shouting distance."

"But he didn't go far enough to need his bug-out bag."

"Not according to the video," I replied. As I spoke, a thought occurred to me. Brow crinkled, I walked over to the monitor that had turned on the day before. It was dark — still shut down.

Electra, who had followed me, asked, "What are you thinking?"

"I made an assumption about the video file that was flat-out wrong yesterday. It just occurred to me that maybe I overlooked something else, but the machine isn't turning on this time."

"So what turned it on yesterday? Did one of us inadvertently flip a power switch?"

I shrugged. "Who knows? Almost everything in here was designed and built by Mouse from scratch. It may not necessarily conform or operate in a way we expect."

"So what now?"

"Well, I guess we—"

I was cut off by the sound of my phone ringing. Pulling it out, I saw that it was Alpha Prime calling.

"Hey," I said upon answering. "Where are you?"

"Outside the gate," he answered.

"Okay, we'll be there in a sec," I stated before hanging up. I then told Electra, "Alpha Prime's waiting on us. We'll have to pick this up later."

She gave me a nod and I teleported us, taking us just outside the gate of the embassy. As expected, Alpha Prime was there, sitting in the driver's seat of the SUV. To my surprise, however, there was someone in the front passenger seat as well: Smokey.

"Oh, man — I'm sorry," I began apologizing upon seeing him. "I completely forgot—"

"Don't worry about it," Smokey interjected, opening the door and stepping out. "I stayed an extra night like we talked about, hung out all day yesterday, and then Vestibule volunteered to take me home."

"And then I found him wandering around the halls of HQ," my father added. "Didn't think it would hurt to have an extra pair of hands on deck."

I frowned but didn't immediately comment on my father's statement, while Smokey and Electra exchanged greetings. Following this, Smokey opened the rear door of the SUV, obviously planning to relinquish the front seat to me.

"Hey," I suddenly said to him, "why don't you keep riding in front?"

He gave me an odd look, then glanced at Electra. Suddenly a light bulb seemed to come on in his mind.

"Oh yeah," he blurted out as he gave the two of us a sly look. "Sure."

With that, he quickly got back into the front seat while Electra and I got into the back. A minute later, we were on the road.

ISOLATION

Electra immediately began asking Smokey about his trip to the West Coast. I used the opportunity to open a telepathic channel to my father.

<You sure this is smart?> I asked. <Bringing Smokey along on this?>

<You don't think he can handle it?> Alpha Prime shot back.

<It's not about him being able to handle it. The issue now is that you've got three teens tagging along on a mission that may have global implications. If we needed another pair of hands, I'm wondering why you didn't snatch up another full-fledged, card-carrying member of the League.>

<Because they're all on duty, smart guy. A good number are out on assignment, but anyone who isn't has been given a duty post at HQ in case Mouse comes back. We have to be prepared. Plus, I know Smokey is a good sounding board for you, and since you're still our best shot at finding Mouse, it made sense to have him with us.>

I hated to admit it, but Alpha Prime's reasoning came across as sound. I stated as much to him and then broke the connection. I spent the next few minutes pondering everything that had happened and was trying to figure out what, if anything, I might have missed when a question from Electra cut across my thoughts.

Focusing on my father, she asked, "So, where are we going?"

"DTG," he replied.

I raised my eyebrows in surprise, as did Smokey and Electra.

"DTG?" Smokey repeated. "They're one of the largest tech companies in the world."

"Not just tech," Alpha Prime corrected. "They're a huge conglomerate that owns everything from casinos to manufacturing plants."

"Yeah, they're massive," Electra added. "They've got something like a thousand-acre corporate campus just outside the city."

"And that's where we're headed," Alpha Prime noted. "After we make one quick stop."

"Where?" I asked.

My father glanced at me via the rearview mirror and winked, saying, "Breakfast, of course."

ISOLATION

Chapter 41

Like the day before, we stopped at a fast-food place for breakfast. Personally, I didn't have nearly the same appetite this time around and thus ordered far less. After we got back on the road and began eating, Electra brought everyone up to speed regarding my theory on Mouse's bug-out bag.

After mulling over what Electra had said, my father asked, "So if you don't think he went far, where's he most likely to be?"

The question was seemingly directed to me. I shrugged in response, saying, "I don't know. If you remember, League HQ was practically razed to the ground last year."

No one commented, but it was unlikely anyone had forgotten the prior attack on the Alpha League, which had actually been orchestrated by one of our own.

"Mouse actually oversaw the reconstruction efforts," I continued. "He could have had any number of secret rooms or hidden chambers built."

"So he could be hiding right under our noses," Smokey surmised.

"It might explain how he seems to appear and disappear at leisure," Alpha Prime added.

There was further speculation by the other three, but I stayed out of it. I didn't like the notion of Mouse scurrying around like his namesake, performing sneak attacks on his colleagues, or plotting to take over the world. None of it felt right.

The others were still bandying about theories when we reached the DTG campus, a boundary marked by a large stone wall on which the corporate name was cast in six-foot-tall metallic lettering. Driving past it, we soon found ourselves on the sprawling grounds of the company, which contained not only stylish, modernized buildings, but also an unexpectedly expansive amount of green space. There was even a waterfall next to an adjoining garden. Simply put, the place was beautiful.

Eventually we ended up in the parking lot of an interconnected cluster of futuristic-looking buildings, the most notable of which was a structure that was designed to look like a cube floating between two other edifices. My father pulled into a reserved parking spot that was clearly intended for VIPs and turned the engine off.

"Let's go," Alpha Prime said as he opened his door.

A moment later, we were headed towards the entrance to one of the buildings.

Once inside, we found ourselves facing a number of speedgates that utilized card readers to allow further access to the building. Next to the speedgates was a security desk, which Alpha Prime began walking towards.

There were three guards behind the desk, and the nearest one looked up as my father approached. Reaching into his back pocket, Alpha Prime pulled out what looked like a plastic card and handed it to the guard.

"I need to get in," he declared. Almost as an afterthought, he hooked his thumb at me, Smokey, and Electra, adding, "They're with me."

There was a scanner of some sort close at hand, and the guard swiped the card in front of it. Almost immediately, a diode on the device flashed red. Frowning, the guard swiped it again, and then a third time. Each attempt, however, produced the same result: a flashing red diode.

ISOLATION

Turning to a nearby keyboard and monitor, the guard hastily typed something that I couldn't see. Following this, he swiped the card once more, and the diode again flashed red. The guard looked at the monitor for a second, and then looked back at my father.

"I'm sorry, sir," he began, "but it looks like your access has been revoked."

"Excuse me?" Alpha Prime said, displeasure evident in his tone.

"Your access," the guard repeated. "It's been revoked."

"When?" my father demanded. "How?"

"I'm afraid I'm not privy to that information," the guard replied.

My father simply glowered at him for a moment. Even in civvies and without anyone knowing who he was, Alpha Prime could be incredibly intimidating. As evidence of this, all three guards were now watching him warily, and two of them had their hands on the butts of their respective weapons.

Without warning, my father turned and began angrily marching towards the exit. We followed him without needing to be told.

Once outside, Alpha Prime let out a groan of frustration.

"Okay, change of plan," he announced suddenly. "Smokey, you and Electra stay with the car."

As he spoke, he pulled the car keys from his pocket and tossed them to Smokey.

"Will do," Smokey intoned.

"Jim, come with me," my father said, then went soaring up into the air.

ISOLATION

I flew up after him, and it took me almost no time to realize where we were headed: the top floor of the floating cube building. Once there, we hovered for a few seconds outside the window, which was made of reflective glass. For a moment, I simply watched our reflections — the two of us, father and son, suspended in the air — and couldn't help but feel that we made an impressive sight.

"Jim, take us inside," Alpha Prime said.

I phased one of the window panes, making it insubstantial, and flew through it into the building, with my father right behind me. I made the window solid again and then looked around.

We were in a posh, executive office that was at least two thousand square feet in size. Based on casual observation, little had been spared in the way of expense, as evidenced by a sitting area filled with leather furniture, hardwood floors, and built-in, floor-to-ceiling bookshelves. In addition, the walls held several paintings that I assumed to be high-priced, and in one corner stood a piece of avant-garde art that looked somewhat like a man sculpted from metal.

Sitting behind a huge executive desk and talking on the telephone was a young man — probably in his mid-twenties — who looked somewhat familiar to me. Alpha Prime began walking towards him, and I followed.

"Yeah, I'm gonna have to call you back," the man said casually into the phone as we approached. Hanging up, his eyes went back and forth between me and Alpha Prime before settling on my father, at which point he stated, "You don't have an appointment."

"Do I need one, Dave?" my father asked, taking a seat in one of two high-back executive chairs on our side of the desk. Following his lead, I sat in the other.

"Apparently not," said Dave. "But then again, the world's greatest superhero is welcome everywhere he goes."

"*Almost* everywhere," Alpha Prime corrected. "Seems my access here has been revoked."

"Well, that's a shame," uttered Dave, somewhat tongue-in-cheek. Looking at me, he asked, "So who's this?"

"This is Jim," my father said. "Jim, this is David Thaddeus Goodson."

"Dave Goodson?" I uttered in surprise. "The founder of DTG?"

No wonder he looked familiar to me. Dave Goodson was a famed tech guru, hailed worldwide as an idealist and visionary. I must have seen him on television or in the newspaper a million times, but he didn't look quite the same in person.

"No, not the founder of DTG," Dave confessed, as he stood up and reached across the desk to shake my hand. "That said, I do run the place." He looked me up and down for a moment, then added, "So, you're Jim. My brother Dale talks about you all the time."

I was about to ask who his brother was, and then the truth hit me: Mouse's given name was Dale. His full name, in fact, was Dale Theodore Goodson. Dave was Mouse's brother! Looking at him with this new information in hand, I could definitely see the family resemblance — another reason he had probably looked familiar. (I also had a feeling that this was Mouse's corporate connection that Vir had mentioned.)

"Speaking of your brother," Alpha Prime chimed in, "have you heard from him lately?"

Dave shook his head as he sat back down. "No."

"Well, it's imperative that we find him," my father stressed. "From all indications, he's been exposed to something exotic and seems to be taking actions that not only threaten the Alpha League but possibly the world. He's not himself...practically half-crazed. We really need to find him before he seriously hurts somebody — or worse."

Dave seemed to contemplate for a moment. "That's a tough row to hoe," he finally said. "Even half-crazed, my brother's always going to be the smartest guy in the room. I mean, he built this company. I get all the credit, but I'm nothing more than a figurehead. Everything DTG has accomplished is a product of his ingenuity."

"But you're his brother," Alpha Prime stressed. "Surely you've got some notion of where he might be or is likely to go."

Dave sighed. "Here's what I know: my brother is always thinking ten moves ahead. Bearing that in mind, he's not going to tell me anything you want to know, because he already knows you'll come see me. Likewise, you aren't going to find him unless he wants to be found, so if you actually *do* pick up his trail, that means he's ready for you."

"So what are you saying?" my father asked.

"That you can't take my brother on and win," Dave stated. "With his abilities, no one can. Not you, not the Alpha League, nobody."

Alpha Prime frowned. "So your advice is what — to just stand down and get out of his way?"

Dave shrugged. "That's what the smart money says."

Alpha Prime nodded as he seemed to mentally digest this.

"If I'm being honest," he finally said, "that's not going to fly with the rest of the League. Also, some of them may think you know more than you're saying."

Dave's brow crinkled. "What's that supposed to mean?"

"Well, with the resources of DTG at your disposal," my father explained, "you could do all kinds of things to help your brother."

"In truth, it's *his* company," Dave admitted. "So the resources of DTG are *always* at his disposal."

"True," Alpha Prime intoned. "All right, we should get out of here."

He came to his feet as he spoke, and I followed suit.

"Thanks for your time, Dave," my father said, extending a hand.

"Not a problem," Dave assured him as they shook hands. "But on a side note, I'm not going to have to worry about any of your colleagues paying me a visit, am I? Maybe trying to see, as you suggest, if I know more than I said?"

"Pshaw," Alpha Prime muttered disdainfully. "Come on, man. We're the Alpha League — we don't do stuff like that."

"Good," Dave said, "because after this is all over, I'd hate having to explain to my brother how one of his teammates took a shellacking because of me."

Alpha Prime laughed. "I didn't realize you had that kind of muscle."

"Maybe I don't," Dave admitted. "But *he* does."

As he finished speaking, Dave pointed with his chin towards a corner of the room — the area where the weird metal sculpture was. A second later, I was shocked when the sculpture took a step in our direction.

Alpha Prime stared at the object, which was seemingly some type of robot, then turned back to Dave.

"You have Failsafe," he stated flatly. "Mouse was supposed to decommission that thing."

"Well," Dave droned, "at one point, Mouse picked up some chatter about some people maybe wanting to kidnap me, so he gave it to me for protection. Sort of like a guardian angel."

"More like a guardian killer robot," my father shot back.

"Anyway," Dave said, "I've enjoyed the visit. Come back any time."

"One more thing," Alpha Prime said. "Why'd you revoke my access?"

"I didn't," Dave replied. "I assume that was my brother's doing."

ISOLATION

Chapter 42

We left Dave's office the way we'd come in — through a phased window (which I then made solid again).

"Hold up," I said to my father as he prepared to drop to the ground. "I've got a couple of questions."

"And you want to ask them *here?*" he asked, making an all-encompassing gesture. "We're a bit on display."

He was right, of course. Two people floating in the air as we were did make for something of a spectacle.

"Up here, then," I suggested, flying to the roof of the floating cube. My father followed and landed in front of me a second later.

"Okay, son," Alpha Prime said. "What's on your mind?"

"A couple of things," I admitted. "First and foremost, what's Mouse's power?"

"His power?" my father echoed.

I nodded. "Yeah. I've never asked Mouse about it and he's never told me, but I've heard people reference his power on several occasions, and his brother mentioned it just a few moments ago. It occurs to me that if I'm going to help run him down, I need to know what he can do."

My father rubbed his chin for a second before responding. "Mouse has something he calls autogenetic cognizance."

My brow wrinkled in confusion. "What's that?"

"The way Mouse explains it, you can put any piece of technology in front of him — terrestrial or alien — and he can not only understand it, but improve on it. Basically, he can build a better mousetrap."

I blinked, trying to take in what I was hearing and its implications. Now I had a better understanding of why others considered Mouse to have power that rivaled my father's. If what I was hearing were true, Mouse was way more powerful than he'd ever let on. (And that's without taking into account his tactical and strategic genius, among other things.)

"So how'd his brother get into the picture?" I asked.

"Before Mouse joined the team," my father replied, "we'd sometimes run into a technical problem we needed help with — for instance, weapons and gadgets from supervillains that we couldn't figure out. DTG was one of the places we'd turn to on those occasions, and they'd usually find the answer to whatever problem we had."

"And that's how you got to know Dave."

"Yeah, but what we didn't know back then was that if the problem was too thorny for the tech guys on their payroll, they'd hand it over to this specialist who they kept off the books."

"Mouse," I concluded.

My father nodded. "Eventually, we found out, and — after some initial misunderstandings — Mouse joined the League."

"And that robot thing in Dave's office?"

"It's called Failsafe. Mouse designed it to be his personal bodyguard, although it usually stayed out of sight until needed. But trust me, if that thing goes into protective mode, you don't want to be anywhere around. Mouse was supposed to deactivate it, but I guess he found another use for it instead."

"Okay," I droned. "Now what about this world domination thing?"

Alpha Prime gave me a confused look. "What do you mean?"

ISOLATION

"Well, you and the other League members said something about Mouse taking over the world yesterday, but you also admitted that you didn't know what he'd removed from the Vault. Then, just a few minutes ago, you said something about Mouse posing a threat to the world. So what aren't you telling me?"

My father gave me a serious stare for a moment, then sighed. "We weren't completely honest yesterday. We didn't know what Mouse may have taken, but the wall stack he was at? Ninety percent of what it contained are components for devices that can be used to destroy the planet."

"So there's a ninety percent chance that he took something capable of posing a global threat."

"Actually, he took *part* of something that could pose a global threat, but in essence, yes."

"So he did actually take something?" I asked, following which my father simply nodded. "Do we know what it was?"

"The inventory system is still a mess, but our tech guys have narrowed it down to three items," he said. "And as you might guess, each of them is a fundamental element in some type of doomsday device."

"So you honestly think Mouse is constructing some world-destroying weapon."

"I hate to say it, but that's what it looks like."

I spent a moment letting his words soak in, plainly having a difficult time reconciling what I was hearing with the man I knew.

"Okay, son," my father said, "what's really bothering you about this?'

"Huh?" I murmured as his words cut in to my train of thought.

"No one wants to believe this about Mouse, but the evidence is irrefutable. Still, despite what you've personally seen, you can't seem to get on board. So what's holding you back?"

I simply stared at him for a moment, not quite sure what to say, and then I let out a deep sigh that actually seemed to deflate me both mentally and physically.

"He called me," I muttered softly.

"What?" my father said, clearly not understanding.

"Mouse called me, asking for my help, a little while before the incident with the Construct. I missed his calls because I was off gallivanting on the West Coast — going to movie premieres, champagne brunches, and yacht parties. Mouse has always been there for me, the person I could always depend on, but when *he* needed *me*..."

I trailed off, unable to finish.

"You feel guilty," Alpha Prime stated.

And there it was: the plain and simple truth. The truth about why this thing with Mouse bothered me so much. The truth about why I suddenly felt like it was eating me up inside. The truth about why I couldn't just accept that my mentor had gone rogue.

"If I had just been there," I said, "maybe none of this would have happened. Maybe Mouse wouldn't have been exposed to whatever it was. Maybe we wouldn't be hunting him now."

My father laid a reassuring hand on my shoulder. "Son, this isn't your fault. I was right there when it happened. That being the case, I'm more to blame than you, and I feel the same — like I should have been able to do something to stop this. But what happened, happened. Feeling guilty isn't going to change that. All we can do is press forward and try to prevent any more damage from this situation. All right?"

I didn't trust myself to speak, so I simply nodded.

"Good," my father went on. "Now let's get out of here."

Without waiting for me to respond, he then flew over the edge of the building, headed towards the ground. I followed, and a few seconds later, we both touched down next to his parked SUV. Smokey was sitting behind the wheel while Electra was in the front passenger seat. Upon seeing me and Alpha Prime, they both got out, obviously expecting that everyone would go back to their original seats. However, they had barely exited before my father tapped the communicator in his ear.

"It's me," he announced. A moment later, a look of serious concern settled on his face. Looking at me, he stated, "It's Mouse. He's attacking again."

"Where?" asked Smokey.

"HQ," Alpha Prime answered. "The helipad."

He then turned his attention to me. Knowing what was expected, I simply nodded and teleported the four of us.

ISOLATION

Chapter 43

The helipad was located under a retractable dome ceiling on the roof of HQ. When we appeared, it was immediately clear that an intense battle was underway.

There were several blackened and charred areas on the rooftop — indicators that some type of explosive device had detonated in those places. Debris was everywhere, with smoke billowing from several large clumps of twisted metal, evidencing the fact that something (or some *things*) had obviously blown up. On the helipad itself was a large chopper, blades rapidly spinning as it seemingly prepared to take off through the open dome. Standing next to it, near the open door of the passenger area and dressed in his Alpha League uniform, was Mouse.

There were probably half a dozen members of the League present, but most of them were down — including Luna, who was on her hands and knees, and shaking her noggin in a way that suggested she was trying to clear her head. The only League member still on his feet was Feral — an imposing, eight-foot mass of fur-covered muscle who was probably exceeded only by my father in terms of brute strength.

We were still getting our bearings when Feral leaped at Mouse. The latter, seemingly expecting this, nimbly dove away just in the nick of time. Feral slammed into the helicopter, and the two went tumbling away in a twisted mash-up of man and machine.

Off to the side, Mouse rolled and came up on his feet. I quickly debated trying to teleport him and rejected the notion, recalling that it hadn't work previously. Before

I could consider anything else, a brilliant, blinding flash of light burst from the place Mouse was standing.

Instinctively closing my eyes, I groaned slightly in pain at the hurtful light, and I heard Smokey and Electra doing the same. I shut down the requisite pain receptors and opened my eyes, but couldn't see anything. Suddenly feeling vulnerable, I quickly cycled my vision through the light spectrum until I could finally see again in a manner approximating normal.

Glancing around, I saw that everyone else still seemed to be rubbing their eyes or otherwise trying to shake off the effects of the light-burst. Looking to where I'd last seen Mouse, I noticed that he was gone. There was, however, what appeared to be an exhaust trail leading up through the dome and out into the open air. Without hesitation, I flew up into the air, following it.

As I cleared the open dome, I telescoped my vision and immediately saw that the exhaust trail was coming from what appeared to be rockets in Mouse's boots. Turning on the afterburners, I swiftly began closing the distance.

Whether he did so out of caution or because he somehow sensed my presence, Mouse unexpectedly glanced in my direction. A moment later, he was pointing his fist towards me, and I saw that he had once again donned the brace I'd seen in the video.

Something like a pulse of electrical energy suddenly shot out of the brace in my direction. Unbothered, I phased, preparing to let the energy pass harmlessly through my insubstantial form. Unfortunately, nothing like that happened.

Instead of the pulse passing through me without effect, it hit me like a sledgehammer to the chest. All of the air in my body was suddenly, forcefully, and violently expelled, like someone had squeezed it out with a vise. I suddenly found myself not only gasping for breath, but falling; the shock of the blow had been so powerful that my body had seemingly shut down my flying ability in response.

I put all my energy into clamping down on my pain receptors, which thankfully only took a second. I then focused on stopping my free fall and came to a halt in midair a moment later. Next, I focused on expanding and contracting my lungs with my shapeshifting ability, thereby forcing the intake of air. At the same time, I scanned the sky for Mouse, but the exhaust trail abruptly came to an end high above me, as if the rockets had simply shut off in mid-flight. Mouse was gone.

ISOLATION

Chapter 44

Smokey, Electra, and I spent roughly the next hour in the infirmary getting treated. Although I was given a clean bill of health almost immediately, my friends didn't get a green light to leave until their sight came back and they both passed a vision test. While waiting for them, I devoted a lot of time to thinking about the most recent tussle with Mouse — specifically, the weapon he'd used on me.

Upon leaving the infirmary, we retreated to the Alpha League's teen lounge. It was essentially a break room for members of the League's teen affiliate, and as such it contained — among other things — a billiards table, video game consoles, and dart boards.

Of course, since it was a school day, there was no one else there. However, it brought to mind the question: why wasn't Electra in school? Smokey and I were no longer attending formal classes, but Electra definitely was. (And I had been so focused on the situation with Mouse that I hadn't even thought about the fact that she was missing class. If the absence of people in the teen lounge hadn't shined a light on the issue, it probably would have escaped my notice completely.)

"I called in sick," was her answer when I finally put the question to her. "Did it while you and Alpha Prime were inside at DTG."

"I thought parents had to call in stuff like that," I remarked.

"I'll need to take a doctor's note when I go back in order for it to be an excused absence," Electra stated. "As long as they get that, the school administrators don't really care about anything else."

"Well, that shouldn't be a problem," Smokey interjected. "If temporary blindness isn't an excused absence, I don't know what is."

I didn't disagree with his conclusion, but I found the thought of Electra missing school troubling. The League already had two truants in the form of me and Smokey. We didn't need any more — and I especially didn't like the notion of Electra becoming one. The last thing I needed was her dad thinking I was a bad influence.

Thankfully, we didn't dwell on the subject, as around that time Alpha Prime entered the lounge. We didn't have to ask how he'd found us; each of us had a tracker in our phone.

"Great," he said. "You three are in here unwinding. That's good. It's important that you don't dwell too much on things like the attack earlier."

"If I'm being honest," I countered, "I'm still thinking about it. Basically, nothing hurts me when I'm phased, but Mouse was able to. It's hard for me to just put that out of my mind."

"You're going to have to try," my father stressed. "Just put some effort into learning from it, so you'll be better prepared next time."

I nodded in response to his comment as if it were sage advice. Frankly speaking, however, it sounded like anemic psychobabble, but I recognized it as an attempt to help me deal with what was bothering me.

"So exactly what happened on the helipad?" Smokey asked.

My father seemed to ruminate on the question for a moment, then said, "The three of you already know that Mouse took the component for a destructive device from the Vault yesterday. In an effort to throw a monkey wrench in any plans he might have, we were going to move some of the other items he might need to disparate locations. Somehow he found out and staged an attack as we were loading them on the chopper."

"And the rest we essentially know," I interjected. "He foiled the League's plans, took the components, and got away clean."

Alpha Prime nodded. "That essentially sums it up."

"So what now?" asked Smokey.

"Mouse still doesn't have everything he needs — at least, according to our experts. We still don't know exactly what he's building, but we know he doesn't have all the pieces to the puzzle yet."

"So there's going to be another attack?" I concluded.

"Bingo," Alpha Prime said, pointing at me.

"So we don't necessarily have to find him," I surmised. "He'll come to us."

"True," said my father, scratching his temple, "but we'd still rather go on the offensive."

"So you want to keep looking for him," summed up Smokey.

"More specifically, we want *Jim* to keep looking for him," Alpha Prime stated, then looked at me. "After all, son, you know him better than anybody. Your insight about the bug-out bag shows that."

I shrugged. "Maybe, but I'm all out of ideas in the Mouse-hunting department, to be honest."

"Well, as I keep saying, try to relax," my father said. "Play some video games, hang out with your friends, throw some darts... Give your mind an opportunity to unwind — to rest — and maybe something new will occur to you."

My instinctive reaction was to shake my head in disdain at the thought. Maybe relaxing at the end of the day (the way we'd played board games the night before) would be sensible, but it wasn't even noon yet. Hanging out and playing games with my friends *now*, when I needed to be looking for my mentor, seemed…I don't know — callous, maybe? I looked at Smokey, my expression making it clear his opinion was welcome.

"Doesn't sound like a bad idea," Smokey asserted.

"Plus, you're putting yourself under a lot of pressure because you feel you owe Mouse," Alpha Prime added. "But if you don't do something to occasionally ease the strain, you're going to wear yourself to a frazzle and burn out, and that won't do him or you any good."

"It might already be happening," Electra chimed in. "You've practically passed out the last two nights."

I spent a moment looking at all three of their faces, then said, "It feels like I'm getting ganged up on here."

"Well, there's an easy way to avoid that," Electra declared. "Just take our advice."

She then looped her arm into mine and, smiling, began dragging me to the billiards table.

ISOLATION

Chapter 45

Unsurprisingly, hanging out with Electra and Smokey served its intended purpose and helped me relax. It wasn't long before we were laughing and joking — much as we would have been doing if we weren't in the middle of a crisis.

After a while, we broke for lunch. I volunteered to teleport to Jackman's — a grill that was one of our favorite places — to pick up some burgers and fries. Smokey, however, insisted on treating so he came with me. Upon our return, the three of us went to one of the tables in the lounge and quickly dove in.

"So," Smokey droned as we began eating, "where do you suppose Mouse might be?"

"I'm really not sure," I admitted. "The thing with the bug-out bag raises a lot of questions."

"Well," Electra said, "maybe that's—"

The sound of my phone ringing cut her off. Pulling it out of my pocket, I saw that it was Kenyon calling. I was tempted to let it go to voicemail, but he was responding to a request that *I* had made, so it didn't seem right to blow him off.

Standing up and stepping away, I hit the *Answer* button and said, "Hello."

"Good afternoon, sir," Kenyon greeted me in response. "I trust you've been well?"

"I have, Kenyon — thanks for asking. And you?"

"Well enough, sir; well enough. Anyway, you asked about the alarm. Fortunately, the paperwork giving me authority to speak for you is still on file with the alarm service, so they were happy to answer my questions."

"So what did they say?"

"As far as they could tell, there was no glitch. According to their analysis, the system was explicitly activated during the time frame you asked about — meaning that someone turned it on — and a few seconds afterwards, the alarm was tripped. However, the system was properly deactivated just a few moments later, before the alarm went off audibly."

"Wait a minute," I said. "What do they mean the alarm never went off? It was blaring at full volume when I got home."

"Not according to their data, sir," Kenyon retorted. "If they had registered the alarm going off, they would have called to make sure everything was okay."

"Right," I said, suddenly remembering. "They're supposed to call if it goes off, and then I'm supposed to give them a code word to indicate that everything is okay."

Mentally, I kicked myself. I had completely forgotten all of that.

"Yes, sir," Kenyon confirmed. "That's standard operating procedure."

"Well, what about the system being set in the first place?" I asked. "You said it was activated right before the alarm was tripped, but I was nowhere near the control panel."

"The alarm company says it was activated remotely using the primary code."

"Remotely?" I echoed in confusion. "That can't be right, because I'm the only person with the primary code or remote access, and I didn't do it."

"I'm not doubting you, sir," Kenyon insisted. "I'm just reporting what they told me. Is it possible you did it by accident?"

ISOLATION

I spent a moment contemplating. I didn't recall fooling around much with my phone on the night in question. However, people butt-dialed each other all the time these days, and I did tend to keep my phone in my pocket.

"Hang on," I said.

A moment later, I hit the *Mute* button and then navigated through the bevy of apps on the phone until I found the one for the alarm system. I had recently installed the latest upgrade, so now it not only told me whether the alarm was off or on, but also logged whenever it was activated or deactivated.

From what I could see, no recent activity had occurred remotely. In fact, nothing related to the glitching that we were currently discussing appeared on the log for the alarm, and I conveyed as much to Kenyon after navigating back to the phone app and unmuting him.

"That's truly bizarre, sir," Kenyon stated, echoing my own thoughts. "Are you certain no one else has the primary code?"

"Positive," I assured him. That said, Myshtal actually did have a code, but it was designated as "temporary." Basically, it was an alarm code that could be given to guests who were visiting and then deactivated when they left. It was a way to let visitors come and go at their leisure without compromising security to a large extent.

"Well, sir," Kenyon continued, "I hate to say it, but maybe it's time to change the primary code — just in case someone's hacked it or something."

I froze as he finished speaking, my thoughts turning in an entirely new direction. Basically, the notion of hacking a security system immediately brought one person to mind.

Someone who could break into any computer system on the planet.

Someone who could manipulate an app without breaking a sweat.

Someone who could digitally go and do whatever they wanted without leaving a single clue behind.

Mouse.

ISOLATION

Chapter 46

I quickly got off the phone with Kenyon, thanking him for his time and promising to be in touch soon. Afterwards, I simply stood there, thinking — trying to put together everything I'd learned.

If my theory was correct, it seemed that Mouse had hacked the alarm system at the embassy and activated it. But then, like the world's stupidest burglar, he'd set it off immediately afterwards. It was as if he wanted to get caught. (And if that were the case, maybe he *had* gone crazy like everyone was insisting.)

However, following this, he hacked the system again, this time making the security company think the alarm had been deactivated while actually leaving it on. That forced me to come home and turn it off.

But why? Why go through all that? What was the purpose? As far as I could tell, he didn't really accomplish anything. All he succeeded in doing was getting me to come home.

Unless that's what he wanted, I said to myself, the thought materializing almost unexpectedly. *It's the only thing that makes any—*

"Hey, you planning to come back and join us any time soon?" Electra asked, cutting into my train of thought.

"Huh?" I muttered, my mind still elsewhere for the most part.

"Looks like your phone call ended a minute ago," Smokey noted, "so we were wondering if you were just going to stand there brooding all day or come back to the table."

"Sorry," I apologized. "I wasn't brooding — just thinking about Mouse."

"Oh?" Electra intoned. "Did you come up with something new?"

"Maybe," I admitted with a shrug, "but I need to check something out. I'll be back in a bit."

"Wait!" Electra cried out, jumping to her feet. "We'll come wi—"

Her words were cut off as I teleported.

ISOLATION

Chapter 47

I popped up in the embassy, in the same spot where I'd appeared two days earlier, when the alarm was going off.

Okay, I thought to myself, throwing my mind back in time, *Mouse manipulates events to get me here, and I show up like he wanted. Now what?*

In all honesty, I was kind of at a loss as to how to answer that. Basically, what was the point of getting me to come home the other night? It's not like he was waiting to talk to me, or left me a note. He'd been nowhere around when I'd arrived and had left no indication of the fact that he'd been there. Frankly speaking, assuming I was on the right track, I hadn't even known he'd put in an appearance until just a few minutes ago. And then it hit me.

He wanted me to know he'd been here! I suddenly realized.

But for what reason? Mouse was obviously trying to tell me something, but it wasn't clear to me what that was. In essence, simply knowing that he'd been here didn't provide me with any particular insight. Aside from the alarm going off, there had only been one possible indicator of his presence: the open door to Myshtal's room.

And just like that, the scales immediately fell from my eyes. I suddenly knew, with unmistakable clarity, exactly why Mouse had shown up at the embassy. I knew why he'd set the alarm off. I knew why he'd left the door to Myshtal's room open.

He was trying to tell me where to find him. Or rather, *how*.

ISOLATION

Chapter 48

Suddenly excited, I teleported to Myshtal's room and immediately found myself in a spacious suite. Outside of the master bedroom, it was probably the largest such room in the place. As a Caelesian princess and favorite of the queen, Myshtal was undoubtedly accustomed to far larger accommodations, but she had made the adjustment easily and without complaint.

Glancing around, I couldn't help but notice that my titular fiancée kept her room neat and clean: no random assortment of clothes thrown around, no shoes impulsively kicked off and left on the floor, no pillows tossed about haphazardly on the bed. Everything was in its proper place — including a number of items around the suite that I identified as being Caelesian in origin.

After a minute or so of eyeballing her room, I realized that I was out of my depth. I didn't know what I was looking for — or *not* looking for, so to speak. I needed Myshtal — especially if my supposition about how to find Mouse was true.

With that thought in mind, I teleported to my cousin Monique's house.

****

I popped up outside the front door of Monique's home — a beautiful Mediterranean-style house on the beach. I had been inside before, but didn't feel comfortable yet just teleporting to the interior.

I reached out telepathically and found both my cousin and Myshtal inside. I did the mental equivalent of tapping on the door of Monique's mind and then established a mental link.

<Hi, Monique,> I said in greeting.

<Hey, cuz,> she replied. <Where are you?>

<Outside your front door. Didn't want to just pop inside.>

<You know you're always welcome here. Come on in. I'm in the kitchen.>

I teleported inside, appearing in a roomy kitchen with an oversized island counter in the center. Monique, standing nearby and sporting a paisley print sundress, immediately came towards me with her arms open.

"Great to see you, as always," she said as she gave me a brief hug.

"Same here," I replied. "Unfortunately, this isn't a social call. I need to—"

I abruptly stopped speaking as I unexpectedly picked up on a curious warbling sound — a captivating amalgam of fluctuating musical notes that combined to form an enchanting melody. It wasn't excessively loud, but it resonated in a way that I almost felt rather than heard.

"What *is* that?" I wondered aloud, immediately recognizing that it wasn't a bird I was hearing, but the sound wasn't quite like any singing I'd ever encountered.

"Yeah," Monique droned, "I was going to give you a call about that."

I didn't respond to her statement. Instead, I began following the sound, with Monique right behind me. It appeared to be coming from an area that had been designated as the great room; however, when I was about halfway there, it changed, becoming something akin to a bewitching aria. More to the point, I was now able to recognize and put a name to what I was hearing: Caelesian singing.

Upon entering the great room, I saw the source of the singing immediately. As expected, it was Myshtal. A gorgeous redhead, she was currently stretched out on a couch and wearing a white crop top with blue jean shorts. Eyes closed, she continued singing for a moment, oblivious to my presence. Her voice was sirenic, and I probably would have stood there listening to her indefinitely had she not suddenly become aware of my presence.

Apparently sensing someone nearby, she stopped singing and opened her eyes. As soon as she realized it was me, her mouth flew open as her face took on an expression of giddy surprise.

"My prince!" she squealed, coming to her feet. Before I could say anything, she wrapped her arms around me and gave me a fierce hug (which I returned, but with far less ferocity).

"Uh…hi," I muttered, somewhat surprised by her enthusiastic display of affection upon seeing me. Empathically, I felt a broad range of emotions coming from her: anticipation, excitement, anxiety, contentment, adoration… Simply put, her feelings were so wide-ranging that it was difficult for me to get a handle on what was going on with her.

I let my arms drop from around her, anticipating she would step back after the hug ended. Instead, she simply shifted her arms from my torso to around my neck.

"You're a bad boy," she stated almost huskily as she mussed my hair with one hand. "You didn't call me last night."

ISOLATION

I frowned in confusion, as Myshtal continued to teasingly berate me for not maintaining our nightly tête-à-tête. I reached up, trying to remove her arms from around my neck; much to my surprise, she proved to be surprisingly adept at slipping out of my grip and putting them right back where they were.

At the same time, I noticed that her eyes were swiftly going through a broad swath of colors. It was a physical trait of Caelesians: their eyes changed color with strong emotions, although it was something they typically learned to control at an early age. The fact that it was happening to Myshtal meant that something was way off.

Continuing to struggle with her, I glanced at Monique and demanded, "What's wrong with her?"

My cousin sighed. "You know how Avis is always calling me a boring housewife who doesn't know how to have fun?"

"Yeah," I answered with a nod. Avis was always teasing her sister for being content with domestic life rather than using her incredible powers to be a superhero.

"Well," Monique continued, "she sent me some 'choice' brownies from a specialty shop, if you know what I mean. It was meant to be a joke — she knew I wouldn't eat them — but it was her way of telling me to loosen up and have fun. I should have thrown them out, but I was going to send them back to her with a smart-aleck response, but somehow Myshtal found them, and, well…"

She gestured towards Myshtal, whom I was still struggling with.

"Are you kidding?!" I exclaimed. "She's high?!"

"As a kite," my cousin added sorrowfully. "I'm sorry, Jim. I should have been more attentive."

"It's not your fault," I assured Monique. "It's just bad timing because I need her for something right now."

Finally getting a good grip on her wrists, I pulled Myshtal's hands from around my neck and looked her in the eye.

"Hey!" I blurted out. "I really need you to focus. Can you do that for me?"

"Anything for you, my prince," she said with starry eyes, attempting to stroke my cheek with a finger.

"I'm serious," I uttered in exasperation. "I need you to concentrate."

"You are so cute when you're angry," she said, tapping my nose with a fingertip, which made Monique giggle.

"It's not funny," I hissed at my cousin.

"I know," Monique conceded, covering a wide grin with her hand.

"Okay, I need to get her home for something," I told my cousin. "I'll bring her back when we're done and she can sleep it off, detox, or whatever needs to happen to get it out of her system."

Without giving Monique a chance to reply, I then teleported me and Myshtal.

ISOLATION

Chapter 49

We popped up in Myshtal's bedroom at the embassy. Unfortunately, when we reappeared, she appeared woozy for a second. Teleportation can occasionally disorient people, and to the best of my knowledge, this was the first time I'd teleported someone who was stoned.

I immediately put my arms around her to make sure she didn't fall. As before, she responded by putting her arms around my neck.

"So you'll catch me if I swoon?" she asked cheekily. "I'll have to remember that."

Now wondering if she'd feigned being lightheaded, I made sure she was on her feet and then removed her arms from my neck again.

"Look," I began, "you said you'd do anything for me. You remember saying that?"

"Of course, my sweet," she replied.

"Okay, then. I need you to take a good look around this room and tell me if there's anything missing."

"If you insist," she said, sounding more somber than I'd thought possible. Then, just when I thought she was taking me seriously, she stretched out her arms and began spinning in a circle, shouting, "Wheee!"

I groaned aloud in frustration, wiping my face with my hand. This wasn't going at all how I had envisioned.

Stepping towards Myshtal, I firmly (but gently) gripped her shoulders.

"Listen," I said. "This is serious. I really need you to—"

"My ring," she said, cutting me off.

I looked at her in confusion. "Huh?"

"My ring," she repeated. "One that the queen gave me before we left Caeles. It's missing."

"Are you sure?" I asked.

"Yes," she stated with a nod. "I looked while I was spinning around. I usually keep it on the dresser and it's not there."

"Okay, great," I said, as this proved my theory.

Part of the reason Myshtal had left Caeles was that she had some budding superpowers, which Queen Dornoccia had felt would be more properly developed on Earth, where such abilities were more common. One of her talents was the ability to find things.

Of course, there were limitations on this particular power. First and foremost, the thing she sought had to be something she had a close connection to, whether a person or object. In short, she probably couldn't find someone like, say, Smokey, whom she hadn't known for long or developed any kind of bond with. (In fact, it was probably safe to say I was the only person on the planet she had that kind of affinity for.) However, something like a precious heirloom from a beloved family member would be an entirely different story.

Basically, my hypothesis was that Mouse wanted me to find him, but for some reason couldn't directly tell me where he was. Thus, he had set off the alarm to make sure I'd know he'd been in the embassy, and — being aware of Myshtal's power — he had taken an item from her room that he felt she'd be able to trace.

Bearing all this in mind, I then asked Myshtal what was probably the most important question: "Do you think you can find it? The ring, that is?"

She gave me a dazzling smile. "Of course."

ISOLATION

Chapter 50

I teleported the two of us to Mouse's lab. Based on the fact that he'd left his bug-out bag, I had to assume he was somewhere close by. (And if that were the case, Myshtal would find him — or rather, the ring he'd taken.) As before, it was dark when we arrived, but after a few seconds, the lights started coming on.

"Okay," I said to her. "Do your thing."

Myshtal simply nodded as she cupped her hands in front of her and closed her eyes. I watched as her brow furrowed in concentration for a moment, and then a small white spark began to form between her hands.

Having seen her demonstrate this ability before, I smiled in anticipation. In a moment, the spark would become a white flame and then zip away from her hand, leading the way to her missing ring — and presumably Mouse's location — like a bloodhound.

Much to my dismay, however, the spark simply seemed to fizzle out.

"Hmmm," Myshtal droned — more to herself than to me — as she opened her eyes. She appeared to frown in confusion for a moment, then closed her eyes again.

Once more, the spark began to form between her hands; however, just as with her previous attempt, it seemed to wither and die a short time later.

Somewhat frustrated, Myshtal turned to me, saying, "It's not working."

"How's that possible?" I asked. "I thought you were supposed to be able to find anything you had a connection to."

"I *can*," she insisted. "But something weird is going on. It's not simply that I can't locate it. It's like the ring doesn't exist anymore."

I frowned, thinking her supposition sounded ridiculous but not wanting to say anything to distress her. The truth of the matter was that — while she was showing a bit of lucidity at the moment — Myshtal was still high. It was entirely possible that her mental state was affecting her power in some way (or, more appropriately, her ability to *use* her power).

"Why don't we do a dry run?" I suggested. "Instead of the ring, try to find *me*."

"But you're standing right there," she pointed out.

"I know," I agreed with a nod, "but we're just trying to make sure that it's not a problem with your abilities."

She seemed to mull this over for a second, then shrugged. "Okay."

Once again, she cupped her hands, but didn't even bother closing her eyes. Almost immediately, a spark formed, burst into flame, and came zooming in my direction.

"All right, your power seems to be working just fine," I concluded, "but I'm not sure…"

I trailed off as I realized that Myshtal wasn't listening to me. Instead, she was staring at a corner of the room with a fierce intensity, like there was some mind-boggling sight there that only she was privy to.

"Are you okay?" I asked.

The sound of my voice almost made her jump, and she spent a moment with her head swiveling back and forth, looking at me and then the corner again several times in rapid succession.

Still high, I thought.

"Are you doing your twin thing?" she asked unexpectedly.

I gave her a nonplussed look. "Excuse me?"

"Did you duplicate yourself?"

I frowned. Myshtal was referring to a power I had recently developed — basically, the ability to make a second version of myself. In essence, I could create a second Jim, but we were still the same person, sharing the same mind, thoughts, etcetera.

I shook my head. "No. I haven't duplicated myself in a while."

"It's bizarre," she said, "because when I tried to find you, I got the distinct impression there was a second Jim in the corner over there."

Still incredibly *high*, I said to myself, then stated aloud, "Okay, we may have to just try this again later."

I looked at Myshtal, expecting a response, but she didn't say anything. In fact, from what I could see, she hadn't moved since she last spoke. Now staring at her, I quickly realized that she didn't even appear to be breathing. I waved a hand in front of her face, noting that she didn't blink, nor did her eyes track any movement.

I didn't need any special powers to understand that something weird was happening. I didn't know the cause, but it seemed best to get her out of Mouse's lab as soon as possible. With that in mind, I was on the verge of teleporting the two of us when a person suddenly appeared in the corner that Myshtal had been staring at.

I stared at the new arrival in complete and utter surprise, thoroughly amazed and astounded by who it was.

The person who had appeared was *me*.

ISOLATION

Chapter 51

He was older than I was — in his mid-twenties, I guessed. Dressed in the trademark black-and-gold uniform of the Alpha League, he walked casually towards me, eating an apple.

Even though I knew the answer, I couldn't stop the question from leaving my mouth: "Who are you?"

"You gotta ask?" he responded rhetorically.

"I mean, are you the version of myself that I met in the past on Caeles?"

"Yeah," the older me initially responded. "Well, no... I mean, not yet."

"I think I understand," I said with a nod. "So what are you doing here?"

"Just hanging out and eating an apple," he replied.

"I meant—"

"I know what you meant," he said. "I just couldn't help being a wiseacre for a minute. I mean, how often do you literally get to joke with yourself?"

He then chuckled for a moment, but stopped when he saw that I wasn't laughing as well.

"Geez," he groused. "I honestly don't remember being wound up this tight at your age."

I ignored his comment. "You were explaining what you were doing here?"

"Yeah," my older self droned casually. "I'm sorta, kinda moving backwards through time."

"What?!" I exclaimed. "How'd that happen?"

"World in danger, supervillain with a new weapon, yada, yada, yada," he intoned. "I saved the day but got blasted. The weapon turned out to be some kind of temporal displacement device, and next thing you know, I'm flying backwards through time."

I scratched my temple for a moment. "So if you're going backwards through time, why is it that you're here — in *my* present — instead of continuing on past this temporal juncture?"

"Every few years, the journey seems to temporarily halt for some reason."

"Every few years?!" I repeated incredulously. "How long has this been going on?"

"You know I can't answer that," the older Jim said. "But let me be clear, the years I'm referring to are those that are *objective* — the ones that I pass through going backwards — and they can go by in a flash." He snapped his fingers for effect as he spoke.

"And you also can't tell me how many years this has been going on *subj*ectively — that is, from your point of view."

"Absolutely not," he stated. "Anyway, I'm not sure what occasionally causes the stop — whether it's something inherent in the device that blasted me, or some force I encounter, but it seems to happen randomly."

"Well, when will this backwards journey end?"

He gave me a disdainful look. "Really? You think I know the answer to that? Your guess is honestly as good as mine."

While I absorbed this information, the older Jim stared at the apple he was holding. He had continued eating while we spoke and was now down to the core.

"Man," he muttered, plainly talking to himself. "Still hungry."

He then stared at the apple, seeming to concentrate, and moments later, my eyes went wide in surprise as the apple became whole again.

"How did you do that?" I practically demanded.

"What — the apple?" he inquired. "Oh, that's right — you don't have your full slate of powers yet."

"That's amazing," I said, still in awe.

"Eh," the older me droned with a slight shrug, obviously not impressed. "It's not all it's cracked up to be. You have no idea how tedious it is to have to reconstitute and eat the same apple over and over and over again. What I wouldn't give for a burger and fries right about now..."

"Wait a minute," I remarked. "All you ever eat is that apple?"

"Unfortunately, yes," he said with a nod. "I somehow had a seed in my pocket when I started this trip, and I grew the apple from it. According to Mouse, it's all I can eat because it's essentially the only nourishment from my own timeline. I asked him about maybe having just a little slice of bacon or something, but he completely shut me down."

"Really?"

Older Jim nodded. "Yeah, it was all butterfly effect and crap... If I eat a T-bone steak and throw the remainder away, then some dog at the junkyard chokes on the bone, which somehow leads to some nut jumping off the Eiffel Tower in France next month, and as a result some kid who's supposed to grow up and save the world isn't born eighty years from now in Sub-Saharan Africa."

"Okay, that's a lot to digest," I noted. "But speaking of Mouse, it sounds like he knows about you."

"Oh, yeah. I sought him out the minute I stopped moving backwards in time."

"What did he say?"

"He told me to stay in the lab, stay invisible, and stay phased. Don't go see anybody, don't talk to anybody, don't do anything."

"Sounds like Mouse," I noted with a smile. I then gave my older self a hard stare. "You know what's going on with him right now, don't you?"

"Of course," Older Jim acknowledged. "All of this is in my past."

"And you can't tell me anything at all?" I asked.

"Just letting you see me is probably too much. Mouse is going to go bananas when he finds out."

"You're right about that," I agreed. "Mouse wouldn't like it at all."

Needless to say, that brought to mind the question: why was Older Jim letting me see him then? Why was he even talking to me?

Of course — he's trying to help, I realized. That said, he didn't seem particularly eager to volunteer information. However, he didn't appear to have a problem answering questions.

Bearing that in mind, I asked, "So, how long have you been hiding here?"

"I'd argue that's classified," he replied.

"Yeah, but it had to be before Mouse went on the run, because he hasn't been back here since as far as I can tell. That means you've been here every time I've come by during the last few days."

"I can neither confirm nor deny," Older Jim said.

"So you were here when I came in with Alpha Prime, Luna, and Buzz. You were here when Electra and I found Mouse's bug-out bag. You were even here when we got the file off the computer."

As I finished the last sentence, I saw something like acknowledgment flash in Older Jim's eyes.

Something to do with the computer file, I realized. And then I had an epiphany.

"The computer," I said. "The one I couldn't find a power switch for. *You* turned it on."

"Not per se," Older Jim blurted out. "I no more turned that computer on than I turned on the lights in here."

I frowned. Older Jim seemed to be equivocating. Reflecting on his comments about the lights, I looked up.

There was nothing special about the illumination that I was aware of. The lights simply came on whenever someone showed up in the lab — or rather, a body they could detect, since Older Jim, when phased and invisible, didn't seem to count. Maybe the computer operated the same way.

"The computer is like the lights," I surmised. "It comes on when someone enters the lab."

"Oh, you mean like now?" Older Jim quipped sarcastically.

It was true. The computer hadn't come on when Myshtal and I had shown up in the lab — at least, not that I was aware of. Now that my thoughts turned to her, I glanced at the princess and noted that she was still frozen.

Tilting my chin at her, I asked my older self, "What did you do to her?"

"Nothing, I promise," he replied. "I merely put the two of us in a time sheath."

I gave him a befuddled look. "What's a time sheath?"

"Think of it as a bubble around us in which time proceeds normally while being frozen everywhere else," he replied. "It's a little trick I picked up from the Incarnates, but don't ask me anything in that regard because I am definitely not answering any questions about *them*."

"Fine," I grumbled. "Back to the computer coming on. Like the lights, it powers up when people are present, but apparently it's only *certain* people. Thus far, it's only come on when Electra and I were in here together."

I chewed on that last fact for a moment. Why would Mouse require Electra and I to be together for the computer to turn on? If it was just *me*, I could understand: after all, I was his mentee. I hung out with him in his lab practically every day. But Electra? Sure, Mouse knew and trusted her, but they didn't spend nearly as much time together as he and I did. Plus, it was common knowledge that Electra and I had broken up. Mandating that we be together for the computer to power up during a crisis didn't seem reasonable. And if that was the requirement, why hadn't it turned on when Electra and I returned to look for the bug-out bag? And with that thought came clarity.

"It's *me*," I declared to my older self. "The computer recognizes *me* in some way and turns on, not me and Electra."

As I spoke, I reached out telepathically, trying to peek in Older Jim's mind. It was really a reach, as my — and presumably *his* — mental shields had always been first-rate. As expected, that turned out to be the case in this instance: mentally, I hit a brick wall and was rebuffed.

"Ha!" my older self barked. "You had to know I was expecting that. Come on, I've been here before — right where you are, in fact."

"Then you already know exactly what you can and can't tell me," I shot back. "So stop making me play these guessing games."

Older Jim just stared at me for a moment, as if deciding something.

"Fine," he finally stated flatly. "I'll give you *one*, and then we're done."

"Great," I replied. "Whenever you're ready."

My older self let out a sigh and shook his head, as if he couldn't believe what he was doing.

"You're right about the computer," he finally admitted. "It's supposed to turn on for you and only you. The systems in Mouse's lab are supposed to scan the biometrics of anyone present and if you're alone, the computer turns on. If someone is with you, the computer stays off."

"So why did it turn on when Electra was with me?" I asked, then narrowed my eyes as the truth became evident. "You did something. What was it?"

"I suppressed all of Electra's vitals and biometric data, so that the scanners in the lab couldn't detect them."

I had trouble hiding my surprise. "You can do that?"

"That and a whole lot more," he declared. "Anyway, as far as the lab's scanners were concerned, there was no Electra. You were the only person in the room."

"And that's why the computer turned on," I concluded.

"Exactly," Older Jim said. "Now, if you'll excuse me, I'm going back to being unknown and unseen."

"Understood," I stated with a nod. "And thanks."

"If you want to thank me," he shot back, "see if you can get Mouse to let me have something else to eat when this is all over. Maybe some lasagna, or steak, or even takeout. On second thought, scratch the takeout; it doesn't really agree with me."

"Will do," I promised.

Older Jim gave me a curt nod and disappeared. The second he vanished, Myshtal began moving.

"No, I'm ready," she insisted. "We can try it again now."

"Huh?" I muttered, unsure of what she was talking about.

"You just said something about searching for my ring again later. I was just saying that I'm ready to try again now."

"No, I think we're good at the moment," I assured her. "Let me get you back to Monique."

ISOLATION

Chapter 52

I immediately teleported Myshtal back to Monique's house. Still under the influence of the brownies, Myshtal apparently couldn't shake the notion that she had somehow disappointed me. Thus, I made it a point to explain to her that she'd done an excellent job, and I appreciated her efforts. I didn't leave until I was confident that she understood I was being sincere.

Afterwards, I teleported back to HQ, popping up in the teen lounge. No one was around. I was about to go looking for my friends when klaxons abruptly began blaring.

Mouse is back, I surmised, not needing any external source of confirmation.

I teleported, popping up at Command Central — the control room for HQ. Nominally the nerve center of all League activity and information, it was filled with various types of equipment, including computers and monitors, and allowed access to cameras throughout the building.

There were a handful of guards on duty when I appeared. My sudden appearance startled a couple of them, but they quickly recovered.

"Where?" I demanded of no one in particular.

Even though I hadn't bothered to properly phrase my question, everyone present understood what I was talking about. Even better, they all knew who I was.

"Underground parking garage," one of the guards replied. "Level Three."

I teleported, this time appearing — in line with the guard's information — on the third level of HQ's subterranean parking structure. I immediately found myself in an expansive parking bay, with vehicles of various makes and models all around.

There was a fair amount of commotion nearby in the form of shouts and other noise, and I dashed in the direction of the sound. A moment later, I was standing at the edge of an open area, where I saw Mouse facing off against several League members. Unlike previous run-ins, however, my mentor seemed to be receiving the worst of it this time.

Mouse was grappling hand-to-hand with Luna when I showed up. Just as I arrived, she broke his grip and then spun inside his guard, at the same time bringing up an elbow that she used to whack him in the head.

The blow sent Mouse staggering backwards. While he was still off-balance, Luna leaped towards him and spun in the air, landing a back kick on his chest that send him flying.

While he was airborne, a streak of black and gold — obviously Buzz — slammed into my mentor, sending him caroming off to the side. However, he didn't travel far before his motility was arrested, brought to an abrupt halt by the hand of my father catching him around the throat in midair.

Mouse clawed futilely at the hand gripping him for a moment, and then Alpha Prime flicked his wrist, as if swatting at an annoying insect. Mouse went sailing backwards; a second later, he slammed into the windshield of a nearby sedan with such force that he not only shattered the glass that he struck but also blew out the remaining windows.

Walking almost in synchronized fashion, my father, Luna, and Buzz began to close on Mouse from three different directions. On his part, my mentor appeared to be barely holding on to consciousness, and I saw a small trickle of blood at the corner of his mouth.

All of the action had happened pretty fast — in the space of just a few seconds, to be honest. Had one party or the other been comprised of bad guys, I like to think I would have immediately joined the fray. As it was, with me now convinced that Mouse hadn't gone rogue, I had hesitated those first few moments. But the current lull in the conflict, such as it was, gave me just enough time to come to a decision.

"Hey!" I shouted, causing everyone to look in my direction. "Mouse is fine now, I think. He's—"

"It's okay, son," Alpha Prime interjected, cutting me off. "We've got this under control."

With that, he, Luna, and Buzz resumed closing in on Mouse. My mentor, however, apparently hadn't been idle. At some point during the exchange between me and Alpha Prime, he had pulled one of the little silver balls from somewhere on his person. He tossed it weakly at Alpha Prime's face.

My father swatted at the metallic sphere disdainfully, apparently intending to bat it aside. Instead of being knocked away, however, the ball seemed to explode on contact, filling the air around Alpha Prime with a thick cloud of glittering dust.

Everyone froze, and all eyes turned to my father. The dust was too thick to see his face, but you could still make out his frame. He had stopped moving and was standing still. Then, without warning, he started making an odd sound.

"Ah…ah…" Alpha Prime began. "Ah-choo!!!"

It was a sneeze unlike any I'd ever seen before. First and foremost, it was loud as a foghorn, and seemingly magnified by our underground location. Next, it gushed out with hurricane force, sending an entire fleet of cars tumbling away.

Realizing at the last second what was afflicting my father, I had phased myself and everyone else (except Mouse, who had apparently vanished). I was about to make us substantial again when I suddenly recognized that Alpha Prime wasn't done yet.

"Ah… Ah-choo!" he sneezed.

Facing a different direction this time, he nevertheless caused the same amount of havoc by once again sending vehicles flying. Moreover, looking at his face, it became clear that there was more to come.

Deciding to tackle the problem from a different angle, I made Buzz and Luna solid again, then teleported Alpha Prime and myself.

ISOLATION

Chapter 53

I took us to a spot where my father could sneeze to his heart's content: the middle of the ocean. There, about a thousand feet up in the air, he was unlikely to cause any harm.

Because he involuntarily closed his eyes while sneezing — and because the sneezing was continuous — I wasn't sure how much Alpha Prime could actually see. However, I telepathically told him where we were and what I'd done (and not to worry about me because I had phased), and got a mental thumbs-up from him in reply.

The sneezing went on for at least an hour and was a testament to the fact that Mouse had really done a number on my father. He had both incapacitated Alpha Prime as well as turned him into a weapon. Who knows how much damage he would have done without someone there to spirit him away?

Fortunately, I'd had a place to take him to where he wouldn't be a danger to others, and I spent part of our time over the ocean reflecting on numerous things — including the last time I'd been in this particular locale. It had been during a transcontinental cruise that my grandfather had taken the family on several years earlier. Just the thought of that trip made me painfully aware of how much I missed my family.

That said, I spent the bulk of my time thinking about Mouse. He'd obviously been trying to contact me, in a roundabout sort of way. Moreover, he'd been trying to contact *only* me, it seemed. Taken altogether, it implied that I shouldn't share anything I'd recently discovered with anyone else.

ISOLATION

Eventually, Alpha Prime's sneezing came to an end. Once we were certain his sternutation had permanently ceased, I became solid again and teleported us back to Alpha League HQ, at which point my father began rounding folks up for an official debrief. Ultimately, I — along with Smokey and Electra — ended up in the main conference room with Alpha Prime and a bunch of League members.

For the next two hours, I listened to my father drill his colleagues regarding what had happened, how to prepare for the next attack, what leads they had on Mouse's whereabouts, and so on. Frankly speaking, the latest attack had been pretty straightforward; even I, arriving on the scene late, could easily sum it up: Mouse had appeared, and a battle had ensued. The only thing I'd been unaware of was why Mouse had chosen the underground garage for his latest appearance, but it turned out that the League had been planning to move some of the doomsday components out that way via a transport truck.

Other than details about the latest skirmish, however, no one really had any info to share. At some point early on I was asked about where I'd disappeared to when I left Smokey and Electra in the teen lounge. Not wanting to reveal what I'd learned, I had merely stated that I'd attempted to follow a lead that hadn't panned out. (I also tried to tack on my thoughts about Mouse possibly being okay, but nobody wanted to hear that — didn't "jibe with the facts," as someone put it.) Afterwards, I had tried on more than one occasion to excuse myself, but my father wouldn't allow it. He said he needed my insights, but I really didn't add anything to the discussion. Truth be told, I spent most of the time with my own thoughts, continuing my attempts to make sense of everything.

ISOLATION

After what felt like forever, my father called the meeting to an end. Almost giddy, I prepared to teleport home. It felt like I'd been trapped in a meeting of bureaucrats: endless talk, but nothing meaningful had been decided or gotten done. Unfortunately, going home was quickly taken off the table.

"Jim," my father said, "I'd really appreciate it if you would hang around."

"Oh?" I intoned. "Did you want to talk about something?"

"I probably phrased that wrong," he stated. "I meant hang around HQ as opposed to going back to the embassy. It'll make it easier to reach you if something comes up."

"Sure…no problem," I replied. "I'll be in my quarters if you need me."

Alpha Prime gave a nod of acknowledgment, and then I teleported.

ISOLATION

Chapter 54

My quarters at HQ were much the same as those of all members of the League's teen affiliate — essentially, a one-bedroom apartment. When I popped up, I immediately turned the lights on before flopping down on a sofa in the living room. I took a moment to simply relish the solitude; it felt like the first time I'd been alone in days.

In all honesty — despite the seriousness of the situation with Mouse — I had enjoyed spending time with my father and friends (especially Electra). That said, occasionally having time alone did a lot to help recharge my batteries. More to the point, it felt like something I really needed at the moment. Unfortunately, my seclusion was short-lived, as I'd only been resting about five minutes when a knock sounded at my door. Reaching out empathically, I sensed that it was Electra.

Sighing, I got up and opened the door.

"Hey," Electra said, surprising me with a quick peck on the lips as she stepped inside.

"Uh…hey," I greeted her in return. "I'm sorry — I wasn't expecting you."

"Well, the way you vanished after the meeting, it's almost like you were trying to avoid me."

"You're right," I acknowledged. "I should have said something. I've just been so wrapped up in this thing about Mouse that I'm not thinking straight."

"It's okay — you're forgiven," she said with a wink. "Anyway, I brought you something."

For the first time, I noticed that she was holding a brown paper bag, which she now held up.

"What's that?" I asked.

"Dinner," she said.

I frowned. "It's a little early, don't you think?"

"I admit it's only a little after five," she said, "but you never finished lunch so I figured you were probably hungry."

"Honestly, I don't have much of an appetite," I confessed truthfully. Even without tweaking anything internally, I simply hadn't felt hungry.

"All the more reason to eat," Electra insisted before heading to the kitchen (although it was really more of a kitchenette).

I was tempted to argue with her, but simply decided to relent. Thus, I followed in her wake and found myself in the kitchenette a few moments later.

"No, no, no," she said, suddenly shooing me out. "I'll prepare the plates. You just go kick your feet up."

"Uh, okay," I responded uncertainly, heading back towards the living room. As with the pizza the previous night, this kind of behavior wasn't typical for Electra. I could only assume that she was doing it because she thought I was under a lot of pressure.

Unexpectedly, a fanciful thought entered my head: me and Electra once again a couple, but with her constantly waiting on me hand and foot. I snickered to myself, knowing that it was something that would never come to pass, but it was fun to imagine.

A soft musical ding suddenly interrupted my thoughts — the sound of the microwave going off in the kitchenette. I assumed it meant Electra had finished warming up the food.

As if reading my mind, she unexpectedly called out, "Almost ready. I'll be out in a minute."

Taking that as my cue, I began heading for a small breakfast table near the kitchenette, which was where I usually ate when staying in my quarters. I took a position behind a chair on one side of the table, deciding to wait until Electra joined me before sitting down.

She came out of the kitchen area a moment later carrying two plates. She placed one on the table in front of me and the other on the opposite side. It was my first time actually seeing what she'd brought, and I noticed that it looked like some kind of fried rice, and that Electra had already placed a fork in it for me.

"When did you order this?" I asked out of curiosity.

"While we were sitting in that debriefing," she replied, and I had a sudden recollection of seeing her play with her phone a few times in the meeting. "I thought you might enjoy some takeout, so I got one of the guards to go pick it up."

I fought to keep my face impassive, but sirens immediately started screaming in my brain. Several pieces of a mental puzzle unexpectedly fell into place, and I suddenly realized I was quite possibly in a very dangerous situation.

"You know," I intoned, trying to sound casual, "I'm actually not that hungry."

"What?" Electra blurted out. "No, you *have* to eat."

"I'll just get a power bar or something from the pantry," I countered.

"No, no, no. I went through the trouble of getting this for you — the least you can do is eat it."

"I'll get some later," I promised.

"No, not later. I want you to eat it *now*."

I gave her a hard stare. "What's the big deal about eating it *now*?" I asked.

Electra merely stared at me for a moment, looking vexed, and I felt frustration and anxiety starting to roll off her in waves.

A moment later, she sighed and said, "Look, I miss you, okay? I've enjoyed being around you the last few days and I was simply hoping we could have dinner together, like we used to. So could you please just sit and eat with me — even if it's just a few bites?"

"Sure," I said with a nod. "It actually sounds a lot more enticing when you put it that way. Just let me run to the bathroom."

"Okay," she said with a coy smile, "but hurry up."

"For you, I'll go at super speed," I promised with a smile. I then shifted into super speed and went into motion, but was back in place probably before she knew I was gone.

"All right, let's eat," I stated as I sat down.

"Wow, that really was quick," Electra admitted as she took her own seat.

"I aim to please," I shot back as we began to eat.

I took a quick bite of the food on my plate and discovered it was actually rather tasty.

"Mmmm," I droned. "This is really good."

"Agreed," Electra stated with a nod. "So, where exactly did you go when you left us in the lounge earlier? I don't believe you ever said."

"Just to check out a lead. Like I said in the meeting, it didn't pan out."

"What kind of lead?"

I shook my head. "Nothing major — turned out to be a waste of time."

"Hmmm," Electra muttered, clearly not satisfied with my answer.

ISOLATION

As we ate, Electra continued to ask detailed questions about where I'd gone and the lead I'd been following. I gave generic responses to all her questions, which she plainly didn't care for. However, after eating about a quarter of her food, I noticed that she was starting to yawn. By the time she'd eaten close to half, her eyes were starting to droop. In essence, she looked like she was incredibly tired and sleepy. In fact, she was in the process of raising her fork to her mouth when she suddenly pitched forward, unconscious, and face-planted in the middle of her food.

More like face-plated, I said to myself as I dropped my own fork and stood up from the table.

I stared at her for a moment in absolute disgust. I now understood why I'd practically passed out the past two nights: Electra had been drugging me.

How does it feel to get a taste of your own medicine? I thought.

Of course, it had been the older version of myself who had tipped me off. He had mentioned "takeout" — specifically, not wanting any — and just a few hours later, Electra brought me takeout. It had seemed too spot-on to be mere coincidence. Thus, when I had asked why it was so important that I eat, I had telepathically peeked inside Electra's mind.

Unlike a lot of other telepaths, I can't do a deep dive into another person's brain and root out any info I want. I can only see surface thoughts and what they willingly want to share. The good news, however, is that when you ask someone a question, the answer usually comes to the fore of their mind — even if they verbally lie about it. In this instance, I saw what Electra had planned for me. Ergo, after I shifted to super speed, rather than go to the bathroom, I had instead switched plates. Result: one knocked-out ex-girlfriend.

Despite having figured out what she was planning, I was still in the dark on a lot of things — like why she was drugging me in the first place. Was this even the real Electra? From all indications, it was, which made her actions all the more confusing. Somehow, though, I knew it all related to Mouse. I needed answers, and there was only one place I thought I could get them.

With that in mind, I was about to teleport when I took one last look at Electra. She was still face down in the plate but from what I could see, she appeared to be breathing, so — in my estimation — she wasn't in danger. Still, it seemed kind of insensitive to leave her like that.

Shaking my head at what I was about to do, I reached out and — against my better judgment — pulled Electra's face out of the plate. I then leaned her head gently back, making sure that she was positioned in a way that made it least likely that she'd fall out of the chair.

Satisfied that I had gone above and beyond the call of duty, I then teleported.

ISOLATION

Chapter 55

I popped up in Mouse's lab. As was typically the case, the lights came on a few seconds after I appeared.

I spent a moment looking around. This was the last place Mouse had been seen before allegedly going rogue. This was where he'd left clues for me on his computer. This was the spot where he'd left his bug-out bag (and leaving it implied that he was somewhere close by).

All roads lead to Rome, I said to myself.

Now that I was here, however, I was at a loss with respect to what I was supposed to do. Was Mouse maybe watching or listening in some way? Sure hadn't seemed like it when Electra and I were in here shouting for him. Of course, in hindsight, I had been wrong to trust Electra or have her with me.

Hmmm, I droned mentally. *Did Mouse know that Electra couldn't be trusted?* It sure seemed that way. After all, he'd essentially left clues only for me, rigged the computer to only turn on for me, and so on. Everything was solely for me — or hinged on me being by myself.

At that juncture, an idea occurred to me. It probably wouldn't pay any dividends, but it certainly wouldn't hurt.

Feeling a little foolish, I said out loud, "Mouse, I found your clues. I'm here like you wanted."

I wasn't sure what else to say, so I just stood there quietly waiting. After about a minute, I was ready to give up. This had been my best guess, and it turned out I was wrong. Apparently I needed to go back to the drawing board.

ISOLATION

Feeling exasperated, I wiped my face with my hand as I prepared to teleport. At that moment, however, I heard someone speak.

"You certainly took your time," said a familiar voice.

It had come from behind me, and I swiftly spun around to find myself facing the speaker.

Mouse.

ISOLATION

Chapter 56

He was dressed as he'd been the last few times I'd seen him — in his Alpha League uniform. Unsurprisingly, he had his computer tablet tucked under one arm; he rarely went anywhere without it. It looked like there were bags forming under his eyes, giving the impression that he was tired, but otherwise he didn't look too bad for a guy who had taken on the world's premier team of supers several times in the last few days.

"You've been busy these past few days," I remarked.

"I think the same could be said of you," he replied. "A lot of people, in fact."

"Well, the League has been suffering a continuous string of attacks," I said.

"Is that a fact?" he intoned with something of a cocksure grin.

I frowned. This conversation was kind of odd. Normally Mouse and I quickly fell into an easy banter, maintaining the ability to joke with each other even when the topic being discussed was serious. Our current exchange felt stiff and formal, like Mouse was somehow wary. In fact, reaching out emphatically, that's exactly what I picked up from him: a certain watchfulness — as if he felt the need to be cautious and guarded around me.

If he was somehow suspicious of *me*, it was an indication that maybe he wasn't himself yet. It was entirely possible that — despite appearing fairly lucid and leaving clues for me to find him — Mouse was still somewhat under the effect of whatever the Tristan Construct had done to him. And if that were the case, he might still be dangerous.

"Anyway," he continued, bringing me back to myself, "I'm glad you were able to figure out my clues. I was worried there for a bit that they were too tricky for you."

"No, it was absolutely perfect," I attested. "Whatever the Construct exposed you to or infected you with, it didn't affect your ability to leave a great trail of breadcrumbs."

As I finished speaking, my eyes went wide as I realized what I'd done. I had somehow drifted into speaking casually with my mentor, and thus had slipped up by saying something I shouldn't have. There was a chance that Mouse wouldn't catch it, but one glance at his face told me it was a futile hope.

Frowning, Mouse said, "Excuse me?"

As had happened many times recently, I wanted to kick myself. In telling Mouse he was infected, I had violated a basic tenet of psychotherapy: never tell a crazy person he's crazy. More importantly, I wasn't sure I could fix my blunder, but I had to try.

"I just said you left a great trail of breadcrumbs," I explained.

"No," Mouse said, shaking his head. "You said I was infected."

He looked at me expectantly, waiting for me to say something. I spent a moment considering various things I could try to tell him to convince him he'd misheard or misunderstood me. Ultimately, I rejected them all. Plainly speaking, even half crazy, Mouse was too smart to lie to. My best bet was to come clean.

"Yes, you've been infected," I declared. "The Construct exposed you to something that altered your thinking. You're not yourself."

ISOLATION

Mouse simply stared at me for a moment, and then, to my great surprise, burst into laughter. And to be clear, it wasn't just a few chuckles; it was gut-busting, side-splitting, knee-slapping laughter — the kind that brings tears to your eyes. It was probably a full minute before Mouse regained his composure, but for me, it just seemed to reaffirm the notion that he wasn't himself.

"Oh, man," Mouse finally muttered, wiping tears from his eyes. "I needed that — really, I did. That had to be the funniest thing I've heard in a while."

"Okay, I have to ask," I stated. "What's so funny?"

"The fact that you called me infected," Mouse replied with a grin.

I scratched my temple. "What's so funny about that?"

"Because," Mouse explained. "*I'm* not infected — *you* are!"

ISOLATION

Chapter 57

"They're called the Busuigno," Mouse explained. "They're mid-dimensional beings."

"Mid-dimensional?" I repeated.

"They exist in a space between dimensions," Mouse said.

"You mean like this place?" I asked, making an all-encompassing gesture.

We were currently in a room about two hundred square feet in size, and which was set up like a smaller version of Mouse's lab, with a number of worktables, computers, monitors, and other devices.

"Not quite like this," Mouse said. "This room is an interdimensional product — it actually exists in another dimension outside our own. I set it up, along with several others like it, as a kind of safe house I could get to quickly."

I nodded. "I understand now how you just seemed to vanish during your recent skirmishes with the League. You opened a dimensional doorway and stepped through."

"Pretty much," Mouse admitted, although my statement wasn't really a theory or guess. It was how Mouse had brought us to our current locus after telling me I was infected.

"Anyway, we were talking about the Busuigno," Mouse continued. "They're a symbiotic race — they attach themselves to other beings and take over their hosts, mind and body."

As he spoke, Mouse brought up an image on one of the monitors near us — specifically, a pic of me in his lab just before he showed up. The color appeared washed out, but I knew that was because the image had been captured with a special camera. Other than that, there wasn't anything unusual about the pic — unless you counted the dark mass that looked like an ugly, crumpled cowl draped over my head and shoulders.

"That's a Busuigno?" I asked, pointing at the cowl.

"Yeah," Mouse answered.

"And it's on me now?"

"Absolutely."

"So…it's controlling me in some way?"

"Actually, it isn't," Mouse said. "I don't doubt that it's trying, but you seem to have some type of immunity — probably a result of your singular genetic structure."

I gave him a curious look. "So you knew that I was immune? That's why you left me hints on how to track you down?"

"Well, I didn't *know*," he admitted. "But I had a hint in that direction."

"What kind of hint?"

Mouse seemed to reflect for a moment. "I know someone who has experience with the Busuigno. He suggested that certain people might be immune to their effects and you seemed to have the proper characteristics."

"Oh — the future me," I surmised. He had mentioned how everything that was happening was part of his past, which essentially made him the only person experienced with this situation.

Mouse looked startled. "You met him?"

I nodded. "We had a chat."

Mouse shook his head in disbelief. "That idiot. I told him not to talk to anybody."

"Well, technically, he only talked to himself, so…"

"Really?" Mouse shot back as I trailed off. "That's the argument you want to go with?"

"Okay, I agree that he probably should have heeded your advice, but it's not like he simply revealed himself," I stated. I then gave a brief explanation of how Myshtal's power had brought Older Jim to my attention. "And I'm sure he knew — just like you — that there was no way I was going to ignore the possibility of another Jim being around."

Mouse simply nodded as I spoke. My statement referred to the fact that I'd had to deal with a dangerous clone of myself in the not-too-distant past, so the notion of a second Jim would have been something I might have prioritized even above locating my mentor.

"All right," Mouse finally said. "In that light, revealing himself may not have been as terrible as it appeared at first blush."

"I'm sure the future me will appreciate that," I noted. "So what exactly did he say about me being immune?"

"I basically told him I had an unusual object coming in and that he might want to go elsewhere while I studied it."

"The Tristan Construct," I concluded.

"Yeah," Mouse affirmed. "It's not rooted in our reality — our space-time continuum — so I wasn't sure if it would affect him in some way due to his 'problem.'"

"What was his response?"

"He said he'd stay put — that stuff like that had never affected him."

"So that was your hint that it might not affect *me*."

"Correct."

"That's why you called me and asked for my help. You figured that if anything went sideways, I would come through unscathed."

"Pretty much."

"So how exactly does the Construct fit into all this anyway?"

"Believe it or not, it's actually a prison."

"What?!" I exclaimed.

"Yeah," Mouse continued with a nod.

I spent a moment contemplating. The Construct hadn't seemed very large. It could certainly hold one person — possibly two, depending on their size. Not many more than that, I was sure.

"Who's in it?" I asked.

"The Busuigno, of course," Mouse replied. "Presumably, someone, somewhere got tired of being a marionette, so they locked them all in the Construct."

"So how many are in there?"

"Billions, I'd guess. Possibly trillions. All except the ones that got out when I opened it."

I looked at him with a horrified expression. "Excuse me?"

"Well, how do you think that one got on *you*?"

"I don't know!" I shot back. "You said they were interdimensional beings, so I just thought it came into our dimension and latched onto me. I didn't realize you were running some kind of transdimensional parole board."

"Once again, they're *mid*-dimensional beings," Mouse corrected. "They typically exist in a space *between* dimensions. Not in our dimension, not in some other dimension, but in a space between them."

"Whatever," I said dismissively. "Where are the other ones that got out?"

"Can't you guess?" he replied. "One's on AP. Another's on Luna. Buzz. Solar Surge. Smokey. Electra..."

He rattled off more names, but in all honesty, I stopped listening after he mentioned Electra. Now I kind of understood her behavior to a certain extent; it wasn't *her* who had been drugging me — it was the thing *on* her.

"So basically," I said when he finished, "you threw open the gates of a penitentiary and let a bunch of convicts out. Now the inmates are running the asylum."

"Well, in my defense," he replied, "I didn't know it was a prison at first. I realized that it wasn't rooted in our reality, but beyond that, it was just kind of a lock-box puzzle."

"And you couldn't resist opening it."

Mouse shrugged. "We all have our weaknesses. But I didn't just open it without any thought to what could be inside. I knew it wasn't inherently dangerous — no explosives, no bio-weapons, or anything along those lines. That said, as long as it was on this planet, we needed to have some notion of either what was inside or what it could do."

"Or we could have just tossed it back where we found it, or locked it away."

"You mean closed our eyes to the problem? The way you could have just ignored that there was another Jim in the lab?"

"Point taken," I conceded. "So what exactly happened when you opened that thing?"

"To explain that, I need to give a little more background," he noted. "As I said, the Busuigno exists between dimensions, but they can freely travel from one to another, which is how they find their hosts. That being the case, it took a special type of prison to hold them."

"Some kind of mid-dimensional stockade," I offered.

"Exactly. Being mid-dimensional, the Busuigno —
in their natural form — can pass through steel and stone
like they aren't there. So, any prison built to hold them
can't fully exist in our space-time continuum. It has to
exist, to some extent, in *their* space."

"Okay," I intoned. "I think I get that."

"Anyway, when I opened it, there was some kind
of temporal distortion. It was like a sphere formed around
me and the Construct, and inside it time moved normally.
Outside of it, though, time appeared frozen."

What he was describing sounded remarkably like
the time sheath Older Jim had created, but I didn't think it
wise to mention it at the moment. Instead, I simply asked,
"What do you think caused it?"

Mouse's brow crinkled in thought. "I assume it was
whoever built the prison. I think they tacked it on as some
kind of safeguard, just in case the prison ever, uh,
inadvertently opened. It would provide time to hopefully
round up any escapees, toss them back inside, and bar the
door before they could do any damage."

"How'd that work out?" I asked sarcastically.

"I got the door closed, wise guy," Mouse
countered. "And only a limited number got out.
Unfortunately, they're controlling some of the most
powerful people on the planet at the moment, and they're
dead set on releasing the rest of the Busuigno from
lockup."

"Why didn't they take over you?"

"Believe me, they tried, but it didn't work. I have
certain safeguards against mind control techniques.
Frankly speaking, it's kind of what gave me a leg up. When
one of them tried to control me, I got a glimpse inside his
mind. Not a lot, but enough."

"And that's how you know so much about what you're dealing with."

"Correct. It's funny — if they hadn't tried to control me then I might not have known anything was going on because ordinarily human beings can't perceive them. As it was, I discovered they were there and used the time in the temporal sphere to find out all I could about them and the Construct."

I frowned. "How long were you in there, subjectively?"

"Just a few hours, but it was enough time to figure out what I was dealing with and formulate a rudimentary plan. Fortunately, I had my computer tablet with me."

"So in that time, you managed to lock the prison back up, come up with a way to leave me clues, and formulate a plan to capture the escaped Busuigno?"

"Yeah," he droned. "I admit it's not my best work, but you have to use the tools available."

"And then," I continued, "when the time bubble disappeared, you came out swinging."

"Not exactly," Mouse stated. "I didn't know if anyone else would be immune to the Busuigno, so I gave it a second."

"That's not the way it comes across on the video," I countered. "Looks like you just started blasting."

Mouse frowned for a second, then began tapping on his tablet. A few seconds later, he pointed at the monitor that had previously shown my pic, saying, "You mean *this* video?"

It was the initial footage I'd seen of Mouse going on the offensive in his lab, only this time there was audio.

"Get him," I heard my father say just before Mouse blasted him.

Next, Luna screamed "Die!" as she charged at my mentor.

I turned to Mouse (who paused the video) and said, "There wasn't audio on the clip they showed me."

"You think they wanted you to hear that?" he asked rhetorically. "But there was audio on the footage I left on the computer for you. Didn't you hear it when you played that?"

"Hmmm," I droned. "I kinda didn't check to see if the audio was on...or if the volume was turned up."

Mouse wiped his face with his hand, mumbling, "Why do I even try?"

"Let's just get back on task," I suggested. Glancing back at the paused video, another question occurred to me. "AP said there was some kind of power surge from the Construct that took the camera offline for a second. He also said it was what unhinged you."

Mouse shook his head. "The time sphere was the only thing that seemed to emanate from the Construct. But if you're talking about why they only have that one piece of footage at their disposal, that was *my* doing."

"What do you mean?" I asked.

"When I was in the time sphere, the escaped Busuigno were in there with me. They could see what I was doing. Therefore, I couldn't actually implement everything I wanted to because they'd know what I was up to. Still, I could lay a good bit of the groundwork, as long as I kept it somewhat obtuse."

"So they could see, maybe, that you were planning to reach out to someone, but they didn't know how or when."

"Correct. With respect to the footage, after I escaped from the lab, it was second nature to me to cover my tracks."

"So you deleted the lab footage from the system."

"I *started* deleting it, but at the time, I saw that someone — presumably the Busuigno — were in the system as well, trying to download it. I was curious as to what they wanted it for, so I let them have the portion that they showed you."

I spent a moment reflecting on what my mentor had just said. "What do you think they wanted it for?"

"They obviously used it for propaganda purposes — to get people who weren't under their control to think I'd gone off the rails. But I think the real reason was the Construct."

"What's the big deal about footage of that?" I asked.

"They've been imprisoned in there for a long time — thousands of years, at the least. And during that time, they've been doing their best to get out."

"I get it," I chimed in. "They wanted to see how you opened it."

"Exactly, and I think they got enough of an idea to form a plan."

"So how did *I* get on their radar? Did they see something related to me when you were in the temporal sphere?"

Mouse shook his head. "I didn't give any direct indication of who I was trying to recruit. However, Alpha Prime knew that I had called you, and I assume when the Busuigno took control of him, they saw that. More to the point, they saw what you could do and assumed they could use you. So at some point one of them attached itself to you, but — much to their dismay, I'm sure — you proved unsusceptible to their control."

As my mentor spoke, I suddenly remembered something that had happened around the time I was being recruited to hunt him down.

"The conference room," I muttered.

Mouse raised an eyebrow. "What's that?"

"That first night they told me you'd gone rogue," I explained. "I was in the conference room with Alpha Prime, and I felt this weird tingle at the back of my mind. At the same time, AP looked at me like he was expecting something. I think that's when the Busuigno attached to me."

Mouse shrugged. "Probably. That's similar to what it felt like when it tried to attach to me, but I was able to shake it off."

"So is it somehow reading my thoughts now?"

"I don't think so," Mouse said. "I mean, typically they can access the thoughts and memories of their hosts, but that doesn't seem to be the case with your symbiont. In fact, based on what I can tell, yours seems to be dying."

"What?!" I screeched. "Is that going to affect *me*?"

"Unlikely," Mouse stated. "The Busuigno feed, for lack of a better term, on the psychic and mental energy of their host. In your case, the inability to take control also means that the symbiont can't feed."

"Then why doesn't it just let go — move on?"

"I'm not sure it can," Mouse replied. "My guess is there's some kind of psychic feedback or reaction that prevents it from releasing its grip on you."

"I think I understand," I said. "The way a person who grabs a live wire can't let go because the electricity clenches their muscles, so they end up getting electrocuted."

"Exactly."

"Do the other Busuigno know the one on me is dying?"

"Probably, but it's unlikely they can do anything about it."

"So why have they been drugging me?"

"Huh?" muttered Mouse.

"They've been drugging me," I repeated. I then gave him a quick overview of how Electra had been drugging my food. In fact, I brought him up to speed on everything that had happened thus far.

"Well, I'm glad you figured it out," Mouse stated. "My guess is that they drugged you so that I couldn't contact you."

"That brings up another point," I said. "Why didn't you just come up to me or leave me a note or something?"

"Isn't it obvious?" Mouse asked. "You have a Busuigno on you. I didn't know if you were still *you* or one of them."

"So you left the clues," I concluded.

"Yes," Mouse admitted. "Although the Busuigno can access a person's thoughts and memories, there are certain things that it can't mimic. Your instincts, intuition, gut feeling... those are things that are unique to you and can't be emulated."

"In short, you figured only the real Jim — as opposed to one with his strings being pulled — would figure out the hints you left."

"Exactly."

I frowned. "But you said you came up with the clues while still in the temporal bubble."

ISOLATION

Mouse sighed. "I always assumed that at some point the Busuigno would try to control you. I didn't know if you'd be unaffected, as the older Jim hinted, but I decided early on that it would be too risky to approach you directly. So no notes, no face-to-face, no nothing. Plus, based on what you said, they never left you alone. If you were awake, someone was always with you for the most part, and if you weren't awake, you were drugged into complete unconsciousness."

I shook my head in disdain. "I can't believe how long that went on."

"Don't be so hard on yourself," Mouse said. "These were all people you trusted. You can't be faulted for believing them."

"Maybe," I muttered unconvincingly, "but I should have trusted *you*. All my instincts told me that you'd never do what they were accusing you of without a reason, but I pretty much let them convince me."

"Again, you can't blame yourself for any of that. I mean, you had the rest of the League telling you I'd gone rogue and offering proof of it. And of course, I wasn't telling you anything — at least not directly."

"It's just weird to think that they put on that entire dog-and-pony show just to convince me that you had to be stopped."

"Well, they desperately needed to get you on their side."

"Why? Just to hunt you down?"

"That's part of it," Mouse admitted. "But the primary reason is because they know that, with you helping me, they might as well just march themselves back into that prison."

ISOLATION

Chapter 58

"The people who built the Construct always assumed that the Busuigno might escape one day," Mouse said, "so they prepared for it."

"How?" I asked.

"Any Busuigno who leaves the Construct is marked with an interdimensional tag."

"Don't you mean a *mid*-dimensional tag?"

"No, professor," Mouse shot back, "because it tracks them even if they move across dimensions."

"Oh — kind of like a cosmic ankle bracelet."

"It's even better, because it can be used to pull them back into the Construct."

"So it'll just claw them back like a giant magnet?" I muttered incredulously. "That's great!"

"It would be, but the 'magnet,' as you put it, seems to be offline."

"Can't you fix it?" I asked.

"That's what I've been trying to do," Mouse insisted. "Every time you've seen me battling the League the past few days, it's because I was trying to get components to repair that system."

"Wait a minute," I blurted out. "They told me you were taking pieces of a doomsday device to take over the world."

"And you believed them?"

"I had no reason not to," I admitted. "But if you were only taking parts to fix the Construct, why'd you attack them in the Combat Arena?"

Mouse gave me an odd look. "Excuse me?"

"You attacked a couple of League members, including Luna, in the Combat Arena."

"Not me," Mouse said, shaking his head.

"Yeah, *you*," I countered. "Luna said you…" I trailed off, suddenly feeling foolish. "They lied, didn't they?"

Rather than answer directly, Mouse said, "Are you sure you're not under the Busuigno's control? Because you seem to buy everything they're selling."

Ignoring his jape, I sighed and stated, "Again, it seems like a lot of effort to go through just for me."

"They needed to convince you I was an enemy — make you wary in case I approached you. Faking an attack is as good a method as any."

"Still, I can't believe I fell for that."

"Okay, before you start getting down on yourself, let's just put it out there: the Busuigno are good at this stuff. They've probably had eons to practice how to manipulate others. That being the case, even *I* was wary when I met you in the lab, because I thought it could be a trick."

"Until my ignorance in saying you were infected revealed that I was the real Jim. Or at least showed I wasn't being controlled."

Mouse chuckled. "Why don't we just focus on the task at hand?"

"Fine by me," I replied.

"Good," Mouse said. "Here's the plan…"

****

Mouse's plan for bringing the Busuigno Magnet (as I called it) back online was fairly simple.

"I've got three of the requisite components," he stated. "There are another four we need, but it should be a piece of cake for you."

"How do you figure?" I asked.

"You can teleport in and out in a flash, and with your phasing ability, you won't have to waste time fighting anyone."

"That raises a point I meant to bring up earlier," I said. "When you zoomed away from the helipad and I took off after you, you hit me with some kind of weapon. What was it?"

Mouse looked uncomfortable for a second, like this was a subject he didn't care for.

"Just to be clear," he began, "I haven't made a habit of studying you or trying to figure out your weaknesses. This was something I did based on pure speculation."

"Okay," I intoned. "What was it?"

Mouse appeared to reflect for a moment before speaking. "Since you've been with the League's teen affiliate, you've gotten into a couple of scrapes that led to you requiring medical attention. Of course, any medical information about you is confidential, but as leader of the League, I've seen it."

"Okay," I said with a nod, "but I assume you've looked at everybody's."

"True, but — as has been stated numerous times — your physiology is unique. That being the case, I noticed from your records that you have several unknown organs, one of which — among other things — seems to store an extra quantity of air aside from your lungs. From all appearances, that organ gets a good workout when you phase, because it can siphon air directly as opposed to you breathing it in."

"Let me guess," I chimed in. "You sucker-punched that organ."

"Technically, I irritated the air going into that organ and it reacted — much like throwing black pepper into someone's face will make then sneeze."

"Which is also something you did."

"That actually wasn't pepper," Mouse corrected. "I hit Alpha Prime with something more potent, but yeah — same reaction."

"Well, the point I was trying to get to was asking whether the League has that weapon, since to effectuate your plan, I have to phase."

"Absolutely not," Mouse assured me. "No one has it but me, and I wasn't even sure it would work."

"What about when we were in the Vault? I tried using my teleportation power on you but it didn't work."

"That's because you tried to teleport a hologram — a decoy," Mouse replied. "I was actually on the other side of the wall section, using a device that bent light waves around me."

"And if you can bend light waves around an object, you effectively make it invisible."

Mouse smiled. "I'm glad all those physics lessons didn't go to waste."

"Again, is that something the League has, or is it Mouse-specific?"

Mouse laughed. "I'm the only one who has it, but that's immaterial since it never truly affected your teleportation power."

"Still, I have to ask," I stated. "The two powers you're saying I need to use are the very two you've seemingly been able to circumvent, so I need to make sure no one else can."

"Well, just so you know, I wasn't specifically focused on *you*," Mouse said. "I'm pretty isolated here, with limited resources, and I was going up against the entire League every time I showed my face, so I had to have a variety of tools on hand: flash bombs, frictionless grease, dimensional doors on the ground, dimensional doors in the air... I tried to stay unpredictable."

"And you've been doing all this by yourself?"

"It's not like I had a choice," Mouse declared. "The Busuigno control almost everybody, and anyone they couldn't control, they got rid of. Take Li for instance; he's not human so he's not susceptible to their control. Plus, he doesn't see the way we do, which means there's a possibility he could perceive them in some way. They sent him off on a bogus mission. Same thing with Esper — with her mental powers, she might have realized something was off, so they sent her on a snipe hunt as well. It's the same with almost everybody else."

I frowned, concentrating on his words. "You said 'almost' everybody else. Who's left?"

"Vixen, but she's safe — holed up in another dimensional room like this one. Basically, she's the back-up plan if we fail."

"Thanks for the vote of confidence," I remarked sarcastically.

Mouse laughed. "You don't need a confidence booster. This will be a cakewalk for you."

"What about this thing attached to me?"

Mouse gave me a curious look. "What about it?"

"Won't it tell the others what we're up to?"

"I guess I failed to explain how they communicate," Mouse said. "In their own space, they can speak mind-to-mind, but when they attach to another being, they can typically only use the methods of communication available to their host."

"So basically, they can only communicate using speech," I surmised.

"Correct," Mouse stated. "But that reminds me: some of them do have a low-level form of telepathy, but it typically requires them to be near one another."

"Well, how do we know the one attached to me isn't one of the telepathic ones — even if it *is* dying?"

"It didn't warn Electra that you switched plates, did it?"

"No," I replied. "So I guess we're safe on that front."

"Good," Mouse said. "Now let's get started locking these yahoos back up."

ISOLATION

Chapter 59

As Mouse had predicted, getting the remaining components was a piece of cake for me and required minimal preparation. First, he showed me images of each so that I wouldn't have any trouble recognizing them. (They looked like metallic trinkets of various shapes, although each was no more than a few inches in size.) He also gave me a Y-shaped electronic device that was about six inches long and which served as a tracker, among other things. At that juncture, he turned me loose.

Apparently, the Busuigno had garnered an idea of what Mouse was trying to do early on. However, their attempts to move some of the parts he needed by chopper and armored transport had obviously met with failure. Thus, for the last four items, they had resorted to a strategy of simply guarding the components.

Mouse, of course, had already pinpointed their location. Two were still in the Vault, and it was easy enough to show up there, phased, via a dimensional door that my mentor opened, and simply teleport those guarding the components elsewhere. (To be specific, I dumped them — two teams led by Luna and Buzz, respectively — in the marina where Mouse kept his boat.) The tracker, which doubled as a skeleton key of sorts, opened the appropriate Vault sections — one in the floor and one in a wall — and led me to the items we needed.

The third component was deep underground in a subterranean chamber below HQ that I never even knew existed. I had to fly down an elevator shaft to get there, but once I arrived, it was the same process: teleport those League members present to the marina and take the component. (In this instance, it was in something akin to a wall safe, which the tracker was able to unlock.)

The last item was a little trickier to retrieve. It was in the personal possession of Alpha Prime, who was in his quarters at League HQ. Having been there before, I simply teleported inside. Much to my surprise, he was waiting for me.

He was standing in the living room, dressed in his Alpha League uniform. My attention, however, was immediately drawn to the fact that he had his hands together, holding them in a manner that suggested he was using them to hide something from view. I didn't need the tracker to tell me that what he held was the last component.

"I know why you're here," he stated, "but I was hoping we could talk."

"There's nothing for us to talk about," I shot back, knowing it was a mistake to engage. This wasn't my father I was talking to; it was some *thing* from another dimension or reality controlling him.

"I think you're wrong," he replied. "I have an offer that might interest you."

I didn't bother responding. Instead, I simply stared at his hands. Under normal circumstances, Alpha Prime's position would have been unassailable. There was probably nothing on the planet capable of prying his hands open and forcibly taking what he held. Fortunately, the circumstances were anything but normal.

Continuing to look at Alpha Prime's hands, I turned them invisible up to the elbow. This seemed to startle him for a moment, and also gave me my first look at the component he held — an ebon-colored little doodad shaped like a cube and about one square inch in size. I teleported it into my hand before making Alpha Prime's hands visible again. Then I used the tracker to open a dimensional door and swiftly returned to Mouse's little hideaway.

ISOLATION

Chapter 60

Upon my return, I immediately handed over the doomsday components to Mouse.

"Any problems?" he asked as he took the devices over to a nearby worktable.

"None," I replied, shaking my head as I thought about all the League members — Luna, Buzz, etcetera — who I'd dumped in the marina. "I mean, Alpha Prime tried to make me an offer, but I ignored him."

Mouse gave me an odd look. "What kind of offer?"

I shrugged. "Don't know. As I said, I ignored him."

"Hmmm," Mouse droned, obviously thinking.

A moment later, he seemingly put the thought aside and turned his attention to the doomsday components. In essence, he put on a pair of what I referred to as "mad scientist goggles" with telescopic lenses, and then began using various tools (including a miniature laser) to work on the items I had retrieved. I watched him in silence, openly curious.

After a few minutes, Mouse — continuing to work without looking up — finally said, "Go ahead and ask."

"Ask what?" I responded.

"Whatever's on your mind. I can feel your curiosity building up like a volcano about to erupt."

"I'm just wondering what you're doing."

"I'm making modifications to the devices you retrieved."

"I can see that," I countered. "I'm just wondering why."

"What — did you think these components came magically designed to work with the Construct?" he asked

295

rhetorically. "I have to adjust and tweak them so they'll do what we need."

I let this sink in for a moment, then stated, "That raises another question: the Busuigno have been trying to keep you from getting these little doohickeys, so presumably they know what you're up to."

"Probably," Mouse agreed. "As I said before, they're not stupid."

"Then why didn't they just destroy the components? That would keep you from turning on the Construct Magnet and revoking their parole."

"I'm guessing they didn't want to risk blowing themselves up."

"What?!" I uttered incredulously.

Mouse continued to work without looking up. "These components come from doomsday devices, and a couple of them pack quite a punch — could leave all of HQ a smoking crater, in fact."

"I thought all that stuff was disarmed when it got put in the Vault."

"It was dis*assembled*," Mouse corrected. "There's a difference."

"Apparently so," I quipped.

"Look, if it makes you nervous, just go in a corner and phase or something," Mouse suggested.

"Thanks," I replied. "Maybe I will."

****

I didn't phase, but I did step back and give Mouse room to work in peace. A short time later, he removed the goggles and set aside the equipment he'd been using.

"Okay, I think we're ready," he announced.

"Great," I said. "I'm ready for this thing to be off me."

"I'm sure it's eager to detach, seeing as how otherwise it'll die," Mouse noted. "Anyway, the next step is for you to simply attach the components to the Construct."

"Attach?" I queried, raising an eyebrow. "Do I need to glue them on or something?"

"No — bad choice of words on my part," he admitted. "They'll adhere on their own, but you have to put each one in the right spot to kick-start the Construct Magnet, as you call it."

"Well, where exactly do they go?"

"I thought you'd never ask," Mouse said with a smile before pulling up an image of the Construct. "Now, pay attention…"

ISOLATION

Chapter 61

It took about ten minutes for Mouse to feel that I could properly recall where to place all seven doomsday components. In truth, I actually had it memorized well before then, but my mentor insisted on drilling it into me over and over. Given the stakes, I couldn't say I blamed him. At some point, however, he pronounced me fit for service, which finally gave me a chance to ask some questions.

"After I get all these contraptions on the Construct," I began, "how long before the Busuigno are back where they belong?"

"Should be just a few minutes," Mouse said.

"Any reason I can't just teleport the Construct somewhere off the grid and do all this stuff with the doomsday components?"

"Again, it's not grounded in our reality. As a result, it's sensitive to abnormal spatial distortions."

"Like teleportation," I surmised.

"Yeah," Mouse said with a nod. "I think it views anything like that as a prison break. It will go into lockdown mode, and the Construct Magnet will be useless."

"Okay, no teleporting the mid-dimensional prison," I noted. "Regardless, it's nice to know this will all be over soon."

Mouse stared at me for a moment, plainly contemplating something.

"Look, Jim," he finally said, "I know it seems like we probably have this situation under control, but I need you to be just as careful and vigilant as always."

"I know," I assured him. "What makes you think I wouldn't be?"

Mouse shrugged. "Sometimes people in your situation have a tendency to get ahead of themselves, and it creates problems."

"My situation?" I repeated. "Are you talking about the Busuigno attached to me?"

"I'm talking about the future you," Mouse explained. "Because you've met him, you may be thinking that somehow everything turns out okay. I need you to understand that that's not necessarily true. The future isn't set. It's not fixed. It's variable, and the decisions you make can easily change things — alter what you think is a set course."

"Honestly, I hadn't even thought about that," I admitted. "It hadn't occurred to me to consider what the future Jim might mean in that context."

"Good, because you need to approach this as you would any other mission, bearing in mind that the fate of the world is at stake."

"No pressure there," I muttered.

"You ready?" Mouse asked, chuckling.

"If I said I wasn't, would it make a difference?"

"Not at all," Mouse assured me with a grin.

ISOLATION

Chapter 62

I came through a dimensional gate that opened on the helipad, which was the place Mouse had pinpointed as the location of the Construct. Needless to say, the Busuigno had lied to me about moving it to another location. When I appeared, it was sitting in the middle of the helipad, unguarded, as though waiting for me.

A few minutes before I'd arrived, Mouse had gone to another part of HQ to create a diversion by wreaking general havoc (as he'd done the past few days). It was supposed to send almost everyone scurrying to his location, but common sense said that *someone* should have remained with the Construct. Thus, the fact that the helipad was deserted was somewhat bizarre.

All of my instincts screamed *Trap!* However, when I stretched my empathic and telepathic senses, I didn't pick up on any other presence nearby. Of course, that didn't mean anything. Someone like Buzz could cover miles in seconds, as could Alpha Prime. With that thought, I took note of the fact that the retractable roof was open.

Maybe they threw in the towel, I thought, but found it extremely unlikely. Considering everything they'd done thus far — everything that was at stake for them — I couldn't see the Busuigno simply chalking this up as a loss. Still, there was no use wasting time. If there was a trap here, I'd find out soon enough.

I shifted into super speed and raced over to the Construct. Surprisingly, nothing and no one tried to stop me. Once there, I opened up a leather satchel Mouse had given me, which contained the doomsday components. I then began placing them in their appropriate positions on the front of the Construct.

ISOLATION

Triangular doodad in the upper left corner... I said to myself. *Black cube goes dead center...*

Keeping in mind Mouse's instructions, I placed each item from the satchel in its proper spot. Based on what my mentor had said, I'd garnered the impression that some action would begin immediately after the components were in place. That being the case, I stood there, waiting with bated breath.

Nothing happened.

Something was wrong. I spent a quick moment glancing around, trying to determine if the Busuigno were somehow interfering in some way. Again, I saw and sensed no one nearby. Turning my attention back to the Construct, I doubled-checked my handiwork and concluded that I had done everything as Mouse had instructed.

Did Mouse do something wrong? I wondered. *Did he make some mistake?*

I quickly dismissed the notion; Mouse didn't make mistakes. That meant it was something on *my* end — whatever was wrong sprang from a gaffe *I* had made. I mentally began retracing my steps, recalling everything I'd done since arriving at the helipad — and then almost laughed as I suddenly realized what the problem was.

The issue was *me*! I was still moving at super speed. That's why nothing seemed to be happening from my perspective.

I shifted back to normal speed, and immediately began to see action with the Construct. One of the attached components began to glow with an azure light. Another started to hum, while a third crackled with electricity. Basically, each item I'd placed on the Construct began to do something.

ISOLATION

I stood by, watching excitedly, thankful that this particular nightmare was about to be over. Thus, it took me by surprise when I suddenly heard my father's voice.

"Jim," Alpha Prime said. "Don't do this, son."

His voice seemed to come from all around me, and I realized that he was using the League's PA system. That said, it didn't sound like he was at HQ; there was a rush of air in the background, giving the impression that he was outside.

I kept my mouth closed. This was not the time to be distracted. Instead, recognizing that this might be — and probably was — a trap of some kind, I phased and became insubstantial.

"You never heard me out about my offer," he continued. "What I'm putting on the table is your father."

I frowned. *Was the thing on my father trying to say it would kill him if I didn't stand down? Could it?* I didn't know — my father was practically invulnerable. Still, the thought of the Busuigno threatening him made me clench my fists in anger.

"Don't you want dear old Dad back?" he asked.

"I'm getting him back!" I uttered in fury before I even realized I planned to speak.

"I'm not talking about the old Alpha Prime — the one who stayed away most of your life — or even the one who's been taking baby steps in getting to know you. I'm talking about the Alpha Prime of the last few days. The one who's made constant overtures to bond with you. Going to breakfast, playing board games, eating pizza… You can have the father you always wanted."

"None of that was real. It's you controlling him."

"It was real," Alpha Prime countered. "I have access to his memories; I know his feelings for you and can

302

manifest them, and much more. Plus, he's not gone — he's still in here. It's like he's asleep, for lack of a better term. Moreover, all of the bonding we've done lately are things he wanted to do but didn't know how to initiate. I took those steps for him, and now you see the kind of relationship the two of you can have."

"You mean the *three* of us," I shot back.

"Perhaps. But again, the emotions being reflected are truly your father's — just like Electra's emotions were at the fore when you were with her."

"What?!" I practically screeched.

"Think about it. In addition to Alpha Prime, you can also have the ideal girlfriend. One who showers you with affection, willing to wait on you hand and foot."

"That's not Electra," I said. "It never will be."

"Does that matter? Like your father, the Electra you knew is still in there. And again, the affection she feels for you is sincere and that's what would be broadcast and displayed. Wouldn't that be worth it?"

"Not in a million years," I stated flatly. "Keep talking all you want, but all you're doing is convincing me that you belong locked up in the Construct."

There was silence for a moment, then Alpha Prime said, "All right, you've forced my hand. Look up — almost directly above you."

My gut instinct was to ignore him, but somehow I found myself doing as he instructed. I looked up, but initially didn't see anything. Bearing in mind that I still couldn't detect anyone nearby, I telescoped my vision and then I saw him, maybe half a mile up in the air.

I also saw what he held: Cat.

ISOLATION

Chapter 63

My mind blanked for a moment.

Cat? I thought. *How..? Why...?*

I couldn't form a coherent thought. I had no idea she was involved in this — couldn't imagine why it had happened or how it had come about.

Although still trying to get a handle on the situation, I noticed that Alpha Prime was holding her aloft by one wrist, letting the rest of her body dangle. She appeared to be unconscious (which was probably a blessing, because otherwise she'd surely be screaming her head off).

"I didn't want it to come to this," Alpha Prime declared. "We're not a violent species by nature."

"No, you just take over other beings who don't have the means to resist," I countered. "You're like a mugger robbing someone at gunpoint, then claiming you're nonviolent because your victim didn't fight back."

"Be that as it may, we Busuigno are fighting for our lives."

"No you're not," I shot back. "Being imprisoned in the Construct isn't a death sentence. Maybe a *life* sentence, but not death."

"For the Busuigno, there's no distinction. We can only experience the universe — and life, as you know it — through others. Take that from us, and you may as well kill us. So as far as we're concerned, this *is* a fight for survival, and there are trillions of us still imprisoned in the Construct."

"And with good reason."

Alpha Prime suddenly looked angry. "Enough talk. Stop what you're doing, or I drop her."

ISOLATION

He shook Cat by the wrist slightly for emphasis. It would have given his gesture greater effect if she'd been awake and wailing in terror, but the message still came through loud and clear.

"No comment?" he stated a moment later. "So be it." He released his grip and Cat dropped like a stone.

Of course, I'd been expecting this and had kept my eye on her. Within a second or two of Alpha Prime letting go, I got a lock on her with my power and teleported her into my arms. At the same time, I teleported Alpha Prime, sending him back to the middle of the ocean where he'd had his sneezing fit.

Thankfully, Cat hadn't fallen far enough to build up a lot of momentum, so catching her was a lot like catching a cheerleader jumping off a pyramid. I then brought my vision back to normal and gave her a once-over, trying to get a sense as to whether she was okay. To my surprise, however, she opened her eyes.

"Easy," I said to her. "I've got you."

"And *I've* got *you*," she replied, pressing a hand to my cheek.

Almost instantly, I began screaming in pain.

ISOLATION

Chapter 64

It was a lot like when Mouse's device had knocked all the air from my body, except this time, it felt like far more was wrenched out — and things that went well beyond the physical: vitality, energy, verve... It was all violently wrung from my body. (Later, I would say that it was like a thousand tiny bombs exploded inside me simultaneously, forcing everything out.)

Wailing in anguish, I dropped to my knees as my bones turned to jelly. My grip on Cat loosened as my arms flopped uselessly to my side; she rolled away for a second before scrambling to her feet.

"Thanks, cutie," she said, giving me a wink. "We knew we could count on you to do the right thing."

We? I thought as I managed to stop screaming. Of course — Cat was under the control of the Busuigno.

"Wow," she murmured, opening and closing her fists as if squeezing a couple of imaginary balls. "This is incredible."

Suddenly she vanished, reappearing a few feet away, then returned to her original position. She had either teleported or moved at super speed, I didn't know which. Then I understood: Cat hadn't just sapped my vigor and stamina. She had drained my powers.

"You should be ashamed of yourself," she said as she floated into the air a few feet and came back down. "It's a crime not to showcase this array of powers."

"They're...*my* powers," I managed to painfully squeak out. "My business...how I...use them."

"Well, they're *my* powers now," she declared. "At least temporarily."

ISOLATION

I tried to move, but only managed to groan in pain. I began trying to tweak my systems to stop the pain, but found limited success.

"Oh, cheer up," she admonished. "I didn't drain you completely. You still have your powers; you're just too weak to use them — like a bodybuilder laid up with the flu. He's still got his muscles and physique, but just lacks the stamina to do anything."

"Thanks," I muttered, trying to get to my feet and failing, while at the same time continuing my efforts to stop the pain. "You're a...real...humanitarian."

"That's actually kind of prophetic," she retorted. "Anyway, I can't stand here jawing with you all day. I've got work to do."

With that, she stepped over to the Construct. I couldn't see exactly what she was doing, but it appeared as though she was moving the doomsday components around.

"We really need to thank you and your friend Mouse," Cat said as she fiddled at the Construct. "It would have taken us quite a while to open this thing up on our own."

"Ha," I groaned weakly. "We're...closing it. Sending...you back."

"You *were*. But did you know that if you realign some of these articles, the exact opposite happens? It's kind of like reversing the polarity on a magnet, so that instead of attracting, it pushes away. In this instance, instead of sucking Busuigno in, it's going to push them out. *All* of them."

I had trouble keeping my mouth from dropping open.

"Are you shocked?" she asked with a grin, stepping back from the Construct and turning towards me. "Of course we knew what you guys were up to, but what you didn't know was that we *wanted* you to take those components — wanted you to reconfigure them to interact with the Construct. I mean, we're smart, but your friend Mouse is in a league by himself. It might have taken us years to do what he did in days."

"You're lying," I uttered hotly. "You tried to stop Mouse every step of the way."

She shook her head. "No, once we figured out what he was up to and knew we could use him to help us, it was all we could do not to giftwrap those components and hand them over. However, we knew that if we made it too easy, your friend would get suspicious, so we feigned trying to stop him, and—"

Her words were cut off as I suddenly rocked back on my heels and leaped at her. I hadn't been able to stop all the pain, but had eliminated enough of it to be somewhat mobile again. More to the point, my lunge seemed to take her by surprise.

I didn't make any attempt at truly trying to engage with her. Instead, I simply used my momentum to thrust her aside and sent her sprawling. I then turned my attention to the Construct, and began hastily trying to move the components back to their original positions.

However, I hadn't managed to shuffle more than two of them before I felt a hand grip my wrist, and once again I screamed in agony as it felt like my soul was being sucked out of my body. It wasn't as bad as the first time, due to the fact that I had deadened a lot of nerve endings, but it was impossible to stop altogether because much of the torment I was feeling wasn't at the physical level.

ISOLATION

It seemed to go on forever, but was probably no more than a few seconds, following which I felt myself forcefully shoved aside — probably telekinetically. I landed in a heap on the floor.

"You should really be thanking us," Cat declared as she began reorganizing the components on the Construct. "After the Busuigno take over this planet, there will be no more wars, no more poverty, no more injustice."

"No more *people*," I added as I struggled up to my hands and knees.

"There'll be people," Cat countered. "They just won't be quite as you remember them."

"What about me?"

"There are bound to be some like you and your friend Mouse," she said, turning in my direction. "Those who are immune or whom we can't control. But don't worry — we'll find a place for you."

I didn't respond, as her words seemed to nudge something at the back of my brain. A moment later, it came to the fore, giving me the rudiments of a very basic plan. I wasn't sure if it would work, but it wasn't like I had a lot of options.

As quickly as I could, I executed a maneuver similar to what I'd done before, drawing my feet under me with a little hop and then charging at Cat. This time, however, she was ready for me.

I came at her with hands outstretched. That said, I must have been far weaker than even I thought, because she simply grabbed me by the wrists. Afterwards, she simply held me there, like a petulant child, as I tried yanking my hands back and forth in an effort to break her grip.

"You must really have a death wish," Cat noted as I struggled. "You simply aren't going to be happy until I drain you dry." She seemed to contemplate for a moment, and then stated, "Fine then — wish granted!"

As before, I wailed as I suddenly felt my very essence being siphoned out of me. However, I had been expecting it, and at the very moment it began, I opened a telepathic channel and shouted, mentally, as loud as I could into Cat's brain.

My telepathic yell appeared to startle her, because she blinked several times as if caught unawares by something. She then appeared to shake her head for a moment, as if trying to clear her thoughts.

At that point, with my strength almost gone, I flopped to the ground, although Cat still gripped my wrists, holding them up above my head. Somewhere in the background, I heard a woeful wailing and realized it was me. A moment later, I didn't even have the energy to give voice to my pain as Cat continued draining me. Apparently, my plan had failed. Completely demoralized and exhausted, I let my head droop as my eyelids fluttered and then closed.

Then, unexpectedly, Cat said, "Stop it."

She still held my wrists, and I could feel my power continuing to flow into her, but something seemed off.

"Stop it!" she repeated, raising her voice. "Stop it!"

All of a sudden, I felt my arms being yanked back and forth, like the hand levers on an elliptical machine.

"Let go, you stupid girl!" I heard Cat screech. "Let go!"

The tug-of-war with my arms became more violent, then all of a sudden Cat screamed, "No! No! No!"

A moment later, the yanking on my arms ceased, and I felt myself being lowered gently to the ground. Struggling mightily, I opened my eyes and saw Cat standing next to the Construct. I tried to speak, but no words would come out.

Apparently hearing my efforts, Cat glanced at me for a moment.

"It's okay, Jim," she said with a smile. "Everything's going to be fine."

Unable to hold it together any longer, I passed out.

ISOLATION

Chapter 65

I came to in a bed in the League infirmary. Looking around, I was surprised to find that I wasn't hooked up to anything: no IV drip, no monitor, nothing. That said, there must have been a scanner of some sort in the room, because a few minutes later Mouse came in, carrying his tablet.

"Great — you're awake," he said without preamble.

"Hello to you, too," I responded. "How long have I been here?"

"Twelve hours, give or take. There really didn't seem to be anything physically wrong with you — you just seemed incredibly exhausted — so we figured just tossing you into a bed was enough. Plus that girl we found on the helipad with you—"

"Cat," I interjected.

"Yeah, Cat. She said to just let you sleep and you'd be good as new."

"And the word of a teenage girl passes for medical advice these days," I stated dryly.

"Well, Alpha Prime vouched for her — once he got back from his ocean excursion, that is — so I didn't feel any need to question it."

"It's okay — I'm just yanking your chain," I admitted. "Where is she now?"

"Cat? I think Alpha Prime took her home."

"Okay," I droned, "now the big question: are we still a planet of people or a world of Busuigno?"

Mouse laughed. "We're still a planet full of greedy, selfish, conceited individuals solely focused on material possessions and monetary gain."

"So we won," I surmised, causing my mentor to chuckle again.

"Yeah, the Busuigno are back where they belong."

As proof, he put his tablet in front of me, showing me an image of myself at present. It was the same washed-out type of pic I'd seen previously, but this time I wasn't sporting the ugly cowl.

"Score one for the good guys," I said.

"Yeah," Mouse concurred, then appeared to grow somber. "So this girl, Cat..."

"She's a friend," I stated as he trailed off. "She helped defeat the Busuigno."

"By draining your powers, as I understand it."

"Something like that," I confirmed. "But I'd prefer to keep that part confidential."

"So is the great Kid Sensation ashamed of being saved by a girl?"

I shook my head. "No, but I think she prefers to avoid the limelight. I just want to respect her wishes."

"I can understand that," Mouse declared with a nod. "So, you want to give me a brief rundown of what happened? I mean, I talked to Alpha Prime and Cat, but I'd still like to get your version."

"Sure," I said, and then gave him a quick overview of everything that happened up to the point that Cat first siphoned my powers. "Basically, the Busuigno were banking on us doing most of the heavy lifting for them in terms of finding a way to open the Construct. Then they just needed to get me out of the way, and they found a means of doing that with Cat."

"I still can't believe how badly I slipped up," Mouse said. "Occasionally, I get tunnel vision, and I was so focused on fixing my mistake in letting the Busuigno out

— so dead set on locking them back up — that I failed to fully consider what else my efforts could be used for. How my work could benefit the enemy."

"It's not your fault. You didn't know that the doomsday components could also be used to open the Construct."

"That's just it – I *did* know," Mouse contritely confessed. "But in my arrogance, I didn't think anyone else did…didn't think anyone else was smart enough to figure it out. And my hubris almost cost us the planet."

"Well, the good news — as you often say to me — is that it all worked out in the end."

"Not without some luck."

"Well, cats are supposed to bring good luck," I said with a smirk.

"Apparently the Busuigno didn't know that when they took control of your friend."

"So it seems," I agreed. "They basically needed a way to negate my powers, because — with my ability to phase and such — challenging me directly was doomed to fail."

"Well, they certainly gave it the old college try in terms of getting a work-around."

"Yeah, but that's also where they slipped up," I noted. "The Busuigno controlling Cat made a comment about how they'd handle people who were immune to their control. It suddenly gave me the idea that if Cat could siphon my powers, maybe she could draw on my immunity, too. So the last time the Busuigno in her tried to drain me, I telepathically shouted at Cat to wake up as loud as I could."

"And apparently, it worked. Cat got your immunity, regained control, and then put the components back in the right configuration on the Construct. Next thing you know, it's 'Adios, Busuigno.'"

"Good riddance," I added. "So what's going to happen to the Construct?"

"We're going to find a hole to bury it in, bury it, then bury the hole."

"Works for me," I said.

ISOLATION

Chapter 66

Mouse and I chatted a few minutes longer, then — after giving me Myshtal's ring to return to her — he took his leave, saying there was a line of people waiting to see me. In actuality, the line turned out to consist of just two people: Alpha Prime and Smokey.

The latter only stayed a few minutes, saying he simply wanted to check up on me. Truth be told, Alpha Prime was practically broadcasting the fact that he wanted a father-son discussion, and Smokey easily picked up on it. After saying he'd swing by again later, Smokey left me alone with my father.

Alpha Prime was silent for a moment, then stated, "I probably should have said it when I first came in, but you did good, son. Great, in fact."

"Thanks," I said. "But how are *you*?"

He seemed to dwell on the question for a second. "I'm good. Physically, of course, I'm not having issues. Mentally, it's still a little weird to know that I was under some other being's control."

"What was it like?"

"Honestly, it was like being in a dream. I could see things that were happening and understand the events taking place, but there was a surreal quality to it."

I nodded. "I think I understand."

"Anyway, one of the things that stuck with me was the time we spent together when…"

He trailed off, but I understood what he was trying to say. "When the Busuigno was controlling you."

My father nodded. "It wasn't lying. The time we spent together — when it was in control — those really were things I wanted to do. But I was out of your life for

316

so long that I...I worry about being overbearing or smothering. I'm still feeling my way around in terms of this parent thing, and I don't want to run you off."

"Honestly, we're both still learning our way around this thing, but you won't get rid of me that easily."

"Seems likely when you consider that some interdimensional creature did a better job of bonding with you than me."

"Mid-dimensional," I corrected.

"Huh?" muttered my father.

"Nothing," I said. "In my opinion, you've done fine in terms of trying to bond. For instance, when you called me at brunch and asked me to dinner, were you under control of the Busuigno?"

Alpha Prime shook his head. "No."

"Then there you go," I said. "You're doing fine on the bonding front."

"Thanks, son," Alpha Prime said with a smile.

"But speaking of that brunch," I continued, "I know you went to see Cat's mom."

My father's mood suddenly turned more serious. "It was important enough that I felt it necessary, so I had a friend who's a teleporter take me there shortly after we spoke. Now that you've seen some of what Cat can do, hopefully you understand my concern."

"Honestly, I still don't quite understand what the big deal is."

"That's because you don't quite understand what she is. Basically, she's—"

"No," I interjected. "Don't tell me."

My father looked at me in surprise. "You don't want to know?"

"I do," I confessed. "But it's something Cat needs to tell me. I no more want you telling me her secret than I'd want Capri telling people I'm Kid Sensation."

"She won't," he assured me. "She could occasionally benefit from having a gag in her mouth, but she'd never reveal anything like that."

"How'd she even know I was your son?"

"She's friends with your cousin Avis. I don't know if you ever saw it, but a while back Avis posted on social media that Kid Sensation was her cousin. It wasn't hard for Capri to put two and two together after that. She also seems to have gotten some info from her niece, Vestibule."

"Nice," I muttered sarcastically. "Everybody knows all about me."

"It's a small circle of people, son — your friends, for the most part, and nobody who wishes you ill. If staying low-key is a big deal for you, I don't think you have much to worry about. After all, they've kept it under their hats this long."

I spent a moment thinking about it, then said, "You're probably right. I'm just used to flying under the radar."

"Well, that may not last much longer," he stated. "Kid Sensation is a big deal, and will only get bigger in the future."

I didn't immediately comment, as his statement brought to mind something I'd almost forgotten: my future self. I considered mentioning it to Alpha Prime but immediately rejected the idea. According to Mouse, *I* wasn't even supposed to know about Older Jim. He'd have conniptions if I told someone else.

"Anyway," my father went on, "I know you haven't been back on your feet for long and I don't want to tire you out, so I'm going to go."

"Hold on," I said as he began walking towards the door. "I don't know how long they're planning to hold me, but — assuming I can check myself out — you want to grab dinner tonight?"

"My calendar's wide open," he said with a smile.

****

Not long after my father left, Electra came by. I was a little surprised, as I had assumed she'd be in class.

"I've been under the control of some extra-dimensional thing for the past few days," she said after I posed the question.

"Mid-dimensional," I interjected.

Electra frowned. "What?"

"Never mind," I said.

"Anyway," she continued. "Bearing in mind that I only just became myself again in the last twelve hours or so, school is probably a wash for this week."

"Understandable," I remarked.

"I'm glad you approve," Electra stated. "But you want to know what's *not* understandable? You drugging me. Not cool, dude."

"Uh, if anything, you drugged yourself, lady."

"Well, you gave me a plate of drugged food. However you slice it, a guy serving up his ex something like that just doesn't pass the smell test."

"Even if she drugged him the two nights before?"

"Two wrongs don't make a right, Jim. Surely your mother taught you that."

319

I laughed. "How about three wrongs, then? Your two and my one."

"Still a fail," Electra declared.

"Fine," I said. "I apologize for letting you eat the drugged food that you meant for me."

"I appreciate the apology, but I'm afraid it's not enough."

"Okay, then how do you propose I make it right?"

A sly smile formed on Electra's face. "I would like for you to get me a plate of *non*-drugged food."

"No problem. I'll have some takeout sent to your house. Just tell me what—"

"Not good enough," she stated, cutting me off. "I want to see how your face looks at mealtime when I'm *not* being drugged."

I frowned, trying to make sure I understood what she was saying. "Electra, are you…are you asking me on a date?"

"No," she declared fervently. "It's not a date and we're not back together. It's just dinner."

"Okay," I said. "But what happened to not doing stuff like that?"

Electra stayed silent for a few moments, and it wasn't clear that she was actually going to answer.

"I miss you," she finally said. "Of course, it wasn't me in control these past few days, but I could see what was going on, and it just made me acutely aware of all the fun we used to have — not just as a couple, but also as friends."

"I understand," I said. "And if it means anything, I miss you, too."

"That was a given," she announced, tossing her head haughtily. "You could have saved your breath."

"Next time I will," I said with a chuckle, causing her to punch me playfully.

"You still need to fix this thing with Myshtal before we can get back together," she said, "but I think we can hang out as friends until then."

"You sure?" I asked.

"Not really," she confessed. "But, in all honesty, the alternative hasn't really been my cup of tea."

ISOLATION

Chapter 67

I threw a party that weekend in honor of Myshtal coming home. Calling it a party, however, was a bit of an exaggeration since it was really impromptu and involved just a few close friends: Electra, Smokey, Vestibule, and Cat. I had been slightly worried that — after her time with my cousin Monique — Myshtal would be burned out on social events. However, I had completely forgotten that, as a Caelesian princess and favorite of the queen, she went to galas and balls all the time, almost as a requirement. In short, it appeared that "burned out" wasn't in her vocabulary. More to the point, she actually liked socializing.

"Oh no," she assured me when I made the suggestion shortly after she returned (at which time I also handed over the ring Mouse had taken). "A party sounds great. But I think we should probably clear the air first."

"About what?" I asked, although I had a pretty good idea.

"My behavior when you came and got me."

"You were high," I insisted. "Don't worry about it. You weren't yourself."

"The drugs only removed my inhibitions," she said. "Let me express how I feel about you. But you already knew, didn't you?"

I sighed. "Yes, but I didn't want to say anything. This situation is complicated enough without additional emotions getting involved."

"Well, you can rest assured that I don't plan to act on my emotions. I know how you feel about Electra and give you my word that I will never be a barrier to your relationship."

"Wow," I muttered in surprise. "That's more than I was anticipating."

"I just feel the need to be honest. If you and I are meant to be together, then it will happen in time. I don't need to do anything to hasten or force it."

I frowned as she spoke, thinking. The temporal rogue I had encountered on Caeles at one point revealed to me and Myshtal that — in the future — the two of us would be king and queen of the Caelesian Empire. Hearing her now, it appeared that Myshtal believed what we'd been told and would be content waiting for that future to unfold.

"I suppose that's true," I finally said. "If it happens, it happens."

After that, with Myshtal on board with the idea, I had made the requisite calls to my friends. As part of the invitation, I gave everyone the option to bring a plus-one, but the only person who took advantage of it was Electra, who came with Dynamo. She insisted, however, that it wasn't a date.

"He was just going to spend the evening sitting at home alone," she told me at one point during the evening. "I felt bad for him."

"No worries," I told her sincerely. "I hope he has a good time."

I was extraordinarily pleased when Cat showed up with Vestibule. Given how she'd felt about me knowing about her powers, I was worried Cat would avoid me now that I'd seen her in action. Surprisingly, she sought me out shortly after arriving.

"You want to take a walk?" she said.

"Uh, sure," I replied.

With that, we had gone out a sliding door at the back of the embassy that opened onto an extensive loggia and pool area. It was dark out, but the loggia was well-lit, and the illumination spread out onto the grounds, revealing, among other things, a parterre garden and a gazebo.

"It's lovely out here," Cat said, walking towards the edge of the loggia.

"Thanks," I replied, as I strolled next to her. "I really don't come back here enough."

She turned to me. "You wanted to know about my powers. I'm sorry you had to find out the way you did."

"It's okay," I assured her. "I know that wasn't you in control. I'm just happy you came through in the end."

"Me, too," she said with a smile. "It was like I was sleeping — dreaming everything that was happening — and then I heard you screaming my name, telling me to wake up."

"And you did. But I'm curious about something. How'd you know what to do with those components on the Construct when you finally gained control?"

"Maybe you don't remember," she answered. "You were trying to speak but couldn't, and then I found I could look inside your mind. That's where I saw what to do."

"Well, I don't know if anybody told you, but you saved the planet."

"So I've heard. It just feels surreal — like maybe I'm still in the dream."

"I can pinch you if you like," I offered, making her giggle.

"No, thanks," she decided. "But there is something you can do for me."

"What's that?"

"Tell me how you found out about me."

"Sure," I shot back with almost no hesitation. I then explained to her about the surge of power I'd felt during brunch.

She looked away when I was done, seemingly embarrassed. "I'm sorry — that wasn't supposed to happen. I usually have more control than that."

"Okay," I droned. "Frankly speaking, though, I still don't know what happened."

"I'll tell you, but it'll probably help if I first explain about my power." She paused for a moment, took a deep breath, then blurted out, "I'm a kitsune."

I frowned. "Isn't that, like, a magic cat?"

"A magic *fox*, actually," she replied, laughing. "Still, that's pretty good. According to legend, a kitsune is a fox or fox spirit with various powers, such as shapeshifting, flight, invisibility—"

"Are you serious?" I interjected, suddenly feeling odd because she was actually rattling off a list of *my* powers. "You can do all that?"

"That's what the kitsune of legend can purportedly do," she explained. "They can also, supposedly, draw on the life-force of others."

"And *that's* what you can do," I realized. "And if they have superpowers, you can siphon those, too — gain their abilities for yourself."

"Only temporarily," she clarified. "But typically, it only works on the opposite sex. And if I take any of their life-force, guys have a tendency to become obsessed with me. They're basically fixated on and drawn to me because, on some level, they know a part of them is inside me. But — unless I draw from them on a regular basis — eventually it fades, for lack of a better term, and everything goes back to normal."

I spent a moment mulling over what she'd just said and reflecting back on the period of time after I'd first felt her power. Back then, I actually hadn't been able to stop thinking about Cat and her abilities for hours.

"My mom says it'll pass," she continued. "She says it's just a phase – this fear of people knowing about me – and things will be better when I'm older and in full control of my powers."

"She's like you," I stated.

"Yeah, but why do I get the feeling you already knew that?" she inquired.

Ignoring what I assumed to be a rhetorical question, I asked, "Do you think she's right?"

Cat shrugged. "She doesn't seem to have any issues with *her* powers. That said, it probably doesn't hurt that – under certain circumstances and with proper control – the siphoning can also give an exquisite kind of, uh…*pleasure*."

I stared at her for a moment, not understanding. And then, recalling the conversation between Capri and my father, the truth hit me.

"Oh," I muttered, while Cat looked away, slightly embarrassed. "Anyway, I think I understand now why you don't want people to know about you."

"If people knew I could drain their life-force — and sometimes do it slightly by accident — they wouldn't want to be around me," she explained. "It's happened in the past. Family members are afraid to hug you. Friends don't want to be near you. Guys don't want to hold your hand."

"Not everyone is like that, I'm sure," I said.

"Most," she argued, "so I've just learned to keep that part of myself under wraps."

"Well, feel free to unwrap that part around me."

"You say that *now*," Cat retorted, "but after you've had a chance to…"

She suddenly trailed off as I reached over and took her hand. It was an act that took her by complete surprise (and me as well, since I had done it without consciously thinking about it). For a long time, she just stared at our clasped hands, like it was something she had never seen before. I realized then that — perhaps aside from her parents and Vestibule — actual human contact with someone who knew what she was (and the power she had) was something Cat probably hadn't experienced in quite some time. After maybe a minute, she looked at me and gave me a warm, bright smile.

****

Cat and I stayed outside simply holding hands for perhaps another fifteen minutes. There was nothing romantic or implied in the act — it was a purely platonic gesture on both our parts. However, even without my empathic abilities, I could tell that having human contact in that way — with someone who wasn't afraid of her or what she could do — meant the world to Cat.

At some juncture, my phone rang. Noting that it was Mouse calling, I excused myself and hastily stepped away for privacy.

"Hey," I said upon answering. "You need me for something?"

"How quickly can you get to the helipad?"

"In about a minute."

"Okay," Mouse replied. "But you need to hurry or you'll miss it."

With that, he hung up, leaving me puzzled as to what he was talking about.

Quickly returning to Cat, I said, "I've got to take off for a minute. Will you tell the others I'll be back as soon as I can?"

"Sure," she said. "Be careful."

"I will," I promised.

Cat then turned to head back towards the embassy, but had barely taken a step before she suddenly spun back in my direction, impulsively throwing her arms around my neck and giving me a big hug. Caught a little off guard, I recovered enough to hug her back. Again, it was platonic, but I understood it was something she needed, especially when she whispered "Thank you" in my ear before stepping back.

I gave her a short wave and then teleported.

ISOLATION

Chapter 68

I popped up on the helipad, noting almost immediately that the spot that would normally be occupied by a chopper now had another craft sitting there. It was sleek and streamlined, with a futuristic design that made it look space-worthy. A moment later, I realized it actually *was* space-worthy. I was looking at a Caelesian shuttlecraft.

Confused, I quickly scanned the place and saw Mouse nearby talking to two people. One was the Caelesian guard I'd spoken to on the rooftop of the diner. The other was Older Jim — the future version of me.

Confused, I began walking in the direction of the trio. Seeing me approach, Mouse quickly broke off his conversation with the other two and headed towards me.

"What's going on?" I asked when we drew close.

"The other you is leaving the planet," Mouse replied.

I was dumbfounded. "You're sending him to Caeles?"

"Why not?" my mentor almost demanded. "This whole temporal issue he has going on is their fault. That being the case, he can go *there* and screw up *their* timeline."

I frowned as his words sank in. The Caelesians were somehow involved in Older Jim's predicament? It was news to me, and showed how little I actually knew of what had happened to him. Rather than ask a bunch of questions, however, I simply said, "I'm surprised the Caelesians went for that."

"It wasn't for nothing," Mouse assured me, glancing at the guard.

My brow crinkled for a moment, and then the truth hit me.

"No," I muttered. "Tell me you didn't let them bug Alpha League HQ."

"It's a small price to pay to get the future you off-planet," he said. "Besides, they're not going to hear anything I don't want them to."

I was pretty confident that Mouse knew what he was doing, but still found myself shaking my head in dismay. I simply wasn't wild about letting someone bug HQ — even if said someone did address and treat me like royalty.

"Come on," Mouse said. "Let's go say our goodbyes."

Mouse started heading back to the other two, and I followed. We were just reaching them when their conversation seemed to draw to a close.

Turning to me, the guard inclined her head, saying, "Highness."

I acknowledged her greeting, at which point she simply headed inside the shuttle and took a seat in the cockpit — presumably the pilot's chair.

"Well, I guess this is goodbye," Mouse said to the older me, extending his hand.

"That it is," Older Jim said, "although I still think a burger and fries would have been fine for the road."

"Eat your apple," Mouse retorted, "and be grateful."

Shaking his head in mock frustration, Older Jim looked at me and said, "Try to get him to loosen up, okay? I really don't remember him being this strict."

"I'll try," I assured him. "You gonna be okay?"

"Of course!" he stated matter-of-factly. "I like Caeles, so this will be a nice visit."

<Anything I should know?> I asked telepathically.

"Hey, you two," Mouse suddenly said. "Let's keep this exchange limited."

"Chill, man," Older Jim admonished. "We were just saying goodbye. How often do you get a chance to see yourself off?"

"One is too many," Mouse groused. "Now get going."

"Fine, I'm leaving," Older Jim declared in mock anger. "It's not good to spend too much time around this place anyway."

As he spoke, he glanced around at our surroundings, making it clear that his last statement was in relation to HQ. Grumbling something about my mentor being a grouch, Older Jim then went into the shuttle and took a seat next to the guard. He waved goodbye, and within a few seconds, the craft started to rise. Moments later, ascending far faster than I'd assumed it would, it had cleared the roof, and in less than a minute was lost to sight.

I was still looking up when the roof started to close, presumably as a result of something Mouse did.

"So," he droned, "what did you and the other Jim talk about?"

"Huh?" I murmured.

"That little telepathic exchange at the end."

"Oh, uh, we were just saying goodbye. Also, he called you some names he probably couldn't say out loud."

"Hmmm," Mouse droned, plainly contemplating something. "Anyway, you should probably get back to your guests."

"Yeah," I said. "This party-hosting thing is more work than I figured."

With that, I said goodbye and teleported home.

ISOLATION

When I reappeared at the embassy, everyone was at the breakfast table, playing a board game that worked in conjunction with a phone app. They offered to start over so I could be included, but I told them I'd join the next game. Standing off to the side, I simply watched, noting that the game appeared to be a lot of fun. More importantly, everyone seemed to be *having* fun, and it was great having most of the people I was close to here.

As I was thinking this, Smokey got eliminated from the game. Laughing and joking, he got up from the breakfast table and came over to stand next to me.

"Bad luck," I said of his elimination.

"I'll get them next time," he promised. "Since you're joining in the next game, I don't suppose you'd be interested in an alliance?"

"Of course," I stated with a grin.

"Cool," Smokey said. "Oh, before I forget, my car's in the shop so I had to catch a rideshare here. Any chance you can get me back to HQ after the party?"

I was about to respond in the affirmative, when I was hit with a sudden inspiration — partially as a result of something Older Jim had said before boarding the shuttle.

"Why don't you stay here?" I asked.

"You mean crash overnight? Uh, sure, that sounds like fun."

"No, I mean *stay* here. Move in. It's just me and Myshtal, and we've got plenty of room. I mean, I'll have to clear it with Myshtal since it's her home, too, but I'm sure she'll be fine with it."

Smokey frowned. "I don't know, man. What would your mom and grandparents say?"

ISOLATION

"They'd ask why I'm letting my friend stay by himself in a cold and uncaring place like League HQ."

He chuckled. "'Uncaring' is a bit harsh, but it can get a little quiet with practically no other teens around."

"You mean it gets lonely," I stated in a tongue-in-cheek fashion.

"Hey, man — I'm a *guy*," he shot back. "We don't get lonely. We prize our solitude, just so you know." I chuckled at his statement while Smokey paused to take a breath. "That said, the, uh, 'quiet' does get to be a bit much sometimes."

"I get it," I assured him, still grinning. "But it just occurred to me that you really should be staying with family — if not the one you're related to by blood, then the one you chose via friendship."

Smokey appeared to mull this over, then nodded. "Okay, why don't we give it a whirl on a trial basis — maybe a week — and reassess then."

"Sounds good," I stated. Glancing at the breakfast table, I noted that the game was still going strong. "The others may be playing for a while. If we head to League HQ now, you can grab some things and we can pop back without missing a beat."

"That works," Smokey declared flatly.

Shouting "We'll be right back" to the table in general, I wrapped Smokey in my power and teleported the two of us, mentally thanking Older Jim for planting the notion in my brain (and wondering if it had been a subtle hint about the future).

THE END

Thank you for purchasing this book! If you enjoyed it, please feel free to leave a review on the site from which it was purchased.

Also, if you would like to be notified when I release new books, please subscribe to my mailing list via the following link: http://eepurl.com/C5a45

Finally, for those who may be interested in following me, I have included my website and social media info:

Website: http://www.kevinhardmanauthor.com/

BookBub: https://www.bookbub.com/authors/kevin-hardman?follow=true

Amazon Author Page: https://www.amazon.com/Kevin-Hardman/e/B00CLTY3YM

Facebook: www.facebook.com/kevin.hardman.967

Twitter: https://twitter.com/kevindhardman

Goodreads: https://www.goodreads.com/author/show/7075077.Kevin_Hardman

And if you like my work, please consider supporting me on Patreon: https://www.patreon.com/kevinhardman

ISOLATION

Glancing around, I saw that everyone else still seemed to be rubbing their eyes or otherwise trying to shake off the effects of the light-burst. Looking to where I'd last seen Mouse, I noticed that he was gone. There was, however, what appeared to be an exhaust trail leading up through the dome and out into the open air. Without hesitation, I flew up into the air, following it.

As I cleared the open dome, I telescoped my vision and immediately saw that the exhaust trail was coming from what appeared to be rockets in Mouse's boots. Turning on the afterburners, I swiftly began closing the distance.

Whether he did so out of caution or because he somehow sensed my presence, Mouse unexpectedly glanced in my direction. A moment later, he was pointing his fist towards me, and I saw that he had once again donned the brace I'd seen in the video.

Something like a pulse of electrical energy suddenly shot out of the brace in my direction. Unbothered, I phased, preparing to let the energy pass harmlessly through my insubstantial form. Unfortunately, nothing like that happened.

Instead of the pulse passing through me without effect, it hit me like a sledgehammer to the chest. All of the air in my body was suddenly, forcefully, and violently expelled, like someone had squeezed it out with a vise. I suddenly found myself not only gasping for breath, but falling; the shock of the blow had been so powerful that my body had seemingly shut down my flying ability in response.

ISOLATION

Kid Sensation Series
Sensation: A Superhero Novel
Mutation (A Kid Sensation Novel)
Infiltration (A Kid Sensation Novel)
Revelation (A Kid Sensation Novel)
Coronation (A Kid Sensation Novel)
Replication (A Kid Sensation Novel)
Incarnation (A Kid Sensation Novel)
Isolation (A Kid Sensation Novel)

Kid Sensation Companion Series
Amped
Mouse's Tale (An Alpha League Supers Novel)

The Warden Series
Warden (Book 1: Wendigo Fever)
Warden (Book 2: Lure of the Lamia)
Warden (Book 3: Attack of the Aswang)

The Fringe Worlds
Terminus (Fringe Worlds #1)
Efferus (Fringe Worlds #2)
Ignotus (Fringe Worlds #3)

Boxed Sets
The Kid Sensation Series (Books 1–3)
The Warden Series (Books 1–3)
Worlds of Wonder

Short Stories
Extraction: A Kid Sensation Story